COPPER
Moon

Donna Taylor

No part of this book may be reproduced. Any similarities
to actual events or people are coincidental.

ISBN: 0692426582
ISBN-13: 978-0692426586

DEDICATION

This is for my amazingly supportive husband.
He believed in me even when I didn't.
Thank the good Lord he likes to cook or
we would have starved to death.

PROLOGUE

10 Years Earlier

My family was really good at keeping secrets, big ones, small ones, and everything in between. Today, I was going to add another one to my own personal list.

My gramps was the best. He totally got that at fourteen, I was old enough to make it to the movies by myself. It was only three streets over from where he'd be hanging out at the feed store. What could happen in three blocks? Besides, it wasn't like Copper Ridge was a huge city or something. Sure, there were plenty of strangers in town, as summer was in full swing, but most of them would be at the lake or on one of the rivers during the day. Tourists didn't waste sunshine hanging out at the movies, especially at the weekend. Matinees were pretty much locals only on a Saturday. Which was great, 'cause that made it the perfect place to meet friends.

"Now Sis, you go straight to the show and don't make no detours. As soon as it's over, you get that skinny hinny back here. Your dad will skin the hide clean offin' me if anything happens to you." Gramps winked as he finished talking.

Gramps planned on sitting in the storage area of the feed store with all the other men, young and old alike, who showed up to swap stories and share the latest gossip. He said it was better than any newspaper for finding out what was going on with anyone who lived within a fifty mile radius of town. I was tickled when he volunteered to pick up the salt blocks for the cattle so I could catch a ride into town with him instead of Dad. Gramps had a million stories which made the thirty minute ride a blast.

If Dad ever found out even half the stories Gramps told me it would get ugly. Moonshine, revenuers, shootouts, and fast cars. Best. Stories. Ever! Gramps knew what he was talking about, too. He was a fifth generation moonshiner, and dang proud of it. Dad had broken with tradition and become a cattle rancher. He had taken the few cattle the family owned as a cover for the real business of moonshine and expanded the herd, until now it wasn't just a front but an honest to goodness ranch. Gramps said that made him even prouder, 'cause times were changing. Said making shine had always been a dangerous business, sometimes deadly, and he was glad to know his son was walking a different path to make a living.

I waved at Gramps, not sure he even saw. He was already swapping tales with a bunch of old guys, walking toward the open bay doors that gave access to the shaded interior. With a grin I turned and headed out for the theater.

Cutting through a back street to knock off some of the distance, I'd just entered the alley that ran alongside the theater when a truck thundered past me. Music screamed out the open windows. The bright red four-by-four with monster tires made it easy to identify who the owner was—Billy Wayne, the sheriff's boy and schoolyard bully. The truck came to a screeching halt at an angle just past me. Typical for BW and his crew. Big time showoffs. The music cut off as the doors opened and the boys spilled out, laughing and knocking into each other the way guys do. All the boys were older than me but I still knew each one. I wasn't too worried about them, since they'd never paid any attention to me at school or anywhere else I ran across them. I kept walking; doing my best to ignore them.

As I went to pass where they were all horsing around, BW stepped in front of me, bringing me to a halt. The other two guys maneuvered to flank me on either side. I felt the first stirring of nervousness at being surrounded by the likes of BW and his buddies. They were still talking trash to each other, but I knew it would soon be me they turned on to tease. They'd probably talk some dirty crap, impressing nobody but themselves.

Boys had started paying more attention to me this summer. Grow some boobs, have the braces come off, and guys suddenly started seeing you. Whatever, I'd been learning to do a pretty good job of tuning jerks out. But this time it felt different. Uglier. Staring at BW I tried out the best mean look I had.

"Get out of my way." My stink-eye didn't seem to have much effect other than to set off hooting and mimicking of my words by the two on either side of me. BW just smiled. He had a better mean look than me, even when he was smiling.

"Ain't you Moonshine's granddaughter?"

"Don't call him that!" Nerves fled and anger took its place. Now I knew how this was gonna go. I'd been dealing with it ever since I got old enough to have guys start trying to get me to sneak booze to them. Sometimes they just wanted to taunt me about what my grandpa did.

"What? Ain't that what everyone calls him?" BW spread his arms wide and shrugged like he was surprised by my anger.

Trey was quick to chime in, as though he was puzzled, "Man, you mean that ain't his name?"

Not to be left out, Robbie snickered, "Shit, I'm pretty sure that's what my old man calls him."

Standing as straight as possible, trying to make myself look taller and tougher, I glared at each of the morons in turn. "If you don't let me by I'm gonna start screaming. Someone'll hear me. Then you'll be in big trouble."

"Whooo, that's scary, boys. We better back off or we're gonna be in *big trouble*." BW pitched his voice high on the last three words, mocking me. He stepped aside and waved me through. Guess I should have known he was letting me go too easy, but all I could think about was getting the heck out of there. If I made it to the end of the alley there'd be people around and these jerks would have to leave me alone.

Taking a cautious step forward, I kept a wary eye on BW. He still had both hands in the air, as though he honestly meant to let me go. I flicked a quick glance at Robbie, then over to Trey, to see if they were also gonna let me get away. They both had puzzled looks, as though wondering why the heck BW was letting me leave, but they didn't appear to be getting ready to grab me. That was all the encouragement I needed. Gathering myself I went to dart around BW, ready to make a run for it. I moved quickly, but BW was quicker. His arm snaked out as I passed and a hand tightened painfully around my upper arm.

Jerked to a halt, BW dragged me up against his overgrown teenage body. I knew I was trapped when his other arm wrapped across my chest, pulling me in tight. I let lose a scream, which was quickly cut off by the hand that had first grabbed me. I exploded into a mass of kicking, twisting fury.

BW was spitting out the f-bomb and yelled at his two hooting and laughing partners, "*Grab those damn legs.*"

Eager to jump into the tussle, Trey and Robbie maneuvered into position. Trey bent to make a grab for my right leg, which gave me a perfect shot at his face with my foot. While I'd been busy trying to kick him in

5

the head his buddy, Robbie, went for my other leg. The feel of blunt nails scraping a trail down my shins, as their hands tried to get a firm grip, ignited real fear in me for the first time in my life.

I managed to land a heel to Trey's chin, but Robbie had gotten control of my left leg. His fingers dug in savagely. BW's beefy hand more than smothered my screams, it cut off what little air I managed to pull into lungs squeezed tight by the arm he'd wrapped across my upper torso. All the fight in me was slowly being crushed, along with my ability to breathe. I knew it was just a matter of time before Trey would get control of my one remaining flailing limb. Fear jacked into terror as BW's arm began to shift across my chest until he was able to grab one of my breasts and squeeze painfully. One second of frozen shock was all Trey needed to capture and give a vicious twist to my leg. Payback for the face kick.

"Carry her over behind the truck." BW ordered, a sick excitement threading through his words. I continued to buck as best I could, but that only seemed to slide my short tee higher and expose more of my body by the second. There were no real thinking involved on of how I was going to escape what was happening. All that kept firing off in my thoughts was I had to keep fighting.

"Turn her lose you sons-a-bitches." Barely controlled rage thrummed through the bite of those words.

Whoever was coming to my rescue scared the crap out of Robbie and Trey. They dropped my legs in their scramble to back away. My sandals had been lost in all that wild twisting, so when my legs were dropped my bare feet scraped the broken ground. BW released me so quickly there was no time to catch myself to keep from falling. Pitching forward, my knees smashed into gravel. Luckily my hands slapped the ground before my face did.

The meaty thud of a fist contacting flesh registered as background noise, my brain was fighting off terror and my lungs were dragging in huge gulps of oxygen.

My mind was screaming at me to *get up*. Trying to push to my feet ground small rocks even deeper into the palms of my hands and the tender flesh of my knees. Gritting my teeth, determined not to let the bastards know I was scared and hurting, I managed to get to my feet. Trying to get it together gave me time to watch Jase Rydan pull BW up off the ground. Staring at Jase, I now knew who had saved me. The blood streaming out of BW's nose also made it pretty obvious who'd received a face full of fist.

Little chicken shit wasn't even trying to fight back. Jase looked disgusted at the fear in BW's eyes as he growled at him, "You, and your little fucked-up friends, need to get your puckered asses out of here before you end up having to scrape them off the ground."

I'd no plans on sticking around to see what was going to happen next. Turning around, head up, back stiff, I started limping back in the direction I'd just come from. Praying the whole time...*please, just let me get out of here.* The humiliation of being caught in a situation like that, piled on top of the fear and anger, had my eyes burning from holding back tears. My throat felt like I'd eaten crushed glass but I couldn't stop swallowing compulsively. In my desperation to flee the spot where my childish illusions of safety and invincibility had been shattered, I didn't even stop to thank my rescuer. Though Jase called my name, I just kept on walking.

The sound of boots thudding behind me, then a hand landing gently on my shoulder had me whirling and knocking the light touch away.

* * *

Jase tried to look as non-threatening as possible. Charlotte Donley, the young girl standing in front of him, had her teeth bared and the wild look of a cornered animal. He had the feeling one wrong move would have her tearing down the street away from him.

Her ponytail was a bedraggled mess of barely contained scarlet strands. Furious blue eyes dared him to take a step closer. He had to admire the fact she was obviously still in defense mode and not quivering in terror.

Hell, she'd been fighting her three attackers with the ferocity of a feral kitten as he drove by the ally. Jase had a feeling she was damn lucky he'd noticed what those little bastards were up to. He scanned down her thin frame, trying to determine if there was any real damage.

Blood oozed sluggishly from a dozen tiny scrapes on both the palms of her hands and caps of her knees. There were four nasty looking scratches on her left shin. The sight of them had him regretting having let those three little cocksuckers run off. Her bare feet reminded him he was holding her sandals in his hand.

"Charlotte, I'm not going to hurt you. You know me and my family. We're the closest thing you've got to a neighbor in our neck of the woods." Jase tried to calm her. "All I want to do is help you get back to your parents. Are they here in town? Bet they let you walk to the movies all by yourself, right? Kid, you can't run off without your shoes. At least hang around long enough to get your shoes and let's see if we can clean you up a bit." His voice was low and soothing, lips curled at the corners in a tiny smile. Hands in the air, palms up, in a non-threatening show of peace. Sandals dangled by their straps from one of his fingers.

* * *

I wasn't an idiot. Of course he wasn't going to hurt me; he'd just saved me. And duh, everyone knew who Jase Rydan was. It kinda surprised me that he knew who I was, since he was so much older. But right now the thought of anyone touching me was a no-go. I felt pretty desperate to get out of there before I started bawling right in front of him.

All I could focus on was getting back to the feed store, climbing into the truck without anyone seeing me, and then coming up with a believable story as to why I had shredded hands and bleeding knees. Last thing I wanted was my gramps or my parents finding out what had happened.

It was the sight of my shoes, held aloft by Jase, that had me really taking a good look at myself. Crap! No way was I going to come up with a story to cover the way I looked right now.

"Come on, Charlotte, let me help you. I've got some old towels and water in the truck. We can knock some of that blood off you." Jase's cajoling tone brought my attention back to him. "Then we'll go find your parents."

Taking a deep breath, I realized I was going to have to take his offer of help to clean up but that was it. Afterwards, I needed to figure out way to keep him from telling my gramps what had happened. I still had hopes of lying my way out of this.

"Thank you." Why was it so hard to grit that out? Trying to choke back sobs I held out my hand. "Give me my shoes. Please."

Jase handed over the sandals. "Wait here. I'll go wet a couple rags. You'll need to clean off those feet." He took off for his truck parked at the entrance to the alley.

I sat down in the middle of the alley and began brushing at the bottoms of my feet. I tried to bring my jack-rabbiting heart under control, as well as slow my gulping swallows of air.

Jase was back quicker than I'd expected. Instead of handing over the wet cloth he squatted beside me and took the foot I'd been examining in one of his large, warm hands. Looking up at him warily, I reluctantly let him clean the sole of my foot. He was extremely gentle, and when he'd completed the rock and dirt removal he picked up the appropriate sandal and slid it on. Jase then turned his attention to my other foot.

While he went carefully from one blood, dirt and rock encrusted area to the next, I studied him. His dark hair was short, with not much peeking out around the edge of his sweat-stained ball cap. I couldn't see the color of his eyes because of the way his head was lowered while he concentrated on cleaning dirt out of cuts, but figured they were the same gray color his brother's were. His eyelashes were crazy long for a guy, but they didn't make him look like a sissy. Looking at his lips made me feel kinda funny. To be honest I'd never really looked at a guy's lips, or thought much about them. But Jase's sure were interesting. Kinda full without that gross puffy look.

He wasn't pretty, like a few guys at school, and he wasn't handsome like my dad. Somehow he was just more and better than either pretty or handsome. I was tall for a girl my age. Even taller than a lot of guys in my class, but Jase was way taller than me.

He wore a t-shirt that hugged his arms and chest. Man, he had some big muscles in his arms, and though I couldn't see, I'd bet my next week's allowance he had what the kids at school called a six-pack. Heck, Jase

11

probably had a twelve-pack, and I wasn't even positive that was possible, but if anybody could do it, I bet he could.

I knew to him I was just a kid, what with him being twenty to my fourteen, but the way my heart had started picking up the pace sure didn't make me feel like a kid. Where BW's hands on me were revolting, Jase's were having a weird effect. Goosebumps were dotting my arms and legs while a heat I'd never felt before rolled into my stomach. A flush was creeping up my neck, spreading a pink tint across my cheeks.

"There, not great but at least it doesn't look as bad as it did." He settled back on his heels and gave me a once over, as though checking to see if he'd missed anything. "Now, let's go find your parents."

"No." That came out a lot louder than I'd intended.

Jase cocked his head sideways not saying anything, just stared at me.

"I really am glad you came along, but please, don't tell anyone about this." Well that certainly sounded a lot like begging. Okay, I *was* begging, but if that's what it took to keep this a secret between us, that's what I'd do. Since Jase had cleaned me up I figured I had a real shot at making my family believe I'd tripped and got skinned up. All I needed was to add back a little bit of the dirt Jase had washed off.

"Don't you think your folks should know what BW and his buddies did?" Jase sounded curious, not like an adult trying to guilt a kid into doing the right thing.

"No. It would just make my folks mad, and Gramps might do something crazy that could get him in trouble. Besides, I don't want everyone else knowing what happened." Yeah, lots of pleading going on now. "This could just be our secret."

Jase kept staring at me for a long minute. His eyes narrowed to slits as though he were thinking things through.

"If I don't tell your parents you have to let me tell Evan, so he can watch over you for me. Make sure those kids don't pick on you because of what happened here. That's the only way I keep my mouth shut." The firm words and hard look let me know there would be no compromising on this.

Him wanting to tell his brother, Evan, had me squirming. Evan was a couple years older than me. He was younger than BW and crew, but not by much. Not what I wanted to happen, but if Evan could be counted on to keep his mouth shut, how bad could it be? At the most he might check up on me for a couple weeks once school started, then he would let it slide.

"Can you promise Evan won't tell anyone?"

"Yeah, it won't be a problem. I've got enough crap on him to keep him in line." Jase flashed a wicked smile at me. Seeing that look made me happy not to have an older brother.

"You can tell Evan, but you can bet your ass I won't ever let those three catch me alone again." Guess it was my cussing that had him trying to hide a grin.

I started to push myself up, but Jase got a hold of my arm and pulled me up as he stood. It was hard hiding my grimace as abused skin stretched over skinned knees. My body felt more than a little stiff from the frenzied struggle I'd put up.

Jase got a real mad look on his face when he saw my expression, and worried me that he might try to renege on the deal.

"I'll drive you to wherever your parents are." Yep, his voice sounded pretty darn angry.

"You can't. I came into town with my gramps, and he's at the feed store. If he sees you driving up with me he's gonna ask a million questions. I'm fine now. Really. I'll walk back to the store and wait in the truck." There I was. Back to begging.

Jase's lips tightened, making it obvious he didn't like it one bit. His curt nod had me breathing out a sigh of relief, but I'd been a little hasty thinking I'd won this point.

Turning away, I once again began limping back to the feed store. Jase's truck fired to life behind me and to my annoyance he kept a slow pace as he trailed me. At least he stopped before actually getting to the feed store. He parked about a block away, and I could feel his eyes follow me until he was satisfied I'd reached the safety of Gramps' truck.

From that moment on, Jase was my hero. The subject of countless fantasies, where the ending turned out far differently than it actually had. As I grew older I tried to put that silly childhood crush out of my mind.

But as with all heroes, Jase proved to be a hard man to forget.

CHAPTER ONE

Present Day

Pulling about a quarter mile into the woods, I threw my truck into park alongside an old beat-up Ford and flashed a grin over at Ruger. Tongue lolling, body wiggling, my boy was cranked and ready to go. I opened the door and it was a tussle to see whose feet were going to hit the ground first. I won, but by a small margin.

Once freed from the cab, Ruger took off, streaking down the trail, heading off into the deep woods. I followed at a much slower pace, wanting to enjoy the early morning freshness before the heat of the day burned it away. It was a short walk on down to the spring, and I wasn't in any hurry.

My smile widened as delicious adrenaline spiked through my veins at the thought of where this path would take me. Happened every time I made a trip out to

16

Gramps' moonshine still. It was the knowledge of doing something not only illegal but potentially dangerous that fed my high.

I rationalized my thrill with some of Gramps' words of wisdom: *We have a long history of not playin by the rules in our family, might as well be proud of it.* I'm convinced both my parents and Granny cursed the day my granddad shared that little bit of family heritage with me. Lord knows there had been a few times I'd lived up to tradition.

Stepping off the trail into the center of the still site wasn't as dramatic as it sounded. Gramps had followed in the steps of generations of moonshiners and was a master when it came to concealing a working site, or numerous working stills as was the case here.

Several living arbors, made of live saplings growing and anchored to a crude framework, dotted the woods. They'd been constructed to house the workings of each individual still. Walking past each arbor, I noticed most of the fire boxes were cold but a few were still being fed. A clear sign this run of whiskey was about finished.

Finding my gramps was easy. All I had to do was head in the direction of Ruger's excited barks and the quarreling voice of an aged man.

"Hey, Gramps, whatcha up to?"

"Charlotte, call your dog. He's about to lick all this hard earned dirt clean offa' me." His scolding did nothing to hide the affection he felt for Ruger.

"If you're that dirty this early in the day he's doing you a favor." I teased right back. "Looks like you're about through with the latest run of whiskey. Are you going to be tearing down soon and move over to Sow's Bed for the next setup?"

At my casual question a strange look crossed his face. He detached himself from Ruger and turned back to the still he'd been working on. The fire box was no longer being fed under this particular pot. Gramps reached down to pull the plug stick out of the slop arm. Clearly he'd completed the run from this particular still and was getting ready to do a clean out.

"Colin and a few of the boys that's lent a hand over the years are gonna be here directly to help start the tear down on the ones gone cold. The last of the shine will be run off by tonight, and we'll be able to start clean out on 'em tomorrow as long as the pots and caps cool off by then. Probably take a couple days to clear everything out." Gramps had talked while he'd continued working, but now he stood to face me.

"I figured on letting Colin have his pick of the stills for his own use. He's young, but he's worked me long enough to know the ins and outs. Course, he'll have to move them over on his own land, iffin' he even cares to work at makin' shine anymore. I plan on keepin' one for our own personal use. If there are any left, I aim on selling them off to some of the fellers that's been pestering me about wantin' one over the years." He delivered his plans with a pinch of defiance, as if expecting a protest from me.

Okay, I'll admit his announcement certainly painted a surprised look on my face. Don't get me wrong, it thrilled me he was finally going to give it up. Come on, the man was eighty; tough as a pine knot, but still eighty. He should've quit years ago. I knew that. But it still came as a shock to hear he was going to shut down a business that had been in his family for five generations.

"So this is it, huh? No more Copper Moon made by a Donley?" There may have been a smidgen of skepticism in my tone. My dad had opted out of the family moonshine business to raise cattle. When he took a pass on following in his daddy's footsteps it was the beginning of the end of Donley whiskey making. Right now it looked like I was staring the true end square in the eyes.

"Now, ain't sayin' I'll never make shine in the future, Sis. Jest not to sell." Gramps' irrepressible smile was back as he winked at me.

"Lordy, Gramps, you had me worried. For a minute there I thought you were gonna start playing by the rules." I forced a smile.

What was wrong with me? I should have been doing a happy dance instead of feeling all kinds of unsettled. Ever since I been old enough to know about the family secret, I'd known about the dangers Gramps flirted with every day.

But the dangers had never felt real to me. They were what added spice to the illicit excitement I experienced on every trip to one of the sites. More than that, those dangers went hand and foot with the forbidden stories he used to tell me whenever my parents, or Granny, weren't around. Here he was, quitting, and *now* I got antsy? What was up with that?

"What can I do to help?" Best way to work through emotions, according to Gramps, was, of course, work. It was also his answer to boredom, sassin' and tears. Work was a miracle cure-all for anything that might ail a person, according to Gramps.

"Well, Sis, iffin' you wanna help the best thing you can do is run by the feedstore this mornin' and pick up that mineral order I placed yesterday. I'll probably have more help than needed here." He let loose a derisive snort. "You know how those ole' boys go at things. They'll get the work done, shor' 'nuff, but it'll take a lot of storytelling, a lot of lying, and a lot of samplin' the last of the runs. Colin's gonna go with me to make the last few deliveries later tonight, so everything's been taken care of here."

No matter how easy he tried to make it sound, the next few days were going to be rough on him. I also knew the men would cuss, spit, tell jokes *not fit for woman nor child*, and generally make this easier on him than I ever could. But still...

On impulse, I blurted, "Let me go with you to make the deliveries. This is my last chance to be part of a history I'd heard stories about all my life."

I'd never been on a delivery to meet with the different runners. It was a rare client who would show up to collect their merchandise themselves. Most of them sent runners to make the pickups. Anyone brave— or stupid—enough, depending on how you looked at it, to become a runner made big bucks for the risks they faced.

Gramps let out his big booming laugh while shaking his head. "Little girl, I'm already due a butt kickin' when I face your daddy again someday." He stopped laughing and looked as serious as I'd ever seen him. "My boy may not have followed in the footsteps of the men in our family. Still, he used the land that's been the Donleys' for as many generations as the whiskey has. And he made a shor' 'nuff damn good livin'. Jest as generations of Donleys before him did on this here same land. I'm jest as proud of you for makin' your own dreams come through with that jewelry shop of yours."

A sadness settled on him. He seemed to age before my eyes. "I'm ashamed to say you've been stronger than me with the deaths we've been cursed with over the years. I didn't do right by you or the ones we lost."

"Gramps, that's not true." I stepped up to so I could slip an arm around his shoulders to give a little squeeze. Shoulders that felt frailer than I remembered. When had he started to weaken? Had I ignored the changes in him in the hopes of slowing down the rush of time?

"Without you and Granny I'd never have gone on to college after high school. You gave me the push I needed to make something of my life after Mom and Dad died. My shop would've stayed a dream without your support."

"That's jest it, Sis. My Maggie was here to carry both of us when we needed her. When we lost her, I didn't pull my weight. I buried myself with working the moonshine. You're the one who tried to take care of me. Jest like Maggie, being the strong one." Gnarled fingers gently framed my face, and faded blue eyes peered into my misty ones. "I'm too old for all this here foolishness. Time for you to stop fussing over me, and find a good man to fuss over you." Gramps was finished with anything serious.

I did as expected and grinned back. Telling it like it was, we never talked like this. I'd been raised to believe hardships were private matters. Grief was to be shared only among family and loved ones. We were not to wallow in sorrow, or throw ourselves in the grave with those who had passed. We were to show our respect by going on with life, the way they would want us to.

"After tonight I'm officially out of the moonshine business. And, Sis, your daddy never wanted you to have nuthin' to do with the shine. You managed to talk your way into visiting the stills, but that's where it stopped, and where it's gonna stay stopped."

Squashing my disappointment at not being able to go on the delivery, I mustered up a smile in a show of understanding. "Okay, but we're going to celebrate your retirement tomorrow. Don't you dare sell all the Copper Moon tonight. It's only right we commemorate the occasion of your retirement by drinking mass quantities of our family's special recipe." Brushing a kiss on his leathery cheek, I backed up. "I gotta get going. I've got a box full of commissioned pieces that need to be shipped to Brianna before the Post Office closes. I'll run by the feed store right after and pick up those minerals."

"I'll walk you back to your truck. I need to bring another box of quart jars down to catch the last of the runs cookin' off. Besides, I'd hate for you to trip over them big words you like to use on your way back up the hill and me not be there to see it." He snorted at his own joke.

We talked as we made our way back up the hill. Gramps promised he'd have Colin come over in the morning to unload the minerals. When we reached my pickup he opened the door for me. Ruger hopped in first, and I climbed up after.

On impulse I turned to Gramps before he shut my door. "Come for breakfast in the morning, and I'll make your favorite. Biscuits and gravy. You can tell me all the wild foolishness y'all get into today." There was a whisper of pleading in my words.

"Sis, you got yourself a deal." If Gramps heard any hint of concern he didn't let on. He just closed the door, slapped my truck, and walked away with a final wave.

CHAPTER TWO

"Here's the plan." Ruger stared at me with the intensity only a Blue Heeler can achieve. "You stay here, guard our truck. As an extra bonus you become the perfect excuse to escape if Miss Lori corners me and starts in with one of her inquisitions."

I took his tail wag as an indication that the plan met with his approval. Giving his head a final pat, I grabbed the box from the backseat and headed for the Post Office.

Shouldering my way through the door into the lobby, I did a mental fist pump. Miss Lori and her work station were surrounded by several elderly ladies. They were all twittering excitedly. There was a pause in the lively discussion, which was most likely about someone else's business. Heads covered in every shade of old-lady-hair, from the brightest cotton white to something that closely resembled steel wool, swiveled to check me out. Giving a tiny wave, I made my way toward Ben Luther's end of the mail counter.

Having satisfied themselves as to whether I was a crony or the next victim up for dissection—I was definitely the latter—they went back to their meddling session. Small town gossips...*bless their little hearts.*

"Mornin' Char." Ben nodded in greeting as he took control of the box placed in front of him. "Biggest container you've shipped yet. Business must be good." He was politely curious but never pushy.

"Things have been going great. All caught up with my commissions, and I plan on taking a little break for a few weeks." Look at me, all friendly and sharing.

Ben shot a look of mild surprise at me. Not that I went out of my way to be unfriendly, it was just rare for me to share extra information with anyone. But I'd caught the name Jase Rydan coming from the chattering horde at the opposite end of the counter.

Pretty pitiful, when all it took was to hear the man's name and suddenly I'm starting up a conversation as reason to linger. All in the hopes of finding out what the women were buzzing about.

It had been ten years since a twenty-year-old Jase had stepped into that alley and rescued me. From what, I wasn't sure of, even to this day. At the time it had felt sinister on a downhill slide towards horrific. Enough to have me imagining the worst for years and fuel a few nightmares. From that point on I'd had a fascination with all things Jase Rydan.

Leaning closer to Ben across the counter, I quietly whispered, "What's up with Jase Rydan?" Then I did a tiny head jerk in the direction of the gray brigade. I couldn't help thinking, *real subtle, Char.*

Ben causally looked their way, then he too leaned closer to me, like a co-conspirator. "Rumor going around has Jase moving back to Copper Ridge. Know that big house he built, down on the lake, a few years back?"

At my nod of encouragement, he continued, "That's where he's going to live. Seems his uncle, who owns that big construction company over in Rogers, has made Jase a full partner. They're supposed to be opening a branch right here in town, and Jase is going to be the one managing it. Going to be building some big fancy houses on the lakes around here, and down on the river, from what I hear."

"Most of the mommas and grand-mommas are in a tizzy, since he's still unattached and got enough money to burn a wet mule. They're taking his moving back home as a sign he's ready to settle down and raise a family." He nodded at me with a knowing look that said, *Hey, listen up, this is information a single woman like you needs to keep up with.*

Then he asked in an, oh-so-casual voice, "Don't the east side of your land, and your granddaddy's, share a property line with the Rydan ranch? You must see a lot of that family passing on the road and all. Good neighbors to have, if a woman ever needed help for any reason."

"Course, everyone knows you and Evan been good friends for years. People around here," Ben paused to dart a look Miss Lori's way, "always speculated why the two of you didn't take the next step past friendship. Might just be it was the wrong brother." He gave another little nod of, *are you listening?*

Straightening, I gave Ben a brilliant smile. "Oh, hey, Ruger's waiting in the truck for me. I left it running to keep the air going, what with it being so hot already this morning. Guess I better get this finished up and get back out there." Who knew Ruger would be my excuse to escape from a conversation I'd started with Ben and not as a means of getting away from Miss Lori's clutches.

Ben thankfully took the hint and became all business. We finished up quickly and, as I gathered up my change ready to make a break for the door, he made one last parting observation. "There's no shame in a woman going after something she wants in life." He threw in wink for good measure.

Mumbling, "Yes, sir," I made good on my escape. I'm no coward but there are times when the best way to come out the winner is to run.

As I settled behind the steering wheel, I looked over at Ruger. "Buddy, you see me starting up a conversation with anyone at the feed store, do me a favor and bite me."

"Hey, Char. Didn't see you come in. Here for your granddad's mineral order?" Harvey Dubois called across the store to me as I stood checking out the new birdfeeders that had been shelved since the last time I'd been in. Cute birdfeeders were hard for me to resist. Turning, I made my way back to the front of the building where he and his wife, Millie, were checking out customers.

"Yes, sir. Gramps asked me to run by and pick it up for him today." I figured I'd better pay up while there was an opening in front of Harvey. Pulling my checkbook from the back pocket of my denim shorts, I began to do the small talk thing as I wrote. "Something special going on? Y'all seem extra busy today." Good thing Ruger wasn't nearby, otherwise I'd be getting a bite right about now.

"Just a normal Saturday." A lot of satisfaction and pride came through with his answer. "You got your truck backed up to the loading dock?"

"Yes, sir."

"Well, run on back and hunt up Darren, or one of the twins, and let them know you're all set to go." Harvey handed over my receipt and order ticket with a smile, then turned to the next customer in line.

I had always loved the open storage area known as the feed room. Earthy smells assaulted my senses as soon as I entered. The syrupy scent of molasses, in the sweet feeds, competed with the sharp bitterness of the ground-up minerals.

A fine layer of grain dust, from the cracked corn and rolled oats, coated the walls and every support beam throughout the huge space. As I hunted for one of Harvey's boys, I caught glimpses of feline backsides with their flicking cat tails as they disappeared into the towering stacks of feed sacks. They were in search of the mice that always infested feed mills. Ruger was in here somewhere, on his own search and destroy mission against the rodents.

The closest thing we had to a country club was in full swing over in the back corner. It was the main meet-and-greet for all the men in the area, and a bigger gossip center than BettyJo's Cut 'n' Curl. Elders sat on the few chairs that were grouped together, while the rest of the men either leaned against nearby stacked bags of grain or lounged against the wall. A few looked my way and did the head nod of acknowledgment. Doing my own head bob back at the group, I continued my search for one of Harvey's three boys.

Spying the oldest, I waved at him to hold up. "Hey, Darren, your dad said to let you know I'd paid up and you could go ahead and load my truck." I handed over the order ticket.

Darren gave it a brief glance then looked back at me and grinned. "Hope you're not in a hurry. I already have your order stacked but it's gonna be a little bit before I can get to this. The twins are tied up right now too. Promise to put you next in line, though."

"Not a problem." I smiled back then wandered over to where Darren had pointed to my fairly small pile of sacks. It was as good a place as any to wait my turn.

Doing some leaning of my own, I crossed my arms and settled against the wall. Ruger showed up to check on me, then he was off again, happily sniffing out prey to pounce on.

Questions started crowding my head, all of them centered on Jase. If the rumors were true I wondered why Evan hadn't said anything about it the last time he'd stopped by my place.

He'd taken the whole *"watch over Charlotte for me"* order from Jase when we were kids much more seriously than I'd expected him to. Throughout school Evan had kept an eye out for me. He became the proverbial big brother. Since Evan lived only three miles down the road he was also my closest neighbor.

He still lived down the road with his parents, which made sense since he was now the one who ran the vast ranch the Rydan family owned. He'd become a regular visitor when I got out of college and came back home for good. Which made it doubly weird he hadn't told me about his brother.

Maybe it was because any time Evan brought his brother up I acted like it didn't interest me. But I *was* interested. Too much so. That's why I changed the subject every time he brought Jase's name into a conversation. I didn't want Evan running back to Jase and telling him what an enormous crush I had on him. How embarrassing would that be?

But then again, if Jase was moving into his lake house, he would be living close enough to be called a neighbor. That made me wonder if he would start stopping by to be *neighborly*. Bouncing off the wall, as if stuck with a cattle prod, I decided it was time to be a little more productive than indulging in one of my Jase fantasies.

Looking around I found none of the Dubois boys were in sight yet. Since they were apparently still busy, I figured what the heck, I'd help them out by getting a head start on loading the minerals in my truck. Darren had my order in a nice little stack not too far from the loading dock. I mean, really, how hard could it be?

Hands on hips, I sized up the situation. Looked like I could easily pull the top bags off the pile without having to bend over and pick them up off the ground. Those on the ground would be the hardest to load. By the time I got to them Darren, or one of the twins, would be here to finish the job. With my truck backed right up against the dock it was going to be a simple matter of carrying the mineral bags over and dropping them in the bed. Easy-peasy.

Everything was going according to plan, right up to the point where I actually started to slide the fifty-pound sack off the top of the pile. My carefully thought out intentions went to hell, where all good intentions usually ended up.

* * *

Jase Rydan walked alongside his brother, crossing the feed room's concrete floor on their way to the main storefront. They'd come in the back way, as most men did, so they could check who was hanging in the news corner. Evan had come to make some changes to the ranch's standing feed orders, and Jase had come along to keep him company.

Rounding a stack of feed bags, Jase noticed a woman standing several feet away with her back to them. Her thick red hair was caught up in a high ponytail and blazed as if it had its own internal light source. His eyes traveled down her trim form with male appreciation, noting the slight indent before the swell of lush hips.

Those hips were cocked at an angle and had hands planted on them. Denim shorts hugged sweet globes of muscle, and a checkbook sticking out of one of the back pockets seemed to call added attention to the feminine curves. It was hard to move on but he continued his inspection by letting his eyes travel the length of her long tanned legs. One of her sandaled feet was slowly tapping the ground.

Evan started chuckling. "Got something stuck in your eye?"

"Shut-up."

"Don't know who that is, do you?" He was definitely amused about something.

"No. Do you?"

"I'd say so. You've been having me keep an eye on her for the last ten years." Oh, yeah, his brother was definitely laughing at him.

Jase whipped his head around to look at Evan and just as quickly jerked his eyes back to the woman. "Well, I'll be damn. Didn't realize it'd been that long since I'd seen her. How have you managed to keep from going crazy over her?" Jase wondered why the thought bothered him.

He'd seen Charlotte a few times over the last ten years but right now he couldn't remember when the last time was. It had become a habit to ask Evan about her when he was home, but he'd never really thought of her as having grown up. Charlotte had certainly grown up and in all the right places.

"Because she's never been interested. Besides, as protective as you were of her for those first few years, you'd have kicked my ass if I'd made a move."

"You're right. I would have."

Jase turned back to studying Charlotte, this time paying more heed to what she was doing. Even viewing her from the back, he could tell she was concentrating on a problem. He looked beyond her to try and figure out what had her total attention. A small pile of sacks seemed to be what she was contemplating. With a decisive nod she made a move on the stack, and that's when Jase realized she was going to try and pick up one of those fifty-pound bags.

* * *

I was well into my lift on the first bag. All right, it was more of a grab, lift and a wild swing to maintain my balance. In the middle of my turn, I heard, "Wait, I'll take care of that."

The one voice guaranteed to be the last I'd expected had me whirling even faster to get a look at the speaker. Jase arrived just in time for me to slam the mineral sack into his stomach. It wasn't exactly like hitting a brick wall, but close. Guess he must have seen what was heading towards him 'cause he was braced for impact.

I'd been doing a pretty good job handling the minerals until I lost all coordination at hearing Jase. Hammering him was the final tip to my loss of balance. In a bid to keep from following the minerals down to the concrete floor I made a grab for Jase.

There was a sudden expulsion of air from abused lungs followed by a fairly quiet *"Shit."* Then a couple of muscled arms wrapped across my back. It felt like they were trying to squeeze the breath out of me by pressing me up against the type of male chest that caused night sweats in women of any age.

I might've held on a tad too long but those steel bands didn't appear to be in a hurry to turn loose, either. I had a good excuse for clinging. I was stunned by what had happened. What finally penetrated my stunnedness was the explosion of laughter coming out of my savior's companion. Embarrassment had me scrambling, trying to untangle myself from Jase's arms. Arms that tightened for a fraction of a second before unwinding.

His masculine hands slid upwards to grasp my shoulders firmly, helping to steady me as I regained my balance.

"What do you think you're doing?" I hissed out the question in as low a whisper as I could manage and still be heard. Meanwhile my eyes did a swift recon of the feed room to see just how many people managed to catch the show. When my look settled back on Jase, those Rydan gray eyes of his held a gleam of amusement.

"Getting the crap knocked out of me would be my first guess." Taking a step back, he released me.

"Don't be such a princess. I had everything under control. If you'd stayed out of the way you wouldn't have gotten hit." I should have slapped a hand over my mouth at that point, before I had one slapped up the back of my head.

Not that Jase would ever hit a woman, but I darn sure was giving him probable cause. Unfortunately my "princess" comment not only had his eyes narrowing but had set his brother off on another round of howling laughter.

"Yeah, Jase, stop being such a princess." Evan managed to sputter between guffaws.

Jase didn't take his eyes off me as he flipped a finger up at his brother and told him to can it.

Evan didn't seem too worried as he struggled to get out a, "You got it, princess. I'll go check on that delivery and give you two some space. By the way, I'm handing guard duty back over to ya, big brother. Looks like you're off to a great start this morning."

I could hear him chuckling as he walked away. That made it official. It wasn't going to matter if anyone saw what happened or not. Evan would be drinking free off this story for at least a month.

And what the heck did he think he was doing? Talking like he was going to hand me off to Jase. He made it sound like I was some kind of property the two brothers could just pass back and forth at will. Deciding to ignore Evan's parting comment, I sucked it up and offered as sincere an apology as I was capable of at that moment. I also tried to *politely* convey the message that he could leave now. "Look, that was bad of me. Thanks for coming to my rescue. I promise to not attack any more innocent bystanders with feed bags. You can safely leave. I'm good."

"I'm not so innocent, so don't worry about it," he said with a wink. "How about once I finish loading your truck, then *you* can safely leave." Striking gray eyes continued to stare into mine, while his whiskey smooth words raised goose bumps down the middle of my back.

Wait...What? Did he just say he was sticking around? Bad idea. Really bad idea. No telling what other stupid stunts I might pull, or dumb remarks I'd make, if he hung around long enough.

Ignoring my stuttering protest, Jase plucked the sack off the ground as though it were filled with feathers and placed it back on the stack. Then, gathering two bags at a time, he headed out to start loading my truck.

I was left staring at his retreating backside. And what a beautiful backside it was to watch. Tight jeans stretched over one heck of a nice butt. The kind of butt that made my fingers twitch with the desire to reach out and grab a couple hands full of muscled gluteus maximus.

The thump of the bags hitting the bed of my truck snapped me back to attention. While I'd been off in la-la land, Jase had turned and was walking back in my direction. I was now staring dreamily at Jase's package.

In a panic, I checked to see if he'd noticed where and what I seemed to be fixated on. Oh, yeah, he'd definitely noticed, judging by his one raised eyebrow and the crooked slant to his grin. "I think I've just been visually violated."

"What? No...I wasn't staring at your...I was just staring into space, and you happened to walk into the space with your...anyway, I was not staring at your...you know." Yep, not only was I staring at his package, I was gesturing at it as well. Jeez, could someone please explain to me why I either needed to be saved whenever Jase was around or I ended up looking and sounding like the village idiot?

Husky laughter greeted my convoluted explanation. "Tell you what, Charlotte. You stare at anything you want on me, as long as I get to return the favor and stare at anything I want on you." Jase didn't wait for a response. He simply gathered up another couple of bags and headed for my truck.

Once I managed to peel my jaw off the floor—did Jase Rydan just flirt with me?—I wisely kept my mouth shut and my gaze averted.

Jase had a habit of always calling me by my full name. It sent goose bumps dancing down my arms. Whenever we'd crossed paths in the last ten years, it was always Charlotte, never Char. And the goosies always appeared.

While Jase dropped the last of the mineral bags in the bed of my truck, I looked around and whistled for Ruger. I wanted grab my dog, say a quick thank you, and make a hasty retreat. Running away was apparently how I rolled today. The feel of rough callused fingers clasping my chin stopped me mid-whistle.

Jase turned my face up to his. "Next time you pucker those lips around me I hope it's for something better than whistling for a dog."

Ruger's compact body careening into my legs was a welcome distraction. He was wired from his hunt and wanted to share his enthusiasm with not only me, but apparently Jase as well. He'd wriggled his way over to him and was shamelessly begging for attention. Not how Ruger normally reacted to strangers. He was usually very picky about who he allowed to touch me. Instead he was treating Jase like his long lost pal. Even went so far as to entice Jase into give him a good back rubbing. Was it wrong to envy my dog?

"Thank you. You really shouldn't have bothered." *Really...reeeaaalllly* shouldn't have bothered, was more like it.

"Charlotte." Jase straightened from rubbing on Ruger and gave me a look I didn't know how to interpret.

"Uh-huh?" When he said my name like that, I wanted to purr.

"I have a feeling I'm going to be bothered a lot by you now that I'm home to stay." With that he turned and walked away.

CHAPTER THREE

"This is bullshit, old man! I've offered you damn good money for those mash recipes for the last year. Now you tell me you plan on quittin' making shine, and still won't sell to me?" Billy Wayne's question escalated to the shrill notes of a petulant child. He screeched at the elderly Donley, like doing so was going to impress him with the seriousness of the matter.

Problem was, not much about BW impressed Jim Donley. The old man sat on a stump in the middle of woods so eternally dark it would've been impossible to see if it weren't for the row of floodlights fastened to the roll-bar of BW's truck. They lit up the clearing like an outdoor arena.

The softer glow of the lantern sitting on the ground next to Jim gave a much more personal light to the weed-choked ground surrounding him. He looked as comfortable on that chunk of wood as he would've resting in his recliner at home.

Taking his time, while BW ranted, Jim reached into his hip pocket to pull out a can of Prince Albert, popped the lid and then sat it carefully on the ground beside him. As though there was all the time in the world he slid two fingers into his shirt pocket, withdrawing a pack of papers.

After carefully pulling one thin white sheet from the package he returned the rest to his pocket. Reaching down to pick up the can, he began building a cigarette with care, paying no more mind to BW than he would a flitting gnat.

"You're not screwing me on this deal! I've got plans and they're only gonna get bigger." Spittle was beginning to fly with each word out of BW's mouth. Not a pretty sight.

In his agitation, BW paced back and forth in front of Donley. His shadow danced on the trees at the edge of the clearing like demented demons.

"Have your order ready to pick up, but that's the last of it. Your plans mean less than a popcorn fart to me. You think I don't know who you've been buying and running all this shine for lately? You think jest 'cause he has you running whiskey all over the country it makes you part of it? Hell, boy, you're only worth anything to him for as long as your daddy's sheriff. It's the fact that cops won't pull you over that makes you so damn popular with all them fellers you run shine for." The old moonshiner spat off into the dark. "Only way you're ever gonna become a part of anything is if I sell you my recipes. And that, boy, ain't never gonna happen." The deep country drawl rolled out of Donley's mouth, slow and smooth. Even at eighty, age and hand-rolled smokes hadn't weakened a voice that had been charming residents of the surrounding area for decades.

But to BW it was the sound of doom to plans of making a name for himself in the world of illegal moonshine. He'd been contacted a couple years ago, and the offer to buy and run Donley's shine, for a certain person, had been too good to pass up. He'd already been a runner for a few different moonshiners. To get paid to not only run the whiskey but also buy it, now that was a sweet package deal. It gave him ideas. Big ideas.

Donley was the best when it came to making shine, and this particular buyer said Donley would never sell to him directly; that's where BW came in. Now all that money and all his huge dreams were slipping out of his hands. Worse than that, his mouth had overloaded his ass. He'd started making promises to the kind of people you don't double cross or lie to. As he thought about what was going to happen if he couldn't get the old man to change his mind, he went a little crazy.

Donley's calm in the face of his screaming fit was beginning to make him feel real small and worthless. His own daddy was a master at doing that to him. He'd be damned if he was gonna let this piece of white-trash ruin his plans or treat him like he was some kind of dog shit. Something to be scraped off his boots, then walked away from.

Maybe it was time to rethink this. Come at it from a different angle. BW might not have been the sharpest tool in the shed but when it came to self-preservation he could get creative. As his mind ticked through options, his pacing slowed until he was at a complete standstill. He just needed to use the right incentive to convince the old bastard to see the wisdom in looking at things in a whole new light.

Striding up to Donley, he took a wild kick at the tobacco can, sending it flying toward the trees. BW stuck a finger in Donley's bony chest, poking hard. His voice lowered, with a bit of a snarl to it. "I'm gonna make this simple and give you two options. First one is real easy: you smarten up, sell me what I want, walk away with some extra money, and we're both happy as shit.

"Second option is gonna be a lot harder on that pretty little granddaughter of yours. Accidents happen. Jest look at how her momma and daddy died. Now it would be a real shame if Char had her own freak accident. Might not kill her the first time, she'd just suffer...a lot. But a family as accident prone as yours, hell, wouldn't surprise me if the next freaky accident killed her."

At the threat, Donley proceeded to do some growling of his own. "Boy, you don't want to threaten me, or my granddaughter. I'll see you roastin' in hell before I let you get your hands on anything that belongs to my family."

"Fuck you! Don't call me *boy*. I'll do it...I'll have
that little bitch screaming if you don't get me those
recipes. It won't just be me, neither. I've got a partner,
and I ain't talkin' 'bout Robbie. It's the kind of partner
that don't take no for an answer. He's been promised a
steady supply of your shine—not someone else's—
yours. And by God he's gonna get it." He ground his
finger into Donley's chest.

At the sound of his name, Robbie sat up straighter
in the front seat of the truck. He'd been watching the
show from the comfort of the cab, but when he heard his
name his ears perked up. He started paying closer
attention to the goings on.

What had started out as plain-ass funny, watching
BW holler at the old bastard, was turning in to a *shit's
about to happen* moment. Everyone knew BW had a
crazy temper, and the old man was just asking for it if he
didn't shut up pretty damn quick. Last thing he wanted
to do tonight was help BW cover up another one of his
screw-ups. Beating up on a man that old was going to be
hard to hide.

Donley pushed BW's finger off as he rose to his
feet. "You ain't got shit for a partner. Now let me tell
you what's gonna happen, *boy*. You're gonna walk your
ass on over to your truck, climb in, and drive away.
Leave the shine. I ain't selling to ya. Then you and me,
well, we're gonna forget this here ever happened. The
reason you're leaving is because if you don't I'm going
to your daddy, our fine sheriff, who just happens to be in
the middle of a hell of a race to keep his job. When I get

to your daddy, I'm gonna present him with a list of dates, times, and amounts of shine you've bought off me over the years. Then, as an added kick in the nuts, I'm handing over time-stamped pictures that show you paying for the booze then loading it in the bed of your truck, *boy*."

BW snapped. It was as though a switch had been flipped. Manic rage took possession as a beefy fist flashed making contact with a stubborn old thrust-out chin. "I said, don't call me *boy*!"

Caught unawares, Jim's head snapped back, causing him to take an awkward step to the side in an effort to stay standing. BW followed to deliver another blow to the old man's gut. No thought processing was going on in any brain cells; just rage and an overwhelming desire to pound the old man's opposition into the ground.

Doubling over, blackness creeping in, Jim struggled to maintain some sense of awareness, determined to fight back as long as he was able. What was left of his consciousness nagged at him that there was something on the ground he could use, if he could just remember what.

There, a large branch was lying next to the stump he'd been sitting on. What was intended as a quick lunge for a weapon, in reality turned out to be more of a hand stretching slowly toward hope. Age's degeneration of a once strong body, and the shock of two debilitating blows, took their measure, putting an end to any chance he had of saving himself.

He never saw the double-handed fist that crashed between his shoulder blades driving him towards the ground and stump. In the final moments all his brain registered was an explosion of light, a fade to darkness, then nothing.

Cussing, and a persistent pulling on BW's arm, slowly began to penetrate the murderous fog that had overwhelmed him. Twisting his body to take a swing at whoever was jerking on him, his knuckles landed a glancing blow, sliding off a sweaty jaw. A string of "Oh shit, oh shit" was the next thing to worm its way into his consciousness.

Going perfectly still, he blinked a few times, as though coming out of a trance. Fists tightly clinched and upright, BW was ready to rain more havoc on any object that moved. It took him a minute to pull it together and focus on a freaked-out Robbie.

Slowly, looking down at his feet, he saw the too-still form of Donley. There was a widening pool of blood on top of the stump against which his head rested. The reasons for all the "oh shits" started to make sense.

"Shit, man, what are you gonna do? He's dead! Shit, he's dead! You killed ol' man Donley!" Robbie's screeching was ear-shattering.

BW slowly shook his head. He blinked a few times, clearing the last of the madness out of his system. "Shut up! I can't think with you running around screaming like a girl. Just shut the fuck up. Give me a minute to think. Besides, I didn't kill him. Don't say I killed him. It's his own damn fault he's dead. Yeah, he started it with all his

'*I ain't selling,*' and '*no more moonshine,*' crap. All I did was give him a couple little taps. Tripping over his own feet is what killed the ol' bastard. I didn't kill him. He killed himself." BW had started pacing again, while rubbing a shaky hand across a damp forehead.

Robbie stopped moaning about the dead man to stare at BW in disbelief. The word "typical" came barreling into his thoughts.

In all the time he'd known BW, which was all his life, nothing had ever been his fault. Yeah, hearing him blame Donley for his own death shouldn't have come as such a shocker. But this time BW's daddy wasn't going to be able to pull his ass out of the fire like he had all of his twenty-seven years on this Earth.

Robbie had no intention of ending up the sucker who took the fall for this. Out-right murder, when it stared you in the face, wasn't the kind of wild times he'd hung around BW for all these years.

"What're you gonna do?" Robbie asked warily. He kept saying "*you*" and BW kept saying "*we*." *Shit!*

"Nothin'. We don't have to do nothin'. It's an accident. He was out here messing around at night in the woods and tripped. Everyone knows Donley sells shine, and this is one of a bunch of different places he uses to move the stuff. They'll think he was out here to meet someone, but that don't mean they'll think it's us. Hell, I didn't tell anyone about meeting Donley tonight." BW turned narrowed eyes on Robbie. "Did you?"

"Hell no! I didn't tell nobody, BW." The sour smell of his own fear-induced sweat stung Robbie's nose.

"Good, that's good. All we gotta do is make sure we ain't left nothing of ours around here." BW started looking around, wanting to make sure the scene looked like nothing more than a spot where an accidental death had taken place.

Robbie stood frozen in place, not making any effort to canvas the surroundings for anything that could possibly lead back to them. A terrible thought came to him, "What about those files Donley was talking about? What if he's got all that shit he claimed to have?"

"Fuuuucccckkk! Can you not shut up for five minutes and just do what the hell I tell you? He was lying, you know that old bastard didn't have no way to take pictures and he sure as shit weren't smart enough to keep records." BW didn't even buy his own assertion on that last point but he wasn't letting on to Robbie. Leastways not until he was sure there was something to worry about.

"Now go find that can I kicked. I'm gonna check his truck to make sure there's nothing in there that points to him having a meeting with me tonight." He headed over towards the old Ford, planning on doing a thorough search. BW prayed to whatever dark god who would listen that there weren't any files around to point to him.

Robbie slowly began a search of the ground around the stump then off in the direction he'd seen the can fly. He kept his eyes averted from the crumpled form as much as possible. A quiet litany of curses flowed between trembling lips as he scoured the clearing's floor.

When he neared the closest trees, he looked up to gage how far he was from the stump. As his head came up he noticed something in his peripheral vision. Something that looked foreign. Something that sure as hell didn't belong on a tree in the middle of the woods.

Dread had him heading in the new direction to check it out. A sickness began to swell in his belly and slowly worked its way into his throat choking him, making it difficult to get words out around the knot. "BW, you need to come look at this."

"Dammit, I'm busy over here. Just get the can then help me search this truck. No, wait, check Donley's pockets, see if there's anything in them that shouldn't be." BW didn't even glance up as he gave out orders. He was busy searching the glovebox.

"Man, I'm serious, you gotta see this." A calmness had come over Robbie. A stillness not related to relief but more of an acceptance that nothing was going to be all right from this point on. His half-formed ideas to bolt, so BW couldn't involve him any further, vanished. For better or worse—and probably a hell of a lot worse—he was trapped into doing whatever it took to cover this shit up.

Whether it was the difference in the tone of Robbie's voice, or just pure frustration at not having orders followed, BW jerked back out of the truck to glare in Robbie's direction. He started stomping his way over to where the other man stood, staring not at the ground, as expected, but at the tree in front of him.

"What is so damn important? We gotta get this cleaned up so we can get the hell outta..." His words trailed off as he finally got close enough to see what Robbie had his eyes locked on.

BW stared in disbelief. There, strapped to a tree, was one of the best black-flash game cameras on the market. Calm acceptance was not in BW's checklist of emotions though, and when the explosion came it was spectacular. As the screaming, cussing, and tree kicking commenced, Robbie backed slowly out of the way.

"Guess that answers the question about whether he was bluffin' or not." Robbie knew the minute the words left his mouth it was the wrong thing to say.

BW spun, nailing him with a glare from red-rimmed eyes. "Take that fuckin' camera down and go search that body like you were told." He stomped back to the old man's truck to finish his own search.

Hurrying to the tree, Robbie began to release the straps holding the game camera. His mind was reeling with the implications of his find. Looked like old Donley wasn't as stupid as BW thought. And if Donley had pictures, he sure as hell had written records. Robbie didn't think his name would be on any of the files, but his face was gonna be front and center, recorded every time he'd accompanied BW to help load the shine.

After he got the camera down he decided to take a look around to see if there were any more scattered around the clearing. Eyeballing the distance from the stump to where the camera had been located, he estimated it at about forty feet. Taking a circular route around the clearing, he found two more cameras.

This was bad, real bad. No chance there weren't some damn good shots of the two of them meeting with the ol' moonshiner. Dread at having to tell BW about the extra cameras slowed his trek back over to the body.

Robbie had been a hunter all his life; death wasn't anything new to him. But the dead man wasn't some animal he'd killed and was going to brag about to the boys at the bar. This husk had been a living, breathing person thirty minutes ago. A man he'd known all his life. Donley might not have been a pillar of the community but he was a well-known figure who was going to be missed. Those staring eyes seemed to be looking straight at him with accusation as he went through the dead man's pockets.

But if he was to tell the truth, at this point he was more scared of BW than the dead body he was pilfering. There was no telling what BW was going to be willing to do to cover this up. Friendship meant nothing if the choice whether to save his own hide or throw a friend to the wolves had to be made.

Finding nothing of significance in the old man's pockets, Robbie gathered up the cameras with relief. He was happy to be able to get away from those accusing eyes. Hearing mumbled swear words coming from inside the old Ford was a clear tip-off to Robbie that BW wasn't finding anything in the vehicle. BW backed out while double checking to make sure the truck didn't look like it had just been thoroughly rifled through.

Robbie was the first thing he spotted when turning around. The bundle of cameras in his arms was the second. Lips compressed in a tight line, BW just jerked his head towards the stack of cardboard boxes containing the shine.

Silently they loaded the boxes in the concealed compartment built into the bed of the truck. When finished, they climbed in BW's truck. Both of them were more than ready to escape from this nightmare, for the moment, at least.

As the duo drove away there was only one witness left to the crime that had been committed: a small dented can at the edge of the woods, where it had been kicked and forgotten.

Robbie maintained an uneasy silence, afraid to ask the million and one questions making his head hurt and stomach riot. He was pretty sure BW was spending the silent drive coming up with a plan.

That was a terrifying concept. BW was as deadly as a cornered copperhead right now. Whatever he came up with was going to have Robbie ass-deep, smack-dab in the middle.

When BW started chuckling, Robbie swung incredulous eyes to stare at him. What the hell could be so damn funny?

"I've got a plan." BW made his announcement after a few more snickers.

Robbie didn't reply. He was too busy wondering if this was going to be the time when BW finally got him killed or tossed in prison.

CHAPTER FOUR

Leaning against the counter, I stared out the kitchen window wondering what was holding Gramps up this morning. He should have been here at least an hour ago.

Sleeping-in was an unknown concept. Granny used to tease that he liked to get up at the *butt crack of dawn*. He would look puzzled, scratch his chin then ask, "When'd you change your name to Dawn?" She'd always roll her eyes, call him "a crazy ol' coot." But then she'd grin at him with a sparkle in those same eyes she'd just rolled. Man, I missed her.

The promised breakfast should have been enough incentive to get him here at sunrise. Add the fact that even though I hadn't come right out and said anything about being worried, Gramps knew, and he wouldn't leave me hanging.

Heaving a sigh, I pushed away from the counter, telling myself to chill out. I grabbed the pan of biscuits in one hand and the platter of sausages in the other.

Decided I might as well put them in the oven to stay warm. At least I hadn't made the gravy yet. That was one thing that would be hot and fresh.

I was mystified why the thought of him shutting the still down was freaking me out. It would be one less thing I'd have to worry about when it came to him. Maybe I'd finally be able to convince Gramps to move in with me. I snorted at the absurdity of the notion. Talk about your long shots.

He'd loved my grandmother with a devotion that began on the day they met. That love was still going strong, despite the fact Granny had passed two years ago. I'd been trying to get Gramps to move in ever since, but he was having none of it. He stated he'd been born and raised in that house, and his Maggie had loved the life they had built together under its roof. There was no way he was going to abandon it now she was gone. Said, "Where the heart was, the body stayed."

Giving up on him showing without a reminder, I reached for my cell to give him a call. Each ring of the phone reminded me of other times I'd tried to reach him without any luck. Gramps' stubborn refusal to get a cell phone had been one of the few serious arguments the two of us had had, and more than once. He'd tell me he'd lived this long without being tied to a phone and he dang sure didn't plan on being tied to one for the rest of the time he had left. Well, damn it, this was a prime example of why he needed a cell. And he was going to hear it from me again.

What if something happened yesterday? Stories about the dangers moonshiners faced in the past came to mind. Gramps loved to tell stories about the good-old-days of moonshine, and the role our family played, right in the thick of it. I remembered them all. Which wasn't necessarily a good thing. One thing for sure, I couldn't hang around the house waiting for him to show up.

Collecting my keys from the bowl on the counter, I hurried out the back door, Ruger right on my heels. Once in the truck I figured I'd make one more call, this time to Colin's cell. Thank the lord he was fifty years younger than Gramps and believed in living in the twenty-first century.

"Yep, what can I do ya for?" Colin's slow twang and twisted greeting never failed to bring a smile.

"Colin, this is Char. Have you seen or heard from my gramps this morning? He had me pick up some feed yesterday. He was gonna call you to come help unload. It's already eight and I've not seen or heard a thing from him."

"I ain't seen him since I helped load up his ol' Ford to make a run to deliver some...uh, you know...that stuff he needed deliverin'. I didn't go with him last night, and I'm not real shor' exactly where he was plannin' on goin' with it." I could hear the apology in his voice for not being any help.

"Gramps told me you were going with him to make the delivery." This was so not sounding good. "What happened?"

"It all started when Dave got drunker than Cooter Brown. He was stumblin' around, tellin' one of his big stories, flingin' his arms every which a way. Ya know how he can't say nuthin' without making a show out of it."

I also knew there was no hurrying Colin once he started explaining the why of something. Cradling my cell between cheek and shoulder I fired up my truck and put it in gear to head on over to Gramps'.

"We're all hootin' and eggin' him on. He starts getting down to show us just how him and Ida go at it when they're wheelbarrowin'." Colin had to stop and guffaw a second before he could go on. "He drops to his knees planning on demonstratin' how Ida looked when he had ahold of her legs—"

"Wait, wait. What the heck is *wheelbarrowing*?" Dang it, I just had to ask.

The sudden silence on the other end was my first clue Colin was so caught up in his story he'd forgot who he was sharing it with. My question was no doubt a rude reminder.

"Mmmm...I can't rightly say."

Liar.

"Anyway, Dave didn't ever finish whatever he was gonna show us 'cause when he dropped to his knees he landed on that broke mason jar. Stuck a big ol' piece of glass in so far Jim ended up trying to dig it out with his guttin' knife."

"What was a broken mason jar doing lying around?" What the hell had gone on yesterday?

"Dave dropped his shine while he was flinging his arms around, when he started in on his story." Colin sounded a touch exasperated. I wasn't sure if it was because he thought the answer should've been obvious or because I kept interrupting him.

This looked like it could go in circles for a while. Time to get back to the point. "Colin, what does any of this have to do with you not going with Gramps?" I honestly tried to not come off sounding pissy.

"That's what I'm tryin' to tell ya, Char. Your granddaddy couldn't dig the glass out it was so deep. Since we were the only two what was still sober, I had to take Dave home. That's why Jim went on the run by himself." Now he was the one sounding put out because I wasn't understanding. "I begged your granddaddy to let me make the run. Told him he'd be better at taking Dave home to Ida, but he wasn't havin' none of it." Colin sounded down right mournful.

Now *that* I could understand. It was bound to have been plain ugly when Colin showed up with a drunk Dave. A drunk Dave who needed to be taken to the county hospital Emergency Room. Ida was known to have a sharp tongue at the best of times.

"Jim said the feller he was meetin' had to have some things explained to him. Told me he was gonna mention a certain insurance policy he'd been keepin' for years." From the way Colin stressed *insurance policy,* he knew what Gramps had been talking about as well as I did.

Backwoods country didn't always mean hayseed stupid. When Gramps had taken over the running of the stills he'd started keeping records. His insurance policy. The one time I'd asked where they were he'd told me not to worry, and if I ever needed them to just go to the heart of the whiskey and poke around. Then he'd laughed and said it was a wonder I hadn't found them when I was a kid.

Gramps thinking he might have to bring up the insurance policy gave me a definite chill. Why would he think that was necessary unless there was some danger involved with this particular customer?

"I'm heading over to his house right now to make sure he's not outside fiddling with something and time simply got away from him. Did he mention anything about heading back to the still after the deliveries last night?" I told myself that in all probability he more than likely spent the rest of the night with his cronies, camped out at the still. He was just getting around a tad late this morning.

"I'll call some of the boys that were workin' with us yesterday and ask if he showed back up last night." Colin sounded like he was beginning to catch a case of my unease. "As soon as I know something I'll ring ya back."

What little time I'd spent on the phone was all the time needed to drive to Gramps' house. Not seeing his truck anywhere in the yard was a dead giveaway he wasn't there.

"Colin, wait, don't hang up! I've made it to his house and his truck's not here. I'm going to run in to see if it looks like he came home last night." I was breathless from my sprint to the house and growing anxiety. My hurried search confirmed my suspicions that Gramps had never returned last night.

"Char, now don't worry none. We'll find him. If none of the boys have seen him, I'll start checking his delivery spots. It'd be just like that ol' truck of his to break down out in them woods. We're gonna figure this out, girl." His firm assertion was encouraging. Just not much.

"I'm going with you. If nobody's seen or heard from him since yesterday, you come straight to my house, and pick me up. You hear me?" My hard voice left no doubt as to how serious I was about helping with the search.

Colin's heavy sigh was easy to hear through the phone. "I'm not likin' it, but I'll come get you."

A cloud of dust churned behind my truck as I pulled up to my house. There was a truck already sitting in the drive but it wasn't Colin's. And the long stretch of masculine perfection leaning against its side definitely wasn't Colin's shorter, stockier frame.

Slamming out of my truck, I headed in my visitor's direction. "What are you doing here?"

"And good morning to you, too, sunshine." Jase smiled at me in lazy amusement. Straightening, he prowled towards me. Really, there was no other way to describe his loose limbed stroll.

His good humor in the face of my brusque question caused me to pause and try for a less rude choice of words. My heart went through its normal little "Yippee!" routine. It preformed one whenever Jase was near. But this time it just pissed me off that I would even notice his manstud perfection. I'd a lot more serious matters to concentrate on than lusting after Jase.

"I didn't mean to be so blunt, but I'm expecting someone shortly. You caught me by surprise. Is there something I can help you with?" That came out better. I made nice while at the same time letting him know I was busy. At least I hoped that's how it sounded.

"Evan was on his way over to invite you to a cookout Mom's planning. I volunteered to come in his place. Apparently my moving back is cause for celebration." His derisive tone and slight grin was an invitation to join in the self-mockery, but he switched gears before I came up with a reply.

"It's been a while since I've lived here but I don't remember everyone leaving their front door standing wide open." He seemed to be watching for my reaction.

My confusion must have shown on my face.

"Your front door. It was open when I got here. Looked like you might have left in a hurry. Considering the way you just drove up, you're returning in the same hurry. Is there a problem, Charlotte? Does it have anything to do with the person you're expecting to show up?" He asked his questions with a hard voice. His tone left no doubt that if there was going to be a problem with my company, he was more than willing to take care of it.

Jase had been closing in on me the whole time he'd been talking, until he now stood only a few inches in front of me. The man had no concept of personal space. My body was a big fat traitor, getting all tingly just because he was invading mine.

This was ridiculous. Why in the world did Jase think he had any right to concern himself with my problems? Surly to God he understood that Evan was only messing around yesterday at the feed store when he turned guard duty over to him. If he thought Evan was being serious, he could get that notion right out of his head. I didn't need anyone to guard me.

"No, there's no problem. Colin's on his way over and we're heading out as soon as he gets here." I should have stopped there. I intended to stop there. My mouth had other plans. "Gramps was supposed to come by this morning. I've not seen him and he's not at his house. Colin knows a few places to look, so we're going to check them out." Why was I telling him this? When had I turned into Chatty Cathy?

The sound of a vehicle approaching thankfully shut me up. We both turned to check out who the new arrival was. Spying Colin's truck had me huffing out a sigh of relief. Jase was simply going to have to come back some other time to talk about this party his mom was planning. Right now I had an AWOL grandfather to track down.

Rushing around to the driver's door I reached for the handle at the same time Colin was pushing the door open to climb out. He looked surprised when he recognized who was standing in my drive. He called out a greeting to Jase before turning back to me. "Sorry, Char, but none of the boys have seen or heard from him since yesterday evenin'. Shor' wish you'd wait here and let me do the lookin'." Worry lines were etched around his mouth and across his forehead.

"I'm going with you, no arguments." I turned to explain to Jase he would have to drop by later. He was right behind me. For a big guy he could certainly move quietly.

"Colin's right, you need to stay here." Jase didn't even look at me after telling me to stay put. It was like I'd been given my orders, dismissed, and his focus moved to Colin. "I'll drive, you can let me know where we're headed."

Unbelievable. That quickly, Jase thought he was taking charge. I hated to burst his bubble but he wasn't invited on this little hunting trip. And he sure as heck wasn't telling me what to do.

"I'm sorry, Mr. Rydan, I missed the part where someone put you in charge of this search, or even asked you to come with us. As for you *thinking* you can tell me what I can or can't do, it's not going to happen. You're not the boss of me." I stood my ground but inside I cringed. *You're not the boss of me?* I sounded like a six year old. Change that to I sounded like a bitch, who sounded like a six year old.

"You can call me Mr. Rydan all you want, Charlotte, but the minute you made the decision to tell me your grandfather was missing you were asking for my help. Now, if you insist on going with us I won't stop you, but understand, I think it's a big mistake. If you want to get this search started I suggest you get in the truck, because as of right now you're wasting time." Steel laced his voice.

Colin hadn't even questioned his directive. He'd simple headed for the passenger side of Jase's truck. When I began my quarreling at Jase, Colin stopped in his tracks. Right now he looked like he was at a tennis match. His head bounced back and forth between Jase and me.

It was my turn to serve, and I had nothing. Both men were staring at me, and I couldn't think of anything remotely smart to say. So I did the only thing I could. I walked over to his truck—might I say *fancy* truck— opened the back door, called for Ruger—the little deserter was standing right beside Jase—and followed my dog onto the backseat. If I was childishly happy Ruger was leaving dirty paw prints all over the beige leather seat, I kept it to myself.

CHAPTER FIVE

I wasn't sulking in the backseat. No, sir. Every time Jase asked how I was doing, I answered him with, "Fine." Maybe that was the female equivalent of "Screw you," but I figured he didn't know, so we were all good.

To be fair to Jase, he didn't rub my capitulation in my face. No gloating. No little snide remarks. Nope. He adjusted his plans and let my—admittedly tiny—show of defiance slide. Which was, in its own way, slightly infuriating. I consoled myself with the reminder that I'd made it into the truck and had not been left at home to wait as he'd originally wanted.

Also had to admit the man was fully invested in finding my granddad. Jase had even called Evan to have him send a couple of his ranch hands out, one to my place and one to stay at Gramps' house, in case he showed up at either place.

I felt on the wrong side of dumb for not thinking about that myself. It was obvious Jase was used to handling emergencies. When one made an appearance he handed out orders he expected to be followed. Unfortunately, following orders wasn't one of my favorite things to do. But I sure seemed to do a lot of it when Jase was around.

I was beginning to think having Jase as a neighbor was going to be a hard road to travel if he kept showing up at my house with invites and offers of help. Scratch that; it was going to become a serious problem for me. Because through the years, a childhood crush had grown into a woman-sized obsession.

Luckily, I hadn't reached the stalker stage...yet. Then again, if I had too many more examples of his bossiness, it might just cure me. Keep me from making a fool of myself by joining the herd of females who would be vying for his attention.

Colin turned to check on me for about the hundredth time since getting in the truck. My smiles to reassure him were on autopilot.

When we'd first started out, Jase questioned him closely about exactly when was the last time anyone had seen my granddad. Colin had looked at me with a bit of desperation as to how much he could say about the still and the load of whiskey granddad was supposed to deliver last night. I'd just shrugged my shoulders, as much at a loss as to what we could clue Jase in on as he was. Right there was one big drawback in having Jase help hunt for Gramps. What if when we found him, he still had all the moonshine? That would not be good for any of us.

It wasn't that Jase probably didn't realize what Gramps had been up to last night. Heck, anyone that had grown up around here would know what the deal was. But it was like having a crazy aunt you kept in the attic; everyone knew it, but no one ever mentioned her. Same went for a moonshiner for a granddad. You didn't talk to anyone about it unless they were directly involved. Jase was about to end up knee deep in a business I wanted to keep him miles away from.

Yeah, Colin and I both had really dropped the ball on that one. The best we could hope for was the delivery had been made and it was afterward that Gramps' truck developed problems. I refused to allow myself to formulate any other scenario for why my granddad had not made it home last night.

The road we were on made a goat track look like a highway. The constant tossing around had me hanging onto the "oh, shit" bar above the window. I'd even started to feel guilty about the claw marks Ruger was leaving on the buttery soft seat. I pulled him on my lap as best I could to try and save the leather some wear. Of course, that meant my bare legs were taking a beating from his claws. The last thing on my mind was the sundress I'd been wearing this morning when we set out on our search.

The trees that crowded both sides of the path seemed to be thinning. Ahead, the small clearing that Colin said we were looking for appeared. He'd been pretty creative as to why Gramps would've been in such a deserted place at night when he'd directed Jase to this spot.

There wasn't a doubt in my mind that Jase knew exactly why my granddad had been out in the boonies last night. No way was he buying the scouting for deer and wildlife by setting up game cameras story. It was a long time before any kind of hunting season would be open.

At least Jase hadn't called Colin a bald faced liar. Personally, I thought it was dang creative. Better than anything I would've come up with.

Colin's sharp inhalation was my first clue that this spot in the woods was going to be different to the last two we'd been at. Pushing forward to get a better look crushed Ruger against the seat in front of me. He promptly let me know he didn't appreciate it and wiggled off my lap. I let him go, eager to catch a glimpse of whatever had caught Colin's attention.

The back bumper and tailgate of Gramps' old brown Ford came into view. In my excitement at having finally found him, I practically crawled over the front seat on top of Jase. Neither man said anything, but I babbled in my relief, stupid stuff about having finally found the old rascal.

My door was open before Jase even turned the engine off. I hopped out and was about to run to the old truck when a hard arm wrapped around my waist and stopped me. I don't know how Jase managed to move so fast but he had me in a tight grip, and I wasn't going anywhere until he let me.

"Charlotte, look at me." His urgent demand was delivered with rough appeal.

"Let me go, Jase, that's Gramps' truck. He's here somewhere. It's okay now." I craned my neck to watch Colin quick step it into the clearing. He called granddad's name when he was a few paces past his Ford then froze. What the hell was wrong with him? He looked devastated. Ruger streaked past where Jase held me and on around Colin. The sight of Ruger seemed to jump-start Colin back into moving.

"Charlotte, look at me." Jase demanded again, turning me so my back was to both the old truck and the clearing.

What was wrong with him? I was getting pissed. Gramps was here and I wanted to make sure he was okay after having spent the night out in the woods.

Jase slid both arms around my back and pulled me to him. He rested his temple against mine and whispered in my ear. "I'm not telling you but asking, please stay right here. Let me and Colin check on Jim."

It was the oddest thing, but as Jase was whispering it occurred to me that it was unnaturally quiet. Ruger should have been barking in excitement at seeing Gramps. Colin should have been adding his own greetings with a heavy dose of teasing for getting stranded out in the woods like this. But there was nothing. That's when I began to realize something was wrong; seriously wrong. Jase was trying to soften the blow of whatever was going to be found in the clearing.

I had no doubt my Gramps was there. The question was what kind of shape he was going to be in.

"I'm sorry but I can't do that." My voice came out just as faint and very polite. I pushed against his firmness. His arms tightened fractionally, then slowly released.

Tears were in me somewhere but they were locked down so tight they might never find their way to my cheeks again.

When I moved into the clearing what struck me first was the sight of Colin kneeling by Gramps where he lay on the ground. Ruger was there too, quietly staring. My heart wanted to deny what my soul knew to be true. Jase and Colin both tried to shield me from his body. I brushed them off, settled on the ground by the shell of my gramps, and pulled Ruger to me. At my touch, he burrowed his head under my chin.

With a curious detachment I noted the blood coating the top of the stump Gramps' head rested on. Streams had even run down the rough bark on the sides and soaked into the ground.

Colin must have closed my granddad's eyelids when he'd knelt here earlier. Odd; I could almost have made myself believe Gramps was sleeping if it hadn't been for all the blood. I searched his face with no clue as to what I expected to see. What I'd not expected was a massive bruise on his jaw. What that meant eluded me. Didn't matter right now anyway. Nothing did.

Colin was murmuring something to Jase about game cameras. He told Colin to go ahead and check but to be careful not to disturb anything. Colin walked away but Jase never left me. He was standing so close that if I leaned back the slightest bit I could touch him. I really wanted to lean back, but I just sat there, immobile.

After Colin returned, Jase stepped a few paces away to talk with him. Colin sounded angry and started to get loud. It wasn't possible to hear what Jase said to him and while it didn't calm him it did result in Colin going back to little more than a murmur as he talked to Jase.

Only thing I could make out was something about notifying the sheriff's office. Colin was to go wait at the head of the dirt trail to point the authorities in the right direction. Jase may have stopped trying to order me around but he still handed them out to Colin, and he was following them without question.

When Jase and I were alone once more I felt him lower himself behind me. Long fingers curled around my arms then half dragged, half lifted me back to settle me in the pocket of his crossed legs. Ruger was right there with me, since I couldn't bear to release him.

Once Jase had me arranged with my back pressed against his chest he enclosed not only me but also Ruger in his embrace. Thankfully he didn't try to offer any words of comfort. He simply held on.

My emotions may have gone into the deep freeze but my mind was anything but frozen. Memories produced picture after picture of the two other times I'd had to face the death of my family. The first time had been in high school. My grandparents had shown up at my parents' home in the middle of the night to break the news of their senseless ending.

A drunk, driving a jet boat way beyond the legal after-dark speed limit, had cut through the middle of Dad's flatbottom while he and Mom were night fishing on the lake. The bastard had also managed to cut through my mom and dad at the same time. I didn't think my tears were ever going to cease when I found out.

Then, two years ago, Granny had a stroke and passed after lingering a few short days in the hospital. Again, my tears flowed freely. But today, when the last member of my family lay dead beside me, my eyes were as dry as the Sahara. Anguish had burrowed so deep tears were worthless in trying to express my sorrow.

"They're coming, Charlotte." The low rumble brought me back to my surroundings. Releasing Ruger, I wriggled to free myself from Jase's lap. He didn't let go but pulled me up at the same time he raised himself off the ground. As soon as we were on our feet he released me. He may have not been touching me anymore but he was sticking close to my side as we waited for the various vehicles to come to a stop.

CHAPTER SIX

Colin climbed out of the sheriff's car first, which came as a surprise since he'd left in Jase's truck. He was red in the face and looked as though he could spit fire. Sheriff Cantrell rolled out next, hitching pants higher to girdle his generous belly. Following close behind the county car was an ambulance with Jase's pickup bringing up the rear, driven by another officer.

Colin marched over to Jase. "We've got a problem." Voice lowered to prevent being overheard past our little circle. Colin's agitation was obvious.

"Sheriff insisted I ride with him and let Dennis drive your truck. He asked a lot of the normal questions, about how long Jim had been missin' and when we'd found him. Those kinds of things.

"Wanted to know if I'd any idea why Jim was out here last night. Then he told me if I'd any thoughts as to what happened out here I needed to remember just what kind of person Jim was. Said any *known associates* might want to think about just how legal some of Jim's activities were and if they wanted to get caught up in 'em, considering.

"Then he asked if there'd been anything removed from the scene before we called the sheriff's office."

By the time Colin finished talking, the numb disconnect I'd been operating under had vanished and a slow burn was taking its place. What kind of person Jim was? Did the sheriff honestly think I'd be willing to let that kind of shit talk slide? He might not realize it yet but he was about to find out what kind of person I was. Before I could storm over to the asshat, Jase blocked me.

"Don't do it, Charlotte. Let me handle this," Jase said, with firm command.

"I'm not going to let him talk about my granddad that way." Shooting a warning glare in his direction, I practically snarled the words at Jase.

"Neither am I."

Sheriff Cantrell moved closer to the body and was leaning over, paying particular attention to where the head lay against the stump. He must have heard Colin talking to us because he looked up to address him, "Colin, you need to go on back over there and wait." Sheriff motioned for him to move behind us, back to where all the vehicles were parked.

Without acknowledging the demand, Colin stomped back the way he'd come. Cantrell then addressed his officer, "Dennis, come on over here and check out these pockets. Then take a look around. See if anything jumps out at you as not lookin' right."

Dennis quickly knelt beside Gramps and went through his pockets. He laid out his findings on the ground. It was all there: his billfold, the pocket knife he always carried, a few peppermints, some of those rolling papers for his smokes, a lighter and a wadded up handkerchief. All the paraphernalia my gramps never left home without.

The officer tried to pass the billfold over to the sheriff, but Cantrell shook his head, not taking it. So Dennis just laid it on the ground with everything else.

With a last long look down the length of the motionless figure, and then the ground around the body, Cantrell straightened. Finally moving in our direction, the sheriff once again hitched his pants higher. He smoothed a hand back and forth over his rounded stomach, as if wiping dirt off his palm. Not sure why, because he hadn't touched anything.

Jase maneuvered himself between me and the officers, which I wasn't real happy about. Cantrell turned a big smile on Jase while reaching out for a handshake.

"This is unexpected, Mr. Rydan. When Colin phoned this in he didn't mention you'd been in on looking for ol' Jim." Cantrell's big voice boomed with good cheer; gone was the shortness he'd used on Colin.

Jase left him hanging on the handshake. The blow-off seemed to wake Cantrell up to the fact he sounded way too chipper for the occasion and needed to readjust accordingly. The sheriff dropped his hand awkwardly and assumed a more solemn expression.

I wondered if the good sheriff even realized I was standing there, he was so overjoyed to see one of the almighty Rydans. More importantly, did he even care that my granddad lay dead at our feet? I might be having a problem finding my tears but my anger was clamoring to make an appearance.

"I don't know why you'd be surprised, Sheriff. I'm not only a neighbor but an extremely close friend of Charlotte's. My parents, as well as my brother, have always maintained close ties with the Donley family. It would be natural for Charlotte to call me as well as Colin when Mr. Donley went missing." Jase was apparently better at coming up with whoppers than Colin.

I knew what Jase was up to by trying to make it appear as though his important and extremely wealthy family would be interested in how my granddad's death was handled.

"Is that right, Mr. Rydan? Strange you'd be that close to Miss Char seeing how you just moved back and all. As for your family, I'm sure they knew Mr. Donley—hell, everyone knew of him—just never figured your folks would be all that close, considering." Cantrell was puffing up, hooking his thumbs in his belt, and narrowing his eyes at Jase.

Or then again, maybe the sheriff was smarter than he looked. Jase may have laid it on too thick and Cantrell wasn't buying it. Which got me to wondering exactly what wasn't he buying? That Jase and I were close friends, or that the rest of the Rydans could give a good damn about my granddad?

The approach of the EMTs distracted me from the power play Jase and Cantrell were in the middle of. They carried a large black zippered bag, which they laid on the ground next to Gramps. The two of them stood and talked to Dennis for a minute. At his nod they knelt, and it became clear they were preparing to move my granddad. As they reached for him I darted around Jase to confront them.

"Don't lay one finger on him." Threat rolled from every syllable. They stopped all movement to stare first at me and then darted a look at the sheriff. Their appearance was the final spark needed to light my fuse. Turning from them, I challenged Cantrell.

"What the hell, Cantrell! You're just going to let them bag him up and take him out like the trash? Ol' Jim's death isn't worth your trouble to try and figure out what happened here? What about pictures? Aren't you going to take any damn pictures?"

"Now, Miss Char, I know you're upset and ain't thinking straight right now, but there's no sense in making more of this than what we have here. Look around your granddaddy, girl. The ground don't look distributed as if there'd been some big whoop-de-doo. His wallet was still in his pocket as well as a pocket knife. If he'd been robbed, the thief sure as hell wouldn't have left those behind." Cantrell gestured at the objects as if to prove his point. "Your granddaddy was out here where he shouldn't have been, doing something he probably shouldn't have been doing. Now, I ain't gonna start poking around with a stick and stir up a hornet's nest that's gonna end up with you bein' the one gettin' one hell of a stingin'. That's something your granddaddy wouldn't have wanted.

"This here is just what it looks like, and no amount of pictures is going to change a thing. A tragic accident is always hard to accept. You just need to let the boys do their job. They'll take real good care of your granddaddy, don't you worry." He made as if he was going to pat me on the back but I jerked away at the same time Jase managed to insert himself back between us.

I wasn't sure who he was guarding, me or the sheriff.

"Even if you do suspect it's an accident, isn't it your duty to determine that by doing more than looking around some? Is the death of some people in this county less important, all depending on who you are? That's something I think a lot of folks might find interesting, don't you? Officials have been known to lose an election when the right people work on seeing they are defeated." The mild words belied the cold intent behind the focus Jase leveled at Cantrell. Everyone standing in the clearing understood that Jase had just made a promise.

"If it was anything other than what it is, hell, of course we would do a full investigation. This was obviously an accident. There's no need to waste the county's money on an investigation of an accident. That's part of my responsibility to the voters, too. And just remember, I'm trying to do Miss Char a favor here. If you think her granddaddy would thank any of us for bringing the long arm of the law into this then you weren't as friendly with ol' Jim as you claim." The man actually stood there and tried to make what he was saying sound reasonable instead of the pig shit it was.

"That's bullshit, and everyone standing here knows it, Sheriff. Mr. Donley might have not wanted the law poking into his business when he was alive but I think he'd damn sure want his killer to pay. I'll protect Charlotte from any fallout if you have a full investigation." Jase looked Cantrell straight in the eye and spoke without raising his voice.

Cantrell stood his ground, glaring at both Jase and me. Gone was the affable good old boy. Without looking away from either of us, he fired a question at his deputy. "Dennis, you see any evidence this here is anything other than an accident?"

"No, Sir." Snappy answer. Sheriff's little minion obviously knew to toe the line.

Cantrell then yelled over to Colin, "Colin, didn't you tell me Mr. Donley was out here to set-up game cameras? Something about it being a *hobby* of his?" There was a definite sneer when he said the word hobby.

"That's what I told you, but I also told you those cameras were missin'. There's also a fuckin' tobacco can that belongs to Jim near bent double where someone kicked it towards the woods. Jim didn't kick his own fuckin' tobacco can." Colin was frothing by the time he quit shouting.

Everything Colin was saying was news to me but obviously not to Jase. That must have been what all the whispering was about between him and Colin earlier. Jase stepped away from me so he could crowd into Cantrell's personal space.

"You heard him, Sheriff. We've got missing cameras and a dented can where it shouldn't be. I think we've managed to find enough evidence for you to call this something more than an accident, even if Dennis didn't." I would not have wanted that tone of voice being directed at me.

Cantrell didn't step back so I suppose that earned him some points. Just not sure if it was for being brave or incredibly stupid. "Back it up, Mr. Rydan. You want an investigation? I'll give you an investigation. But before I get started, you might want to discuss something with your *good friend,* Miss Donley." Warning was evident in Cantrell's voice.

"First off, if you want to call bullshit on something, how about Mr. Donley being out here with game cameras as a hobby? I start looking for a murderer and I'm going to have to wonder why anyone would murder Jim. That's going to lead to an investigation of his background. We all know what's going to turn up and what it could lead to if I have to involve the Feds and ATF.

"Let's say you don't know what it's going to lead to, let me fill you in on a few facts. If the ATF find the kind of activities we all know they're going to find, they can confiscate all of what is now Miss Donley's property. She doesn't even have to be arrested. But that's not going to help her if she loses her home.

"While you're discussing all of that, you might also want to consider how involved Colin is in all of this. The Feds shor' nuff will. So go ahead and insist I do an investigation. What I don't get is why you don't understand I'm trying to help you out here. I'm trying to do what Miss Char's granddaddy would've had me do—protect her."

I wanted to slap the smugness clean out of Cantrell, because he was right. I did have to consider how this was going to impact a lot of people. Not just Colin and not just me. Thing is, I couldn't let it go. Even if it was in my best interest. There was no way I could allow whoever had murdered my gramps to get off scot-free. But I wasn't going to give up without letting Cantrell know he wasn't my only option on finding my granddad's murderer.

"Charlotte, have the investigation. I'll help you through it. Whatever it takes," Jase urged me with a deadly calm, making sure Cantrell heard him. He was so supremely confident in his ability to protect me from what the sheriff rightfully predicted, Jase didn't even consider how it might impact him.

But I knew better. Gramps had told me enough tales I knew what would happen if the ATF sunk their teeth into a case like this. Not even Jase's last name and connections would be able to protect me. Or anyone associated with me, which included him. All it would accomplish would be to drag his and the rest of his family's name through the mud. Shaking my head, no, at Jase, I then confronted Cantrell again.

"Call it an accident, Sheriff. I don't need you to investigate to figure out who the murderer is. Gramps left me everything I need to find the bastard. By the way, you're wrong calling bullshit on the cameras. He set them up every time he made a trek to the woods. So I guess it could be called a hobby of his, keeping track of all the wildlife he ran across. He had so much fun recording his findings he wrote it all down so there was no question as to what kind of animal showed up."

Walking over to all that remained of my gramps, I leaned down to him one last time. I gently trailed a fingertip down his bruised face, then straightened back up. Without another word I headed to Jase's truck with Ruger to wait for him and Colin.

CHAPTER SEVEN

When Sheriff Cantrell arrived back at his office he lowered himself into his overstuffed desk chair and stared into space. A sickness had settled on him that went to his soul. He raised trembling fingers to his forehead, massaging deeply, working his way down to rotate them at his temples. Digging deep with the tips, he wished he could burrow into the throbbing pain and put it out. Chunky fingers finally dragged down across fleshy jowls to end up slapping his desk top.

What the fuck was he going to do? Was there any evidence at the scene that made Donley's death anything more than an accident? Probably. But then again he hadn't really looked for any, or allowed his deputy to look. He'd tried to justify his actions as protecting Char from the AFT and Feds. And keeping big brother out of all of this did play a large part in his less than thorough investigation. He had other, more pressing reasons to keep it local and under his control.

His boy, Billy Wayne, had called this morning to ask if anything had happened lately in the county that was interesting. He was all casual like with his questions but it wasn't the first time he'd called up checking on criminal activity in the county. It usually happened whenever Billy Wayne had done something and he was wondering if dear old Dad had found out yet.

When Colin had called in old Jim's death a sick feeling had settled in and taken root.

Did he believe Donley's death was an accident? Hell, no. Donley was old but the likelihood of him stumbling around in the dark and tripping was slim to none. Cantrell and everyone else knew damn good and well the old man had met someone in that small clearing last night; to either sell his shine to or have it picked up by a runner.

The likelihood of that runner being his boy was damn good, especially after that call from Billy Wayne this morning. And it was probably him if for no other reason than whatever had happened in that clearing last night had turned to shit. Billy Wayne's only real talent was creating shit.

If Char Donley made good on her promise to start looking for her granddaddy's killer, using some kind of records the old bastard had kept, she was going to stir up a hell of a mess. Say Char did start snooping around? She started asking questions of everyone that had ever bought shine off of Donley, or ran liquor for one of the buyers? It wasn't going to be good for anyone in town.

Oh—wait—there was one person it was going to be great for. That good-looking sum'bitch, Brent Allen. The man that was running against him for the sheriff's office.

He already had half the women in the county panting after him, ready to cast a vote his way. Only experience that little prick had with law enforcement was being a lawyer over in east Arkansas, getting crooks set free. The man made a damn good living at it, both where he came from and now here. Brent had the smarts to realize all he had to do was sit back and let the shit hit the fan over this Donley business.

Now if *he,* being the sheriff, started questioning everyone as to their whereabouts Saturday night, he was going to piss off half the county. If he did nothing, he was going to piss off the other half of the county. As an added ass-kicker, it looked like Char had Jase Rydan sniffing after her.

Jase was making noise about being willing to throw his weight behind getting him kicked out of office if he didn't investigate Donley's death as a murder. The bastard would do it too, if he didn't at least pretend to look into it.

He'd heard stories about Jase not being someone you wanted to have as an enemy. Hell, as a teenager he'd been wilder than a buck, for a while there. Running with some tough ass boys who had grown into some scary sum'bitches.

It wasn't a stretch to believe Jase could be as mean a bastard as the group he used to hang with. Not that the guy ever did anything illegal that he knew of. But he sure had a way of making people ask how high when he told them to jump. No matter how he looked at it, he was facing a major cluster fuck.

Was there anything at the scene that pointed a finger at BW being involved? No. Did he have a gut feeling BW was up to his ass in the affair? Hell, yes. Why? Because he'd spent most of his son's twenty-seven years of life pulling his ass out of one fucked up mess after another. This might finally be the one time he wasn't going to be able to pull that damn rabbit out of the hat. The one screw up that spelled the end for both of them.

What he had to do now was make a choice. Did he stick to his decision to file this as an accident, or was he going to investigate it as a murder, where he would have some control? He'd had the funeral home put Donley on ice for just this reason. If he did decide to classify it as murder he was going to have to send the body off to Little Rock for an autopsy. Once that happened he was going to have the state nosing around in the business. Maybe even the Feds, if they got word about the moonshining part of it. There wasn't a law department in the country that liked it when the Feds butted in.

Fuck it. He'd told everyone at the scene it was an accident and, by God, as far as he was concerned it was going to stay an accident. Let Char do her little investigation. If she did have her hands on some kind of records that old Moonshine kept, well, then good for her. He had a feeling she was going to have one hell of a time keeping control of those records.

There were going to be a few more people wanting possession of them than just the killer. Trying to keep Char safe might keep Jase so damn busy he wouldn't have time to follow through on the threat to see a new sheriff instated come election day.

He felt a tiny pang of remorse that he was more than likely hanging Char out there to get herself killed, but not so much that he was willing to try and stop what was bound to happen. If she started snooping where she didn't belong it would be her own damn fault if she ended up dead.

What did give him a deeper ache was the decision to not help Billy Wayne if it turned out he was involved in any way in the killing of Donley. His wife wasn't going to be too happy about his new rule of "no more pulling Billy Wayne's ass out of the fire." Hell, he blamed Mary Ann for most of their son's problems. He swore Billy Wayne took after Mary Ann's kin on her mother's side. Everybody knew the Wagners were all bat shit crazy and Billy Wayne was loaded up with it.

Yep, keeping the State Police and the Feds from sniffing around was the last bit of help he was willing to give his son. From now on, BW was on his own. He had no intentions of covering up any more of the shit his son managed to step into, year after year. At least not until the election was over with.

The race he was in with Brent was a tight one, and he was going to distance himself as far from his dumbass boy as possible. Shit, that right there would garner him a hell of a lot of votes.

Having made his decision, he picked up the phone and called Fowler's Funeral Home to give them the go ahead to prep the body for burial. He just hoped to hell he wasn't giving the go ahead to more murders over the coming days and weeks. If he was, well, maybe those killings would solve a few more of his problems.

CHAPTER EIGHT

On the drive back to my house, the silence was almost like having another person in the cab with us. One who was sucking out all the energy. No more directions to obscure wooded locations or discussions of where to check next. No more questions from Jase that Colin needed to evade or answer with a lie.

Detached, I sat in the backseat with Ruger clutched in my arms. Colin eyeballed me every few minutes. I knew he wanted to say something to console me, but he was at a total loss on where to find the correct words. It was hard to commiserate with a silent female who stared stoically straight ahead, not a tear in sight. I would've thought the no tears part more of a blessing than a worry. Hell, what man wanted to be around a bawling woman?

Then there was Jase. He still had that hard, flat look that had settled on him with the arrival of the sheriff. He'd pushed hard for me to let him force Cantrell into an investigation. He was so positive he could handle any dirt that might be thrown at anyone associated with an investigation involving moonshine and murder. I wasn't so sure and definitely wasn't willing to put it to the test.

Having failed to convince me to let the officials handle Gramps' death, I was pretty sure Jase had spent the drive back coming up with ways to prevent me from searching for the killer. Not going to happen.

We were definitely a different trio returning than when we'd started out that morning. As we pulled into my drive, any sense of urgency or hurry was gone. When Jase opened my door I slowly followed Ruger as he jumped from the cab. I stared at the ground the whole time I climbed from the truck and started walking towards my home.

The sound of someone calling my name brought me back to an awareness of my surroundings. Looking up, Evan was standing in my path with his arms open. I didn't even hesitate and walked straight into them. I welcomed the warm strength of them as they crossed my back and pulled me gently to his chest.

For the first time that day I felt the sting of tears. A couple of rebels wormed their way past my closed lids and crawled down my cheeks. I drew a shuddering breath, grabbed Evan's shirt in a crushing grip and dug deep, determined to not let any more tears escape my rigid control. Strange that I hadn't realized how much of a rock Evan had become for me over the years. In that moment he felt like a true brother to me, and I allowed myself to pretend, for just a little while, I wasn't the last member of my family.

* * *

Jase silently watched his brother hold Charlotte and murmur words of solace into her hair as he softly rocked her back and forth. Regret at having called Evan to let him know what had happened was selfish, but he had to admit he was damn sure regretting it.

He had this crazy notion of ripping Charlotte out of Evan's arms and gathering her to him instead. Jase thought back to that moment in the clearing, when he'd pulled her on his lap to offer comfort. Charlotte hadn't fought him but she sure as hell hadn't clung to him like she was hanging on to his brother. No, she'd hugged her dog instead and he wasn't sure which of them had given her the most ease, him or the dog.

Standing at a loss, wondering what he should do, was a new experience for him. He couldn't remember ever being this unsettled over a woman because...he never had been before. It was watching Evan console Charlotte that was throwing him a curve.

Looking over at Colin, it was easy to see that universal look of a man ill-at-ease in an emotionally charged situation. But Jase knew his own personal reaction went deeper than simple feelings of discomfort. This was way more complicated than he'd planned on.

Years ago, when Charlotte was just a kid, he'd been there when she'd most needed someone to rescue her. Now that she was a grown woman, he once again wanted to be the one she turned to. Seeing her in his brother's arms was a kick in the face.

While he'd been away, she'd grown into a beautiful woman. Yeah, he'd been the one to persuade Evan to watch over Charlotte while she was growing up; it was just now he wasn't sure it had been such a great idea.

Well, Evan had been given several years to make a move if he was interested in being something more than the protector and friend he'd asked him to be to Charlotte. Time was up. He was back to stay and planned on seeing if there was more to this attraction he felt for a woman he'd rescued when she was a child. Unlike his brother, he damn sure wasn't planning on taking years to find out.

* * *

I wasn't the clingy and needy type, but pulling away from Evan was harder than I'd imagined. He let me go, then ducked down to make it easier to peer into my face.

"You doing all right, squirt?" Concern laced his words and darkened his features.

"I'll get there." It was the best answer I had.

Movement off to the side reminded me we had an audience. Taking another step back from Evan, I pivoted to face both Jase and Colin.

Colin was clearly uneasy but Jase was a puzzle. His body appeared relaxed but the intensity of his stare felt like he was trying to deliver a message to one of us. I couldn't tell if it was Evan or me. Whatever was going on with him, I didn't have time to decipher piercing stares from a broody man.

I'd a million details to handle concerning my gramps' death, and there was no one left but me to take care of them. Gramps always told me, *"Pity parties don't solve a damn thing."* Suppose that meant it was time to suck it up and prove him right.

"Colin, would you mind driving my truck to the barn and unloading those mineral bags for me?" Giving him a job to do was the only thing I could come up with that might make this easier for him.

"You bet. I'll check the cattle while I'm at it." Relief, at having something concrete he could do, took the slump out of his shoulders. Amazing how giving a job to someone could transform them.

Colin left with an eagerness that confirmed my suspicions; he needed to get away. And not just because he wanted to be doing something helpful. He needed some time to sort out his own grief. He'd actually spent more time with Gramps than I had over the last few years, working the shine and helping with the cattle. He was hurting.

Before I could address either of the brothers, Evan began to speak. "Char, why don't you take a break? When you're ready we'll head into town and figure out what needs doing."

As considerate as his offer was, and despite having admitted to myself there were a lot of decisions to make, I wasn't ready to even think about what those next steps entailed. The preparations would signal the finality of my granddad's death. They were going to be put on the back burner until I was ready to accept it. "That won't be necessary, Evan. I'm not leaving, and there's no sense in both of us staying. Whenever Charlotte wants to go in I'll take her." Jase spoke with a firmness that said it was all settled.

I wasn't sure who was more surprised—me or Evan. Once again Jase hadn't asked, he'd simply taken charge and expected everyone to fall in line.

"No one is taking me into town later, and no one is staying here with me either, understand? Tomorrow morning will be soon enough to start in on whatever needs to be taken care of. Which I'll handle just fine on my own. It's not like it's the first funeral I've ever had to plan." My reaction to his announcement was over the top. Even I realized it was way out of proportion to what he'd said but couldn't stop myself. The anger I felt had to go somewhere, and Jase was a handy target.

If it sounded like I'd started blowing a horn at a pity party; well, too bad. All I wanted was a handful of aspirin and a dark room with a bed. Hopefully the combination would erase the pain scraping my eyeballs raw.

Evan was reluctant but knew me well enough to know when to back-off. Jase, not so much. "You forfeited any chance of being left alone when you blasted Cantrell with your intentions of looking for Jim's killer."

"She did what?" Evan barked his question at Jase as he turned, eyes bugging.

"Oh, that's not even the best part. She threw a not so cryptic message at the sheriff and everybody that was there today caught it too. Concerning certain records Donley kept that nobody in this county is going to want to go public. Not the best way to go about starting a hunt for a killer, considering." Jase may have been talking to Evan but he was glaring at me.

"Considering? What's with everyone throwing out freaking *'considering'* every five minutes? Well, consider this! I'm walking into my house and, once my door is shut, feel free to do whatever the hell y'all want, as long as leaving me alone tops the list." Up until that point I'd thought I'd done a pretty good job at keeping my emotions corralled. But they had just jumped the fence and were galloping down the road to crazy town.

Refusing to stay a second longer I made my way to the porch and stormed to the front door. Ruger barely made it through the wooden barrier before it was slammed behind me as I passed through. Not the smartest thing to do, seeing as it already felt like two spikes were being hammered into the top of my skull.

* * *

"What was that, Jase? Char just finds out her granddaddy's dead and you pick a fight with her? What the hell are you doing?"

Jase watched Charlotte stomp off, reluctant to let her walk away alone but knowing she'd reached her breaking point. One he'd pushed on her. She was stubborn, proud, independent, and irresistibly appealing, despite all of that.

"I'm sorry, Evan."

"Char's the one you need to be apologizing to." Evan fumed, looking like he wanted to take a swing with that fist clinched by his side.

"No, you're the one that needs to know I'm sorry if you think you're attracted to Charlotte, because it's not real. You would've claimed her by now if it had been. Your days of being her protector are over. I'm taking her back and it's not going to matter what you *think* your feelings for her are." Jase didn't raise his voice, but he did cross his arms and leveled an intense look at Evan.

"Shit, Jase. Listen to yourself. Char's not some toy you can call dibs on, like when we were kids." Evan snorted in disgust. "I care for Char, but not the way you appear to be thinking. I told you that yesterday. Yeah, over the years we've become close. But she's like my sister. She needs someone who can comfort her right now. Looks to me like all you can manage to do is aggravate the hell out of her.

"Just because I teased Char yesterday when I said I was turning guard duty over to you doesn't mean I'm going to let you show up and screw around with her head." Evan sounded as determined as Jase, if a little less calm. "Right now it sounds like we have a hell of a lot bigger problem on our hands than who gets to keep Char."

Jase decided to take Evan at his word on the level of his affection. He loved his brother and had figured the best way to head off any potential problems between the two of them had been to state his intentions up front. Charlotte might be more comfortable with Evan, but his own plans for her involved a whole lot more than comfort. Those plans were going to have to be put on hold while he figured out how to keep her safe.

"It may take the two of us and then some to keep her on this side of the grass if she's crazy enough to play detective. Once word gets out about those files it's not only going to be the killer we need to worry about. Every bastard in town who thinks he may have something to lose by those documents going public is going to want their hands on them."

"Are you positive Donley was murdered?"

"From what I saw, and what little Colin told me, there's no possible way it was an accident." Jase ran a hand through his thick hair and puffed out a deep breath as he said, "I just have to somehow convince Charlotte to turn over the records to me, persuade her to let me keep her safe, all while I help her search for a killer. Which I'll have to argue her into letting me do in the first place. Piece of cake."

Evan's anger at Jase was replaced with worry for Charlotte. "Count me in on helping keep her safe. Just do me a favor, stop pissing her off and leave me out of anything that involves convincing Char to do something she doesn't want to."

CHAPTER NINE

Having dragged myself through a shower, I threw on a soft tee and panties. Tossing some aspirin back, I drained the glass of ice water I'd brought upstairs with me. Closing the bedroom curtains blocked the late afternoon sun from streaming in, and it came as a blessed relief.

It wasn't until I lay on the top of cool sheets that it hit me what Jase had said about the files. Shit, the man was right. I groaned in disbelief at my stupidity for not only informing Cantrell but everyone else who had been in the clearing as well of Gramps' record keeping.

I had become that girl. The one in the movies who couldn't keep her mouth shut. She tells the villain exactly how she's going to nail him, while I'm sitting there wanting to scream, "Shut up, what *is wrong* with you?" Yep, that was me today. News of the records would be all over town by now. Town...hell...it'd be all over the *county* by now.

The worst part was, I didn't even know where they were. My threats to hunt down the killer were an empty brag, at least until I had my hands on those documents. Giving up on tracking down my grandfather's murderer was not an option. Once I figured out who was responsible I made a promise to myself that I would find a way to make him pay.

Waking to a fully dark room came as a surprise. Rolling my head slowly to the side to check the time on my alarm clock, it registered that the skull demolition had subsided to a dull throb. Thank the Lord for the pills I'd taken earlier. Unfortunately the reality of my gramps' death remained, along with the profound sadness.

Rumbles coming from my stomach clued me in as to why I'd woken up. I hadn't eaten anything all day and my body was letting me know, even if my emotions said I wasn't hungry. The restless, crawly feeling helped me decide food would probably be a good idea. At least it gave me something to do.

Pushing off the light throw, I swung my legs to the side of the bed. Starting to stand, I froze. Light throw? I'd definitely not used a spread when I'd lain down.

How had someone managed to make it into the house to cover me? Thinking back to my demented exit from Jase and Evan, I remembered slamming the front door but not locking it. Having figured out the how still left me with a couple of questions. Who had covered me, and how had they gotten past Ruger to do it?

Having a sneaky suspicion as to the *who*, I finished climbing off the bed and went to my dresser to retrieve a pair of shorts. Ruger pulled himself out of his bed with a stretch and a shake, ready to follow wherever I might lead.

I headed downstairs for food and to see if my suspicions were correct, if he was even still here. Rounding the newel post into the inkiness of the living room, I didn't need the moonlight angled across the floor to make my way across the space into the kitchen.

Once there, I did turn on one of the band of lights located under the cabinets. Between the moonlight and the tiny bit of illumination from the kitchen it was easy to locate Jase's distinct form stretched out on my couch.

His boots were off, as well as his shirt, but he still had his jeans on. I didn't know whether to be mad he hadn't left me alone, or to admit it was reassuring to not be on my own. Going with ignoring the situation until forced to face it, I went about fixing myself a sandwich as quietly as possible.

As I went to gather bread and utensils it occurred to me I'd left the biscuits and sausages in the oven all day. Opening the oven door I bent over to remove the cold pans of ruined food. Taking a step back I bumped up against a warm body. Shrieking, I dropped both pans. Ruger started barking aggressively, when I instinctively started kicking and fighting against the arms that surrounded me.

"Charlotte, stop, it's me, Jase. Calm down, honey. I've got ya. You're safe, sweetheart." Soothing words breathed into my ears from his sleep roughened voice. I stopped trying to fight, but my heart kept on trying to beat out of my chest. My ragged breathing was hard to get under control. The adrenalin coursed through my system.

As soon as I stopped struggling, Ruger stopped barking. His low growls let us know he was still on alert. At least he was until he remembered the food that now littered the kitchen floor. Always willing to help, he dug in and began to clear the mess. Not having the heart to scold him, I just sighed and hoped he didn't make himself sick.

"You scared the crap out of me, Jase." For some reason I was whispering. The darkness, combined with Jase's embrace, contributed to a feeling that anything above a whisper would be wrong.

"Not what I intended." His chest rumbled against my back as he followed my lead and kept his voice lowered. The heat from his bare skin soaking through my thin tee encouraged my stiff posture to soften. "Heard you come down the stairs. Figured since I hadn't seen you eat anything all day you were probably hungry. I followed you in here thinking you could sit while I fixed us both something to eat."

"You don't have to do that. I can handle it." I sincerely hoped my reluctance to move didn't come through as clearly to Jase as it did to me. For a tiny second longer I simply wanted to stay in his arms and lose the feelings of abandonment. Feelings that made no sense, because Gramps certainly hadn't walked away from me. He'd been wrenched from my life by a murderer.

"How about for what's left of the night you let me take care of you? Use me to ease your pain in any way you need. If it's food, let me prepare it. If it's someone to hang on to, I'm here. You aren't going to have to face this alone, Charlotte. Don't fight me tonight." His rough murmur encouraged my back to relax even deeper into the contours of his sculpted chest.

Temptation comes in many forms. The allure of letting go and turning everything over to Jase was irresistible. What would one night hurt? Tomorrow I could pick up the reins and regain control. I was turning into a regular Scarlett O'Hara. That lady had it going on with her whole, *"tomorrow is another day."*

Not willing to vocally surrender, I simply nodded. At my capitulation, Jase tightened his arms a fraction, then released me with a nudge in the direction of the dining table. He headed back to the living room and I watched him retrieve his shirt. After slipping it on he returned to search the kitchen for the makings of a meal.

Neither of us spoke as he moved about the room, preparing sandwiches and pouring milk into glasses. When all was ready and placed on the table, he sat down beside me in a companionable silence to share the simple fare.

It shouldn't have been but for some reason the normalcy of eating with another person was a painful reminder of what I had lost. In four years of living on my own I'd never felt as alone as I did right then. A coldness crept in. I wanted nothing more than to crawl onto Jase's lap, have him wrap me in his embrace and burn the chill from my soul. I wanted him to lie and tell me everything was going to be okay. I needed the human contact to fight off the growing despair of realizing that from this point on I was on my own.

Shame, at so easily giving in to such depressing thoughts, had me rising from the table while still chewing my last bite. Seeing that Jase was also finished, I gathered his plate and empty glass along with mine and carried all the dishes to the sink.

"I'm going to head back upstairs now. Thanks for fixing the sandwiches." My voice came out strong, polite, but distant. Gone was the cozy warmth of our previous whispered exchanges. I flicked off the band of lights and headed for the living room.

Jase was right behind me. Reaching out he gripped my shoulder, bringing me to a halt. I stood there but refused to turn around.

"What happened, Charlotte? Why are you shutting me out all of a sudden?" Jase was still trying to wrap me in the heat of his throaty whisper.

"Why are you doing this, Jase?" Spinning to confront him, I placed both hands on my hips. "Are you confusing me with that little girl you had to save so many years ago? Well, I don't need saving. In case you haven't noticed, I'm all grown up and can manage just fine on my own."

Jase paused before answering. He was studying me like some kind of puzzle he'd thought solved but had become all scrambled again. "I'm doing this because I see a woman standing in front of me who is going to be facing some hard times with the death of her grandfather. Hard times she doesn't have to face alone. We are neighbors and friends, that's enough to start with. For now."

What did "enough to start with" even mean? I wanted to be mad at him, and wanted him to be mad at me, but he was unflappable. Damn him for sounding so reasonable while I came off as that bratty kid I denied being. There was so much anger and sadness brewing in me, and Jase was the only target around to bubble that hot shit all over. No, it wasn't fair, but that wasn't going to stop me from trying to leave a mark.

He brought a hand up to brush some wayward strands of hair back behind an ear, but I flinched back before he could complete the tuck. Taking an extra step back and a deep breath, I stiffened my resolve to not let Jase take on responsibilities that belonged to me. I could—and would—handle whatever the next few days and weeks had in store for me.

Hoping the deep shadows in the room would hide any tiny doubts that might show on my face, I challenged Jase. "We may be neighbors but friends is a bit of a stretch, despite what you told the sheriff, don't you think? Evan is my friend, and Colin is a friend, but I don't recall adding you to my contact list."

If I'd hoped to discourage him with my snarky comment, the tiny lift to the corner of his lips made it pretty clear it hadn't worked. Deciding I needed to be more direct I tried again. "Jase, you need to leave now. You've made sure I'm okay, and I appreciate that. But I don't want you here in my house any longer. I want to be alone."

Jase started walking as soon as I finished talking, but it was back into the kitchen and not to gather his boots so he could hit the road. Wondering what the heck he was up to now, I followed. He walked straight to the counter, where my cell phone lay plugged into the charger. Picking it up he activated the screen, punched in his phone number, hit save then laid it back down.

"There, now we're friends." Walking back into the living room, he sat down to tug on his boots and then finally headed for the door. At the last second he glanced back at me over his shoulder. "Try and get some more rest. I'll be here in the morning. That will be soon enough for us to get a start on trying to sort all this out."

The door closed softly. He'd given me what I'd asked for. I was alone. And it sucked.

CHAPTER TEN

After Jase walked out the door, I spent what was
left of the night on the couch he'd been sleeping on. I
hugged the throw pillow he'd cushioned his head with
and cried. Those pretty little tear drops some women can
manage were not for me. Mine were raw gasps of pain,
with snot and tears mingling in torrents down my face,
all smeared together with each swipe of the back of my
hand.

Ruger whined, while he alternated between trying
to clean my face with his tongue and squirm his nose
under my arms. But my arms were busy clinching that
pillow to my chest like it was a lifeline. Before even
starting I'd promised myself that this was going to be the
one and only time I would allow complete loss of
control. The sunrise would be my signal to end my
unchecked outpouring of grief. Once daylight arrived, I
would pull everything back inside and face what had to

be done. It's what Gramps would've expected of me and what I demanded of myself.

As the shadows in the room shrank from the invading sunbeams, I squinted through swollen and gritty eyelids. The storm of tears unleashed in the early morning hours had taken a toll. At some point in the predawn I'd fallen asleep, exhausted by the violence of my emotional release.

If a good cry was supposed to make a person feel better, then I must have had a bad one. My head felt like it was stuffed with cotton, and my throat ached from my wailing. Propelling myself up with a stiff arm, I used my other hand to drag my tangled mass of hair out of my face. A shower was definitely in order, followed by a huge cup of coffee. Perhaps it would help clear the cobwebs left over from last night. After climbing off the couch I made an executive decision and made for the kitchen instead of the stairs. I decided caffeine was a necessity not to be delayed.

As the coffee dripped into the carafe I saturated a dishtowel with cold water to hold over my aching eyes. Stealing a cup from the coffee maker, I carried both it and my wet towel aiming for the front door. I wanted out of the house almost as bad as Ruger, judging by his dancing wiggles.

My front porch swing was calling my name, and the nearby fields were no doubt calling to Ruger. Settling into the cushions of the swing, I sighed in relief at the chill of the towel draped across my eyes and up over my forehead. My first sip of dark brew was heaven, the occasion made even more perfect by the total absence of any stray thoughts wandering through my mind. Whadda ya know...it lasted for all of two seconds before my brain kicked back into gear.

If I really took a hard look at the different deaths in my life, each one had been a defining point of change for me. My parents' death when I was a child of fifteen had felt like the end of the world. Thing was, my grandparents had been there to continue on as my family. They were my shelter and my hiding place.

Perhaps too much so.

They had to push me into going away to a college in Texas, bully me into following my dreams of turning unique stones and bits of metal into original pieces of jewelry. Thankfully, while at college, I'd met Brianna, who was now my best friend. A best friend who lived in New York. What did that say about my ability to make friends where I lived?

There was Evan, who had been pushed into being my friend by his brother. And Colin had been granddad's friend first. Looking at it realistically, other than those two I didn't have friends. I had friendly acquaintances.

Bri was a huge part of my business success, pitching my designs to her rich family and their friends. It didn't hurt that her parents owned several prestigious jewelry stores up and down the east coast. Bri and my grandparents had been my crutches when my parents died.

Then, when my granny passed, two short years ago, it was a hard loss and I missed her terribly, but Gramps had needed me to take care of him that time around. He'd been right when he'd complained at the still; I did fuss over him. So much so that he and my shop had become my focal points.

Evan was the one who made the push to stay connected as a friend. And Bri breezed in, whenever she could get away, to stir up some crazy times. Otherwise I would've happily settled into a narrow life of looking after Gramps and my work.

Now, with Gramps' death, a hollowness was trying to suck me in, and I wasn't liking it. A ghost going through the motions of a living breathing woman was not going to be my next transformation.

First order of the business: get through the next few days. Once they were behind me, next up was going to be finding those damn records and starting my hunt for a murderer. That was what I needed. A plan. With a plan there was a reason to get up each day.

Crunching gravel and the muted roar of an engine coming down my lane had me heaving a sigh, this time of resignation. Sounded like I'd worked out a plan none too soon.

I pulled the towel off my face and watched for the vehicle about to arrive in my drive. I looked like hell warmed over, but had no plans for a mad dash to make myself more presentable. Anyone showing up this early would have to take me as I was.

Rat-nest hair, puffy eyes and blotchy complexion should teach him a lesson about showing up unannounced. By *him,* I meant Jase. Because I was willing to bet the farm that was who was about to pull up to my house. He'd warned me last night he would be back this morning. Figures he would neglect to say how early.

Was he going to take one look at me and know I'd thrown one hell of a sob-fest? Of course. The man wasn't blind or stupid. Did I care? Nope.

As Jase's now familiar Chevy came to a stop, I took another sip of my coffee and waited for his approach. It was impossible to watch Jase traverse the distance from the drive to my front porch and not appreciate his long-limbed stride. You could practically see the confidence ooze out of the man's pores.

"What are you doing here so early? Another invite from your mom?" No heat to my question, but there might have been a hint of sarcasm.

"The fatted calf is being turned back to pasture for now. I'd promised to be back this morning. Being the good friend that I am, I naturally came early so I'd be available when you needed me." He deserved some kind of award for not blinking an eye at my snark or my appearance. Grudgingly, I had to admit it was a relief Jase didn't bring up the fact I'd obviously had a complete breakdown after I'd kicked him out last night.

"If I delete your name from my contact list will you disappear as easily?" It felt wrong to enjoy this back and forth with a man who was too freaking gorgeous for this early in the day. But it also felt good to think of something other than what the day had in store.

"Darlin', if my name should somehow be deleted I'd naturally understand it was a terrible mistake and simply re-enter it. That's what friends do for friends. We stick through the good times, the sonovabitch times and the occasional accidental delete." Jase leaned a hip against one of the porch supports then crossed his arms as he smiled at me.

He was dressed a bit less casually today than he'd been yesterday. He was still in boots and jeans, but the jeans weren't faded and the boots were more dress than work. His sky-blue button-up shirt did amazing things to his gray eyes.

Okay, I might have been starting to squirm internally at the bag-lady look I had going on when compared to Jase. He could eat dirt before I let him know of my growing discomfort.

"Jase, what are you really doing here?"

"Exactly what I said. Here to help in whatever way you need." His easy smile remained while he let his eyes wander from my bare feet, tucked up under me...across my skimpy shorts—I hoped my ass wasn't hanging out—up my favorite tee to sleep in—he seemed to be focusing a little too intently on my bra-lessness—to finally settle on my less than appealing morning-after-the-storm face. And to complete the picture of wonderfulness, my hair looked like it had been styled with a hand mixer. I refused to fidget under his scrutiny.

"As a friend, I would like to point out you look delectable from the neck down and like hell from the chin up." Jase made his observation in as matter-of-fact manner as a man can get.

"As a friend, acquired through a hostile-takeover, I would like to point out it's none of your business how I look." Yep, I planned on sitting there, looking like hell. Which was a classic case of cutting off my own nose to simply be defiant. Now that I'd had my caffeine shot, all I really wanted was a shower. My head was itching and my skin was fairly twitching at the thought of cool water sliding down it.

"Charlotte, as much as I enjoy looking at the delectable parts on display right now, we both know that when people from the community start showing up, and you know they will, you are going to want to be prepared.

"There are also decisions to be made concerning your grandfather's passing that need to be taken care of sooner rather than later. If there's someone you'd rather go with you into town to help make those decisions, just tell me who and I'll get them here." A lift of an eyebrow and his stare clued me in that he was waiting for an answer from me.

Damn, I hated it when someone I was trying to be nasty to insisted on being reasonable. He'd also managed to hit a sore spot I'd been poking mere moments before his arrival. My lack of friends. Yeah, I could ask Colin—he'd loved Gramps—but he would be useless when it came to planning a funeral. Colin could be counted on when it came to help with the still, the cattle, even in a fight. But when it came to the emotional stuff, he was helpless.

Bri was the obvious choice, and she would have been amazing support. One big problem with that; she was on a plane to Europe with another friend of hers.

She'd begged me to go with them. Thank the lord, I'd refused. By the time she could even arrange to make her way back, the funeral would be over. I'd already made up my mind I wasn't going to contact her about any of this until she returned home in four weeks.

That left Evan or Jase. I was a little surprised Evan hadn't showed up this morning with his brother, but I figured it probably was Jase's doing. As much as I hated to admit it, Jase was the one I wanted pushing me through this. He wouldn't be maudlin and would keep me from becoming so by being himself. Arrogant and bossy.

"Don't you have a million things you should be doing right now to get that office of yours open in Copper Ridge?" At least I didn't bat my eyelashes and simper when I asked. The question was a sure sign of giving in.

Sensing my surrender Jase's smile returned as he answered me. "Not much for me to do, right now. Lawyers are doing their thing and my uncle, in Rogers, is handling the business there. I told you last night to use me however you needed to. If I ever change my mind I'll let you know."

"Coffee's in the kitchen, help yourself. A friend told me I looked like hell, so I guess I need to head upstairs and do something about it." This was as close as I could come to verbally conceding defeat. Climbing out of the cushions, I headed for the door, passing Jase. He moved away from the post to follow me in. I didn't bother looking for Ruger. Little man was off making his morning rounds. "Give me thirty minutes or so and I'll fix us some breakfast when I come down," I said, halting at the bottom of the stairs.

Jase had trailed me over to the steps and was standing closer than I'd realized. Picking up one of the rat tails hanging over my shoulder Jase gave it a tug. "How 'bout you let me handle the cooking while you're upstairs?"

Not willing to fight over every tiny detail, in what was going to be a long day of decisions, I nodded, then turned to ascend the steps. Something told me to save my energy to do battle over more important arguments that would probably rear their ugly heads later.

CHAPTER ELEVEN

"Miss Donley, I'm certain you've heard this a number of times today, but I am truly sorry for your loss. Your grandfather was a much loved and respected member of our community all his life. He will be greatly missed." Brent Allen, candidate for sheriff, was suitably somber and sincere.

In other words, he was in full campaign mode, spreading a thick layer of bullcrap. As far as I knew, he'd never even spoken to my granddad. If he had, I sure didn't remember it. Then again, he could have been one of Gramps' customers, for all I knew.

He cornered me outside the Daisy Shoppe, just as Jase and I were about to enter, and grabbed onto one of my hands. I glanced around to see who he was trying to impress with his grave demeanor. Ahhh, there you go, Connie Winslow was coming up the sidewalk with her momma, neither one looking thrilled to see Jase standing beside me.

Connie was Jase's last local girlfriend before he broke it off and left for college. She was also recently divorced and on the hunt for husband number three. Or perhaps they weren't happy seeing Brent hanging on to my hand. I'd heard he was in the running for the position of next husband to be. But they weren't the only ones moving closer to the spectacle. The old men who occupied the benches on the courthouse lawn were also getting up to mosey in our direction.

"Thank you." Perhaps not the most original comeback, but it was better than *leave me alone.* See, I was working on the new approachable me that made friends.

"I understand you weren't happy with the current sheriff's handling of the matter of Mr. Donley's questionable passing. He labeled it as an accident without a thorough investigation. I can assure you that would not have been the case if I'd been the one in charge." As the crowd around us grew, so did his volume and the flashing of whitened teeth.

The sonovabitch was actually doing this. He was going to use my gramps' death as a way to gather votes. Then the question I should be asking struck me. How did he know about my blow up with Cantrell? And if he knew about my confrontation with the sheriff, it was a safe bet it wasn't the only information being passed around. I tried to pull my hand out of Brent's grasp but he tightened his hold. Seems he wasn't finished using me as a stumping tool.

While I stood there, trying to make up my mind on how to get away without causing a scene, Jase took matters into his own hands. "You're going to have to give her back her hand. We have an appointment, and we're late." Jase latched onto my free hand and started walking. If Brent didn't want to look like he was in a tug of war with Jase, he was going to have to let go.

Sally, the owner of the Daisy Shoppe, must have seen the gathering crowd and stepped out her door. She was checking out the commotion when Jase made his announcement. If she was surprised at his blatant lie she didn't let on. Heck, she jumped right in with her own whopper and loudly proclaimed for all to hear she'd come outside to look for us. Had a feeling just about as many people believed we had an appointment with Sally as believed she was so desperate for business she was out hunting it down in the streets.

I seriously didn't care what anyone thought at this point. All I wanted to do was make my escape from Brent and the audience he'd attracted. Murmurs of displeasure from the group seemed to be equally divided between Sheriff Cantrell and me. The men were not happy with Cantrell's handling of my granddad's death. As for the women, all their unhappiness centered on me. Something along the lines of "how dare I use my grandfather's demise to my advantage in trying to snare Jase?"

Brent gave in and let go of my hand but I'd underestimated his determination in wooing the group surrounding us. "Miss Donley, please feel free to call me at any time if there is any way I can be of service. Every citizen in this county should feel like they have someone they can depend on to look after their interest and keep them safe. Hopefully I'll be that someone in the near future, not only for you, but for everyone." The grave look he directed at me had just the right amount of concern and solicitude.

"That won't be necessary, Brent. I've got this. Charlotte has me to watch over her and make sure she's safe. And I take my job seriously." Jase managed to fire off his remarks to Brent as he pulled me through the door into the quiet of the flower shop.

"What was that?" I asked Jase with more than a hint of temper. Problem was, I didn't have a clear handle on who I was really mad at. Brent was a prick for using my gramps' death as a campaign focal point—boy could that ever backfire on him—but then Jase had gone all big bad bodyguard out there.

"That was me letting everyone know you are not on your own. The way word gets around, hopefully anyone interested in doing a search at your home for *valuable items* will be deterred when they hear you are not as isolated as they might hope. You can thank me later," Jase said, without a trace of sarcasm. "Before the big sideshow out front, you were wanting to complete the arrangements for Wednesday. Why don't we let Sally here do her job and help you?" Jase nodded his head at the hand-wringing Sally, reminding me we were being observed.

Once again I felt like Jase and I were the main attraction at a spectator event. Sally kept darting curious looks between the two of us. Her gaze would linger on Jase the longest in the back and forth action her eyes were doing. Totally understandable.

He had a naturally seductive lift at the corners of his lips when he smiled at her. And the unruly strands scattered across his forehead magnified the contrast between the cool gray of his eyes and the rich darkness of his hair. If his smile was an attempt at soothing her flustered nerves it was an epic fail. On the other hand, if he wanted to give her vascular system a workout, I'd say he nailed it.

Harnessing my aggravation at the world in general, I shifted my attention to Sally. I began to explain what I hoped she would be able to do for Gramps in the way of flowers. Jase lent me his strength by twining his fingers with mine, a small act of support he'd performed at each of the stops we'd made today. As at the funeral home, he remained silent unless I began to falter in a decision, at which point he would lean over to quietly offer a suggestion.

As I signed the order form for the casket spray, I had this crazy thought that I'd never bought flowers for anyone who was alive. Every order for a floral arrangement I'd ever placed, or been involved in helping pick out, had been for someone I loved who had died. Thoughts of all those flowers chosen for loved ones now gone flipped some kind of panic switch.

"I've got to get out of here. Now!" Latching onto one of Jase's hands with both of mine I blurted out my demand in a harsh whisper. I hung on to control by a slim thread.

Breathing became labored, more of a gasping for air than a smooth in and out action. Sweat started to bead my forehead and slick my palms. Last night's hysterics was supposed to have been my only concession to losing control. But right now, if I didn't get away from all of these freaking flowers and stop breathing in the perfume-saturated air, I was going to shatter.

Jase didn't miss a beat. Slipping an arm around my waist, he tucked me tightly against his side and headed for the back of the shop. Pushing open the first door he came to turned out to be Sally's office. After quickly crossing to a chair, half carrying me, he forced my head down between my knees. Jase crouched beside me, rubbing my back and demanding I take slow deep breaths. Sally must have been hovering somewhere in the background because I heard Jase ordering her to leave and shut the door.

After what felt like hours, but was in reality probably only a few minutes, I slowed my breathing and pulled the dramatics back. Embarrassment had color creeping into my cheeks. Talk about an unexpected freak out.

One minute I could handle things just fine and the next I was outhouse-rat crazy. Jase seemed to be taking my looney tunes spectacle in stride though. He brushed damp tendrils of hair off my temple. He looped the heavy swath of red waves behind my ears as I straightened into a sitting position. I wished he would can his inspection of my features, but I wasn't about to start another commotion by complaining.

"You ready to blow this joint?" He kept his voice lowered but a tenderness flavored his words.

Nodding was the best I could manage with the humiliation riding me hard. At my signal of compliance, he helped me stand. He drew me to his side to walk with me to the door. Exiting the room revealed an anxious Sally, again wringing her hands. A look of relief came across her as soon as she set eyes on me. The burn I felt creeping up my neck was a sign my face was about to become a lovely shade of red.

"There now, feeling all better?" Sally's soothing words held no censor. "Don't you go thinking you've shamed yourself, Miss Donley. You're going to find through the coming days and weeks, no matter how strong you are, there are going to be times when it all crashes back in. A stray thought or a forgotten memory will pop up and, sugar, there won't be a thing you can do to stop the storm that'll follow." Not what I wanted to hear. Thing is, Sally owned the only flower shop in town and I bet she'd seen more than her fair share of drama. She pretty much had it figured out.

"We're going out the back." Not sure if Jase was telling me or Sally. He was in full, *I'm the man, and I make all the decisions* mode.

When the door closed behind us, Jase tried to tug me more fully into his arms but I flattened both of my hands against his chest and resisted. I was becoming way too dependent on a man I'd known all my life from a distance but had reconnected with in a much more personal way only three days ago. I needed to get some distance and perspective back. I couldn't let myself fall into thinking he was always going to be there for me. It would weaken me at a point in my life when I needed to be my strongest.

"Is this where you tell me you're all right and you don't need my help any longer?" Jase's question had a bit of an edge to it.

Lifting my chin, I said, "I do appreciate you taking care of me in there, but you're right, I'm going to tell you I'm okay. Because it's the truth. Don't feel sorry for me and act like you're the only one I can ask for help *if* I need it."

"Perhaps you'd rather have Brent take over and hold your hand through this? I'm sorry I dragged you away from all the knuckle rubbing going on between the two of you. My mistake. I thought you wanted away from him. Not to worry though. He still seemed eager enough to be of *service* even after I hauled you off. " The calm formality he used was sorta screwed up by his clenched jaw and sarcasm.

"Where the hell did that come from? I don't even know Brent Allen! But if he's willing to help find Gramps' killer I'll dang sure use him. Just like he used me today, to try and gather votes. I told you last night, and I'm telling you right now, thanks for your help but I can handle it from now on out. Once you get me home you can congratulate yourself on having done your neighborly duty." By the time I'd finished speaking, my fingers were curled into fists, nails digging into my palms. Mainly to keep from slapping Jase.

"Don't tell me you didn't notice, while he may have been drumming up votes he was also eyeballing you like a starving dog with a meaty bone dangled in front of him?" Ice was warmer than the look got from gray eyes gone glacial. "And if you're wanting to use somebody, you can damn well use me." He snapped my body against his before I could blast him with the words trapped in my throat.

Wrapping an arm around my lower back, he pulled me in so tight his belt buckle was going to leave an imprint in my stomach. His other hand fisted in my hair to jerk my head back at the perfect angle for him to swoop in and take control of my mouth.

I had no excuse for not resisting. Jase would've stopped immediately if I'd put up any serious protest to his kiss. Despite all my previous lies to myself—all the rejections aimed at Jase's insistence on us being friends, with hints at being possibly more—I wanted this. Right now, I needed this connection with Jase's warmth to chase away the terrible coldness that had settled into the very marrow of my bones. Regardless of the *I'm okay* shield, donned over the last couple days, nothing was right with my world. Perhaps I'd even pushed Jase into this fierce reaction, wanting proof I wasn't on my own.

What began as him asserting his dominance over my pride and refusal to acknowledge my needing him turned into a sensual assault. Yes, there was a wildness to the nip of his teeth on my bottom lip and his thrusting tongue demanding entry, but once access was granted the beast calmed. The heat of seduction took over. Our tongues began their sliding dance over each other as soon as he gained entry. He enticed mine to follow back into his mouth were he began a slow rhythmic suction, setting up a pulsing pull to the center of my core. I couldn't breathe, but that didn't seem to matter because he was my breath.

While entranced with the wonders of his mouth, the rest of my body was making discoveries of its own. My arms snaked around Jase, and my hands were exploring the long, corded muscles in his back, kneading in one spot, clenching in another. I tried to pull in tighter, to increase the friction between the softness of my breasts rubbing against the firmness of his torso.

A hardening ridge, growing behind a restricting zipper, left impressions of its own, of the wet and heated kind, centered at the apex of my thighs. Jase let his hand glide from my back down to encompass my ass in a firm clasp. Then, widening his stance, he pulled me in even tighter against that ridge and slowly began to rock his hips back and forth in the barest of movements. If my eyes hadn't been closed they would've crossed permanently.

The honking of a car horn slowly brought me back to our surrounds. Or maybe it was because Jase's movements ceased. His mouth, no longer locked with mine, allowed the fog to clear. His forehead rested against mine for half a second before he moved away from me.

"I'm sorry. That should have never happened." His apology came out rough.

What had been to me the most sensual experience in my limited sexual career—pretty sad, since I wasn't a virgin—was an embarrassment for him. The apology hurt but I'd be damned if I let him know that.

"Look, I've been under a lot of stress the last couple days and you've been dragged into it. It's understandable if the frustration just sorta exploded. We got a little carried away. I just need to learn to stay out of alleys. I don't have a very good track record with them. Just take me home and we'll forget this ever happened," I told him, with a self-disparaging, no-big-deal shrug. It was no doubt ruined by the breathy quality to my voice.

"It's not going to work." His hooded look was intimidating. The noticeable growl with each word he spoke wasn't exactly reassuring, either.

"What? You taking me home? I get it. The kiss was a mistake and if you don't want to take me home, no problem. I'll call Evan or Colin to come pick me up. I'm sure one of them would be happy to." If he thought I was going to go all clingy, after that liptastic blunder he regretted, he could think again.

"No. You're not calling anyone else. Yes, the kiss was a mistake. But not for the reasons you've probably got figured out in that convoluted brain of yours. I agree it was sparked by frustration at your stubborn pride. Insisting you can handle all this shit coming at you without my help. While in the next breath, you stand there and tell me you're more than willing to accept some other man's help. Now you're trying to act like what just happened meant nothing. Screw that. You want to handle something, then handle this. You're as attracted to me as I am to you." Jase wasn't yelling but he sure as heck wasn't calm either. "Damn it, Charlotte, I realize this isn't an ideal time for you and me to find out where this can go. But that's the way life works. Ideal times are rare. I'm not willing to wait for the next one to come along.

"Hell, your granddad just got murdered. You need the time to mourn and I want to give it to you. But you start talking crap about looking for his killer and I can't give you time. A shit storm is headed straight for you, and standing back to watch you get caught up in it is not an option. You need me *now*. Not in some distant future that will be perfect." If he sounded intimidating before he was downright menacing now.

Strangely enough, I wasn't scared in the least, but I was confused as hell. On second thought, confused didn't come close to touching on the way I felt. From being convinced he wanted to kick his own ass for kissing me, to being told he wanted me, while sounding like he was about to tear me limb from limb; it was a little hard to wrap my head around all of it.

"So you're saying you think we could have a thing?" Yeah, with all he just laid out that was the only question I had for him.

"I'm saying we already have a thing. You're the one who needs to stop looking at me through the eyes of the girl you were the first time we met. But you've fought me every step of the way, so damn determined to prove you're not the same kid who needed to be rescued. You don't even realize I already look at you the way a man looks at a desirable woman." Jase raked a hand through his hair in frustration.

"I'm seeing you now." Whispered words I wasn't positive he'd heard. Then louder, "I've been seeing the man you are for years. It just never seemed possible I could ever be more than some scared kid you took the time to save and then made sure was protected."

Aggression drained out of Jase and with an exquisite tenderness he cupped my face with both hands. "Honey, all I'm asking is for you to let me be here for you right now. Everything else will work out as it's supposed to."

"I can't promise I won't fight with you, especially when you get bossy." It was only fair he knew what he was getting into.

"Then we're even. I can't promise I won't get bossy." A gentle smile softened his lips.

Searching his face for several heartbeats didn't answer the million and one questions crowding my mind, but I guess that was part of life, too. Moving forward on hope and not on promises. I smiled back. "Let's go home."

CHAPTER TWELVE

Within minutes of arriving back home from making the funeral arrangements, the condolence visits started. They were spaced out, and most of the people didn't linger, but there was a constant trickle all afternoon and into the evening.

It was amazing how Jase talked to everyone who showed up and put them at ease. He even managed to keep those awkward silences from happening. The ones where a person shows up, with the best of intentions but, when faced with saying something after the usual "I'm so sorry," they draw a blank.

I couldn't help but notice a few—okay, a lot—of raised eyebrows when people first saw Jase and the role he took as host in my house. But Jase ignored any surprised looks directed at him. The man was so self-assured it was apparent he didn't give two cents for what anyone else thought about why he was there with me.

By the time the last person left, exhaustion, both physical and emotional, had me feeling like an empty balloon. Even Ruger was dragging his tail but not Jase. He went from shutting the door on the last visitor straight into cleanup. He was walking around the room, gathering Styrofoam coffee cups and picking up paper plates like it was nothing new to him. What guy does that? He should have been right on the heels of Dickson Flatts, the last man to leave, and high tailing it for his house before he got roped into doing exactly what he was already doing.

"If you keep this up I'm going to have to check under the hood to make sure you're male. First you cook and now you're cleaning house. If you tell me you also clean toilets I'm never letting you out of my life." A weary sigh puffed from between my lips.

Laughter burst from Jase, and he deposited his collection of trash on the dining room table. Walking back, he looped his arms around my waist and pulled my hips into his. "Darlin', you are more than welcome to look under my hood any time you feel the need. But, to ease your mind, growing up, Mom made sure Evan and I learned to take care of ourselves. Which meant cooking and cleaning. What can I say? I've been trained by the best."

Tenderness filled his expression. He lifted a hand to trail the tip of his index finger down the ridge of my nose, then continued on down to trace the outline of my lips. "You look done in. Why don't you go get comfortable and I'll gather up the rest of the cups and plates."

"Not this time, mister. We'll do this together if you insist on helping." Tired or not, I was not going to crawl up those steps and leave all this work for Jase.

Jase agreed without a fight, which was a bigger relief than it really should have been. I still had a fear Jase subconsciously saw me as weak and in need of a protector. I could never be attracted to someone with a fragile personality. Just the idea I might be seen that way by him made me cringe.

We made a good team as we worked together clearing the debris left behind. Once everything was back in order an awkwardness began creeping in. At least for me. What now? Did I kick him out like last night or were we going to take up where we'd left off earlier with that kiss?

Were there some kind of rules to follow on how to begin a relationship while planning a funeral? If there were, I wish someone had given me a copy.

"Stop it, Charlotte," Jase said. He walked up to where I stood, searching the room for something else to keep busy with. Large hands landed on my shoulders to hold me in place.

"What?" All right, that came out defensive sounding.

"We have plenty of time to figure out how this is going to work. It doesn't have to happen tonight or even next week. Let's just take it day by day." Jase was treating me like some skittish foal about to bolt. It was embarrassing that he knew I wasn't certain how to act now that our mutual attraction was out in the open.

Deciding I could at least pretend to be as laid back as Jase about our...whatever we had, I casually said, "You're right. No need to jump into anything here. As a matter of fact I'm beat and you have to be, also. Go home and get some rest. I'm going to take a long soak in the tub then head to bed. I promise to call you tomorrow if anything comes up I can't handle."

"Woman, you are going to be the death of me," Jase grumbled. My body stiffened, wondering what I'd done wrong now. My experience with having a steady boyfriend was zero. I'd gone on dates. Even dated the same guy for a few months. But there had never been anyone serious.

Jase dropped hands to my hips then leaned forward and whispered in my ear, "Do you honestly believe the way to get rid of me is to plant a picture in my head of you laying back naked, in a bathtub? Imaging that the only part of your body showing through the bubbles being the peaks of your breasts?"

His words and the husky roughness in which they were delivered had me trembling at the sensual image he conjured up. His words also had me confused again. It was starting to become a common occurrence around Jase.

"Before I decide to follow you into that tub, you need to go on up and take your bath. I've some spare clothes in my truck I'm going to grab for the morning.

Looks like I'm going to have another date with your couch tonight," Jase said, with a rueful grin.

Taking a deep breath I made my offer, "You don't have to sleep down here." Hopefully my eyes weren't as pleading as I had a feeling they might be.

"Yeah, baby, I do." He'd gone all low and hoarse. "Right now is a lousy time to be starting something physical. When we get to that point, I don't want any doubts in your mind it's you, a feisty as hell female, I'm taking to bed. Not some walking wounded you think I feel sorry for."

Disappointment and gratitude mingled in equal portions. Jase was right. I wanted him now, but it wouldn't hurt to give myself some time. Breathing space to make sure this wasn't prompted by a need to fill that hollow spot in the center of my chest created by Gramps' death.

Nodding in agreement, I told him, "You're right. Bad timing. But you don't need to spend the night on the couch. There's a spare bedroom. I'll throw some sheets on the bed and it's good to go. Or what's even better you should go home, Jase. I'm good for the rest of the night. If you want to come back tomorrow I'll be happy to have you here. There's bound to be a few more people stopping by and you handle them better than I do."

"I may not be climbing in your bed, *tonight*, but I'm not going to leave you alone to go through another night like the one you just had. I will take you up on the offer of a bed, though.

"Now, Ruger and I are going to make a trip outside. When we get back in I'll lock up for the night so you won't even have to come back down."

With the decision of whether Jase was going to share my bed or not settled, the weariness from earlier came crashing back. It was scary how grateful I was that Jase would be here with me. "I'll leave the light on in the spare room so you can find it easy. You can open my door to let Ruger in with me when you come up. There are towels in—"

"Baby. Go. Stop worrying. I've got this."

If I'd thought there would be fewer visitors today I'd obviously not factored in the draw of getting the chance to visit the granddaughter of a rumored moonshiner and possible murder victim. Apparently my gramps' death was the hottest ticket in the county. Price of admission—food. Casserole, pie, or cake, have one in hand and you could walk right in.

An overabundance of friends had never been a problem for me, but my granddad must have had legions, judging by the number of visitors who streamed in all day. Jase and I gave up on trying to fit everyone in the house and eventually moved out to the front yard, standing in the shade provided by the giant oak trees. Jase eventually called in Evan as back up in greeting and accepting goodies from arriving busybodies—now I was just being ugly.

Colin had to be contacted to help out by bringing extra coolers and ice to hold the mounds of food being transported in. There was plenty to offer everyone stopping by and plenty of helping hands in passing the offerings around.

Not positive when I began to notice the change in the visitors' ages and sex, but there was a noticeable shift from the crowd of elderly couples and single men of all ages. By the latter part of the day more single women, either alone or with Momma in tow, had shown up, and all of them were clustered around Jase and Evan.

The ladies were suitably shocked at the death of such a *wonderful old man*, who I'd bet my eye teeth they'd never met. They appeared to have forgotten exactly whose granddaddy he'd been. All of their horror at his death was not being expressed to me, but to the two Rydan brothers. Apparently, the death of an old moonshiner wasn't the only draw.

Standing back and watching the show was amusing at first. Jase and Evan handled their adoring fans with the ease of men long used to being objects of pursuit. It stopped being so funny when I recognized a couple of Jase's ex-girlfriends mingling with the crowd.

It became down right irritating when Connie came sashaying from her car, swinging her hips in a tight, white, mini belt—excuse me—skirt. I don't know what kind of bra she was wearing but the dimples on her nipples were showing through the stretch of a pink tank top. All of her non-slut clothes must have been in the wash.

The other women surrounding the two Rydans parted like the Red Sea as Connie never slowed in her approach. When she reached her objective, Jase, she handed off the pie she was carrying to the closest female and waved her hand in a shooing motion.

What was the final spark to my fuse was the way both men stood there with stupid grins on their faces. They kept giving some sort of eyebrow signals to each other.

"Jase, I simply can't tell you what a shock it was to hear about dear Mr. Donley's passing. Poor little Char must just be crippled with grief to resort to calling in a charitable man, such as yourself, to help in what should be her duties to honor her granddaddy. Bless her heart." Her hand on Jase's bicep rubbed and squeezed like she was assessing a slab of prime beef. It was about to be ripped off at the wrist, just as soon as I could get to her. That bitch just insulted me twice and *blessed my heart*!

A hand on my arm prevented me from marching across to Connie to start pulling off body parts. And Jase might have been in danger of me ripping off his eyebrows if he wiggled them in Evan's direction one more time.

"Ignore her, Char. Let her make a dang fool of herself in front of everyone," Colin said, as he stepped in front of me, bringing me to a halt. "Jase can handle her. He knows the score and ain't about to buy what she's sellin'. Besides, I need to talk with you, and while Connie is putting on her show is a good time to get out of here."

Taking one last look in Connie and Jase's direction I decided to shelve my homicidal thoughts. I turned and led Colin away from the crowd. Rounding the back of the house, I checked to make sure we were blocked from anyone seeing or hearing us.

Colin didn't waste any time in getting to the point. "It's already started, Char, and you need to start watchin' your back. Things are gittin' serious a hell of a lot faster than I figured on. There's already been three different men come to me askin' if I'd any notions as to where your granddaddy's records were. They offered some big money if I'd sell to them. A couple of them ol' boys was from town, and jest scared people were gonna find out about them buying shine and reselling it." Colin shrugged in a dismissive way as he didn't think there was much to worry about from those two. Then his whole stance changed. His body visibly started tensing and his fingers started flexing in and out of a fist. "But one of them you know. It was that bastard Billy Wayne. Thing with BW though, was different.

"He first tried to hire me to make shine for him. Said he had someone willin' to pay top dollar for moonshine made from Jim's mash recipes. Acted like we could be partners if I could get my hands on them. Then he started in on if I could get Jim's information on all his customers away from you he'd even give me a bonus on top of being his partner.

"Talked about how those records were gonna make it easy to contact everyone what bought off Jim and let them know their supply would keep right on comin'. I told him there weren't no way I'd be partners with him, and I couldn't, even if I was a willin', since I'd no idea where any of that stuff was kept.

"He got real mean real fast, you know how that ignorant asshole can get. Said I better rethink his offer 'cause the next one wasn't gonna be so friendly. And it might not be to me. That's when I told him if he even looked at you hard I'd kill him."

Anger not fear was my first reaction to what Colin was telling me. There was no doubt in my mind that if BW saw an opportunity to take over Gramps business he would jump on it with both feet. But I couldn't help but wonder if there wasn't more to it. That little cat sack just placed himself at the top of my list of suspects.

"Don't mention this to Jase or Evan." I was not going to have both of the Rydans going into a lockdown set of mind when it came to me. Jase seemed to have me under twenty-four hour surveillance as it was. From that point on I needed some space.

First off I had to find those darn journals to even start trying to figure out who might be responsible for the murder. Jase hadn't asked about them—yet—but he was going to want to check them out sooner, rather than later.

I suspected those records were as much a part of his insistence on staying with me as the not wanting me to be on my own with my grief. The fact I could even believe that of him might be a wakeup call. I needed to admit I wasn't even the tiniest bit secure in his attraction for me.

"Char, do you think it's a good idea keeping anything from Jase? You know as well as me BW was threatin' you. Jase seems real taken with you, and he could keep you safer than just about anyone." Colin's hesitation at keeping Jase in the dark just showed how much everyone worried how Jase was going to react if they did something he might not like.

"Colin, what I'm about to tell you is just between you and me." I searched his face to see if he understood just how serious what I was about to tell him was. "I don't know where the records Gramps kept are hidden. Actually, I was hoping you knew. Now that I know you don't have a clue either, I'm going to need some alone time to search for them. Once we make it through tomorrow, I'm going to get down to some serious hunting. I'd rather do it without Jase breathing down my neck. That's why I'm asking you help me keep a few things private."

Bugged eyes and a hand rubbed back and forth across the top of his buzz cut signaled extreme agitation. Colin obviously didn't think much about my throwing out threats to hunt down a killer with records I didn't even have in my possession. Blowing out a worried sigh, Colin said, "Whatever you need I'm here, Char. But I dang shor' hope this don't come back to bite us both in the ass."

I sincerely hoped it didn't either, but a huge part of me needed to do this on my own without Jase. It was my family who had been attacked. I wanted to be the one to find and settle the score with the killer. And there was a large part of me that felt like I still needed to prove to Jase I wasn't that little kid anymore. The one who couldn't handle the big boys in a fight.

CHAPTER THIRTEEN

Seeing my gramps laid out in that coffin during visitation was devastating. Viewing that body, with stiffly styled hair and heavy makeup, was when I finally realized he was never going to be calling me Sis ever again. It didn't make a lot of sense; after all, I'd seen him lying on the forest floor. No hope it had been a cruel mistake.

No, it was the artificial caricature of my vital, larger than life Gramps that hammered home some hard truths. No more would he tell wonderful stories of way back when. No more teasing about my fancy-pants words, or any of the other hundred-and-one ways he'd filled my life with love and laughter.

Jase stood by me as more formal condolences were expressed from visitors at the funeral home. Hopefully I made the correct responses when addressed and didn't stare blankly whenever people were talking to me. During the drive home, Jase insisted on sleeping in the spare bedroom again, just in case I needed him during the night.

As soon as we made it home I settled on the couch, not willing to face my dark room and darker thoughts on my own. Jase went into the kitchen to get me a glass of water and aspirin, instinctively knowing the need without me having to ask. Once the pills had been swallowed and the glass sat on an end table, he settled beside me and pulled me onto his lap. I huddled against him as he rubbed my back, placed tiny kisses around my face, and softly whispered words of comfort as I clung for dear life.

Jase eventually carried me up to my room where he stood me on my feet. He gave me orders to get ready for bed, then turned to leave. Before he could walk away I grabbed his hand. There was a tenderness in his look as if he already knew what my request was going to be. "Please, I don't want to be alone tonight."

He pressed his free hand to my cheek and caressed it with a callused thumb, then solemnly spoke, "I'll be back to tuck you in."

I'd only been under the sheets a short time when Jase walked in without waiting to be invited. He was wearing boxers and nothing else. As though it were the most natural thing in the world, he pulled back the covers and climbed in beside me.

There was nothing sexual in his touch as Jase turned me on my side then arranged my back to his front. Thick arms enveloped me with warmth and support. Once we were settled to his satisfaction, it was like a dam burst. One that had held back all my thoughts and emotions all evening.

Words spilled out of me in a flood of remembrances, all centered on Gramps. Jase listened, asked a question now and then, and we even laughed together over some of the antics Gramps had pulled through the years. For me, the retelling of his life was a letting go more real than anything that would take place at the funeral. I said my goodbyes as I talked, and talked, until exhaustion pulled me into sleep.

Jase was gone when I peeled my eyelids back way too early to start the day. Staring at the empty spot where Jase had lain, my eyes traveled over the rumpled sheets. I told myself it was ridiculous to feel abandoned but that emotional reaction kept cropping up lately.

Smoothing a hand over the cool sheets up towards where his head had left an indent on the pillow I noticed a note in the little dip. It simply read he would be back later.

The crinkle of paper was unnaturally loud as my hand tightened around the note. I held my breath while reaching out with my senses, searching for any hint there was someone else in the house. My home had that desolate feeling that shouts "you're alone." Funny how I'd never noticed such emptiness before Jase started making it a habit to spend the night.

I refused to give in to the bleakness of what the morning had in store for me without Jase to distract me. Instead I chose to look at this chance to have a few hours alone as a positive thing. I'd not had two minutes to call my own since Gramps' passing. This would be a great opportunity to make a trip out to his house and get a couple hours of searching in before I had to start getting ready for the ordeal of the service at the graveyard.

My climb out of bed was more of a reluctant crawl than a rip-roaring charge to get things accomplished while I had some alone time. Getting dressed was going to be put on the back burner until I'd made a visit to the coffeepot.

After I wandered downstairs I stood in bewilderment, staring at the chaos that seemed to have overtaken my home. Really, I understood everyone had been trying to express his or her concern and sorrow for my loss. But all I could focus on was the mountain of food swamping the counters in the kitchen, old buffet and dining room table.

There were enough baked goods to stock a bakery for a week. I didn't even want to think about the meats and casseroles in the refrigerator and coolers. What the hell did everyone expect me to do with all of this food once they were gone? I was as guilty as any woman from the country of having delivered more than my fair share of casseroles and pies to a bereaved family. The operative word there: family. Something I no longer had.

Coffee. I needed coffee. Caffeine was going to make all of this easier to handle. Hopefully it would also give me the *oomph* necessary to push me into throwing on some clothes and heading over to Gramps'.

A knock on my door had me groaning in disgust at myself for having piddled around so long that I was now trapped until I could get rid of whoever was standing on my front porch. Turning my back on the southern buffet of comfort, I stomped my way over to the door. Flinging it open, provided me with one hell of a shock. I'd been more than ready to give whoever it was a piece of my mind for showing up this early in the morning.

The sight of Mrs. Rydan standing on my porch had me choking over whatever I'd been about to screech. She took one look at me then stepped forward to wrap me in a tight hug. She didn't say a word but so much understanding was conveyed in her tight grip the possibility of tears showing up was a serious threat. After a heartfelt show of sympathy she stepped back and, in a matter of fact voice, she took charge. "You can either sit while I make you some breakfast or you can head on back to your room and start getting ready to face the day. I'm not going to lie. It's going to be rough, but I'm here to help smooth the edges. Jase and Evan are with Colin out at the grave site, taking care of that end of things."

I'm positive she saw me flinch at the mention of the grave but thankfully she ignored it.

"My husband, Ben, will be here in a little bit to start relocating all this food to the church's kitchen. I've made arrangements with the Methodist Episcopal Church for everyone to gather there after the service instead of returning here. Since you very wisely choose to have only a graveside service, an announcement will be made after the funeral so everyone will know to head to the church for the repast, instead of invading your home again. Jase thought that would be what you'd want." It was fascinating she could manage to be so *take charge* with a voice so dulcet.

As I was being sucked into the vortex of Jase's mother's will, I began to understand where his overabundance of dominating authority came from. In all the years I'd known the Rydans this was the first time I'd been the focus of Mrs. Rydan's sole attention. She was definitely a force to be reckoned with.

Luckily, her bossiness was easier for me to stomach than when Jase was doing the same thing. Right now, her take-charge attitude was exactly what I needed. Jase had told me on the day we'd found my gramps I wasn't going to be alone through this. Just hadn't realized his whole family was going to be there for me also. Still, couldn't help but wonder how his parents felt about being volunteered to assist the granddaughter of a moonshiner.

"Charlotte?" A kindly nudge of a question.

Hearing my name snapped me back to reality. I'd zoned out. And how embarrassing was that? "I'm sorry Mrs. Rydan, what were you asking?"

"None of this Mrs. Rydan, call me Martha, and when my husband gets here he's going to expect you to call him Ben. So, which will it be, breakfast or your room?" Commanding she might be, but her questions and orders were delivered with such a musical pitch it came off as soothing rather than irritating.

Opting for coffee and my room, I left her standing in the kitchen making battle plans. Before I left, Martha gave orders for me to take all the time needed to prepare for the day. I knew she wasn't simply talking about bathing and getting dressed. She assured me any visitors who might show up would be put to work. Said it would serve them right if anyone was so rude as to drop by on the day of the funeral. I was proud of myself for not pointing out the irony of that statement. And, despite losing any chance of making a quick run by Gramps', I had to admit the woman was a lifesaver.

Taking Martha's advice, I lingered over my shower and the necessary chore of building the shields that were going to help me make it through the day. In a way, last night felt like it had been my own private memorial to Gramps, and what was going to happen today seemed superfluous.

It was an event for the public that had to be endured, and once it was over I could get on with the business of finding the person responsible for all this pain. Gramps had always demanded I grab life with both hands and not wallow in grief when his time came. But he'd never planned on being murdered.

Even though Martha had encouraged me to take as long as needed before making an appearance back downstairs, guilt niggled at me over the two hours I'd spent in my room. When I did finally make it to the center of the kitchen, it was hard to believe the amount of food that had already been hauled out of the house. Mr. Rydan, Ben, appeared to be getting ready to leave with another load, if the boxes stacked on the dining table were any indication. As soon as Martha saw me standing there, looking a little lost, she alerted Ben to my presence.

He had the same tall stance as his sons. Age had not softened his frame in the slightest. He was an extremely attractive man with a light scattering of gray hair around his temples. Jase may have gotten his dark hair from his mom, but his eyes were all Rydan. Just like his dad's. Those steely gray irises held a warmth of understanding as Ben acknowledged me.

Jase had certainly inherited his dad's square jaw and devastatingly sensual mouth. It was easy to picture how Jase would look in his fifties after seeing his father up close. And it was going to be a good look on him.

"Miss Donley, we've never been introduced and I'm sorry the first time we meet it's such a sad time." Ben's rough cadence sounded so much like Jase's I added it to the list of things passed along to his son.

Ben walked up to stand close but he didn't immediately try for a hug or grab my hand for a shake. He gave the impression he was letting me make the decision on how comfortable I felt about physical contact from a strange male. If only some of the others who had shown up in the last few days had been so considerate. There'd been a few hugs that came close to crossing a line and that was just gross.

Sticking my hand out for a shake I told him, "Please, call me Char. Martha has already told me to call you Ben. I am very grateful for all your family has done and is doing for me."

Ben gave a deep chuckle and my hand a firm shake. "I'm betting my wife whirled in and began organizing both you and your life the second you opened your door and let her in the house. For such a tiny thing she likes to throw her weight around. She has certainly lined me out over the years."

Martha punched her husband in the shoulder. "You love it."

Ben leaned in and gave her a smacking kiss on the lips. "No, ma'am. I love you. Now I better be getting the last of these boxes to the church." He gave me an encouraging smile before he picked up a load and headed for the door.

That's what I wanted, someday. A man who wasn't afraid to show love for his wife after what had to be over thirty years of marriage.

After Ben left Martha turned her attention to me. She directed me to sit at the table, where she preceded to lay out a light meal. "You probably don't think you can eat right now, but it's for the best if you try. The last thing you want to do is give those yahoos who go to every funeral in the country something to talk about if you keel over from hunger." She smiled as she urged me to eat.

CHAPTER FOURTEEN

After choking down as much as possible, without my stomach revolting, I got up and cleared the table. Martha refused any further offers to help pack what remained of the commiserative gifts of food. Giving in, I made a line for the back door. Ruger immediately trotted over to me for some reassurance it was okay for all of these strangers to be wandering around our home.

Squatting down in front of him I took his face in both hands and stared into serious golden-brown eyes. "Don't worry, buddy, they'll be gone soon and things will get back to normal." I was trying to con myself and my dog, because after today, I didn't have a clue what normal was going to look like.

I gave his ears a good scratching, trying to make us both feel better. "Tell you what. If you see one more casserole headed for the front door you have my permission to tackle whoever is carrying it."

Someone clearing their throat was my first indication Ruger and I were no longer alone. Whoever it was, no doubt was scandalized by what I'd just said. Not everyone in the community appreciated my sense of humor. Standing up and brushing at the hem of my dress, I slowly turned to see who had walked up behind me.

The first true easy breath I'd drawn all day happened when I saw it was Colin. It was also the first real danger to the thick wall I'd been hiding behind in order to make it through what was to come. I walked over to someone who was hurting as much as me over the loss of Gramps.

"If you brought a casserole I should warn you, I've given Ruger permission to attack." I hoped he would follow my lead and steer away from anything that would crack the barrier holding my grief in check.

"So I heard." Colin smiled but it wasn't a natural looking one by anyone's stretch of imagination.

"In my own defense for what you just heard, have you been inside my house lately? There's enough food in there to feed a third world country. Mr. Rydan, I mean Ben—jeezz, it feels weird to call him Ben—anyway, Ben has been hauling it over to the church all day. If there's been anyone in the county who hasn't dropped by I'm not sure who it would be. And everyone's had a covered dish in hand." I was babbling, knew it, but couldn't stop myself. "Hell, Colin, ninety percent of these people have never even stepped foot on our property before. I didn't realize most of them even knew Gramps."

Colin's face went all tight and pinched looking. When I finally shut up his mouth twisted in sarcasm. Not an expression usually seen from easy going, fun-loving Colin. "A lot of them there ninety percent are customers scared not to show up."

His comment wasn't a total surprise, since I'd been thinking something along the same line. Having Colin voice the same opinion just confirmed what I already believed. Other than the women who had shown up to scope out Jase and Evan, and the people who'd come simply out of curiosity, the rest had a definite pattern to them. The men who showed up were overly solicitous, and if the wife came she'd mouth the requisite expression of sympathy while at the same time looking like she would rather be sucking green persimmons than having to act sympathetically over my loss.

Heaving a sigh, as if regretting he'd started this line of conversation, he nevertheless continued. "Char, you know Jim had lots of honest to God, good friends. Folks that counted themselves lucky to be able to call him one. You also know a lot of folks looked down on your grandpa for the way he made a livin'. A lot of those same folks, that wouldn't have spit on him if he was on fire, were some of his best customers."

None of it was news to me. I'd lived with it my whole life. I'm not sure if small towns bred more hypocrites and mean bastards than big cities but it felt like we had more than our fair share.

Wanting to change the subject, I asked Colin where Jase and Evan were. He explained how they'd gone back to their places and were getting cleaned up. I then asked him the question that had been rattling around in my brain ever since I'd gotten up this morning.

"I want to ask if Ruger and I can ride with you out to the graveyard for the service and then to the reception at the church afterward?" It meant a lot to me; still, I searched his face for any signs of discomfort over my request. I didn't want to cause him any distress.

"Ain't you gonna ride in the family limo with that great-aunt of yours?" Colin sounded puzzled but at least he hadn't rejected my request right off the bat.

Just the thought of riding in a car that had carried so many grieving family members made my skin crawl. The amount of anguish released in such a vehicle had to have seeped into the seat cushions. I realized how insane it sounded, but logic wasn't going to override my aversion.

"No, I didn't arrange for one. As for Great-Aunt Ivy, her daughter is driving her straight to the grave site for the service then back to my house. They're both going to spend the night with me."

Drawing a deep breath, I continued, "Colin, you loved Gramps as much as me and I need that today. I need to feel like there's someone with me who's going to miss him the way I do." Jase would understand why I wanted Colin beside me. At least I hoped he would.

"You know I ain't much good at this emotional stuff, but I'll dang shor' go through it with you. If that's what you want I'll be proud to do it." He put out his hand for a shake, as if closing a deal. My heart lightened a little at the gesture. This is what I needed from Colin, his awkward genuineness to help me get through the service.

Colin left with promises to return in plenty of time to pick both me and Ruger up for the funeral. Having no wish to return inside, I moved back up onto the porch to get out of the heat of the sun. Standing and staring out across the fields that adjoined my backyard, I heard the slap of the screen door. Turning, I expected to see either Martha or Jase coming to check up on me. Maybe even Evan, although he'd been avoiding me like the plague the last few days.

"Miss Donley, Mrs. Rydan said I would find you out here. I'm sorry, Miss Donley sounds so formal, may I call you Charlotte?" The last person I ever expected to see was standing on my back porch smiling at me. The smooth tones and well-groomed appearance belonged to Brent Allen.

"Char. You can call me Char." I didn't say "no one calls me Charlotte but Jase," but I thought it.

"Char, I hope you will forgive my intrusion, but I felt the need to apologize for the other day in town, and wanted to do so before you laid your grandfather to rest." He reached for one of my hands, with less of a handshake reach, since his palm was facing up, and more of a *knuckle rubbing* one, as Jase had called it. Not really knowing how to avoid it without being obviously rude I let him take my hand. And the knuckle rubbing commenced. "While I'd had the best of intentions in offering you my condolences, unfortunately, I let my zeal for informing the public of my deep-felt conviction all citizens in our county should be treated equally turn it into a sideshow. It was only after Jase had, quite rightly, dragged you away I realized what a very public display of your emotions I'd made. It should have been a private matter between the two of us, and I'm deeply sorry." His smile seemed sincerely regretful.

"Mr. Allen, do you always sound like you're either making a political speech or addressing a courtroom?" This is why I had *sooo* many friends. Fortunately, Allen chose to find my question amusing instead of bitchy.

He grinned at me and replied, "Brent. You've got to call me Brent, since I really hope we can become good friends. I need someone like you around to call me on it when I start laying the bullshit on too thick."

Brent's flip from distinguished candidate to good ol' boy was bizarrely quick. But now he sounded more like a normal guy it was easier for me to see why so many women found him attractive. He wasn't in Jase's league—his hands were too soft when compared to Jase's and his suits too fancy—but there was no denying he was a good-looking man.

"If you think you can handle my…sometimes less than tactful ways, we might be able to manage the friends part." I didn't exactly grin at him but this surprise visit had diverted my mind from the impending ordeal for a couple minutes.

"Now I've delivered my apology and made a new friend I'm not going to hang around. Just wanted you to know I'd figured out what a jerk I'd been. Also, wanted to be certain you'd call if there was any way I could help in your search to get justice for Mr. Donley." Brent pulled out a business card and offered it to me.

"This is a more personal card and has a cell number only close friends have. I want you to have it and know I'm always available to you. It doesn't matter what day of the week or hour of the day." His intense look and change of voice to something more intimate set off alarms that Jase might have been right when he suggested Brent was a little too interested in me. I gave a mental snort of disgust at myself for letting Jase cause me to see things not there. Taking the card I thanked him for dropping by and thoughtfully watched him leave. Brent might prove to be useful in helping me find my gramps' killer. The verdict was still out on him.

CHAPTER FIFTEEN

My hands and shoulders ached from all the handshakes and hugs, first at the graveside, and now here in the basement of the Methodist Episcopal Church. Everyone who had been at the graveside service had come to the church to share in the repast after the funeral was over. Thank God for Martha. She always seemed to sense the exact moment when the person expressing their sorrow for my loss began to be too much for me. She would step in at just the right moment to lure them away by offering something to eat or by dangling the prospect of a conversation with someone who had a juicy bit of gossip. She had a talent for leading away the most persistent mourner.

Her latest victim was Miss Lori. I admired the way she maneuvered between me and Miss Lori with the precision of a Quarter horse, cutting her off and herding her towards the casseroles. As Martha eased her away, I heard her ask Miss Lori for an opinion on whether one of the dishes tasted off and might need to be discreetly pitched. We wouldn't want to offend the person who had brought the food offering.

Not wanting to waste such a brilliant tactical move, I searched the crowd for my great-aunt and second cousin. Hopefully they were as ready to leave as I was. I located them in a crowd of older folks and walked over to check with them.

Standing beside my second cousin, we both listened as her mom enthusiastically exchanged stories with old friends she hadn't seen in decades. After a minute, I quietly explained to my cousin that I was ready to leave but they should stay as long as they wanted. It wouldn't matter how late they were, since I'd be at home waiting for them.

Janet started apologizing almost immediately, saying they had decided not to stay after all, and were going to head back home. It was only a three hour drive, and even though her mom was old she had a strong will. Great-Aunt Ivy wanted to sleep in her own bed tonight, and was determined her daughter was going to take her home.

It was both a relief and kind of sad they wouldn't be staying, but I understood. We were more or less strangers, despite the blood-tie, and from personal experience I knew how difficult it was to change a Donley's mind once it was made up. I said my goodbyes to both, with hugs and promises to do a better job of keeping in touch in the future.

Looked like I had a free afternoon and evening ahead of me. A perfect chance for me to finally make it to Gramps' house to search the place from top to bottom. If I got lucky, maybe the records would turn up fast and Jase would never need to know I'd been stretching the truth a mile about having my hands on them.

Now that I knew this was my chance to begin hunting for the killer, I was impatient to get started. It was time to round up Colin and head back to my place.

When I spied him on the far side of the room, with a group of rough looking men, I took off in his direction. As I neared them it became clear they were a lot more intimidating looking than the average man one usually found in church. One in particular struck me as obviously being in charge. He was also the only one Colin introduced me to.

"Char, this is Sawyer. He wants to talk to you." Colin made the introduction with an apologetic note in his voice as he waved a hand in the man's direction.

I studied Sawyer closely and at the same time he studied me. He was a towering mass of tightly controlled emotions not easily identified. From his penetrating stare to his massively booted feet, he projected an image of "you don't want to fuck with me." Not the best thought to have in church, but he couldn't be described any other way.

There was nothing particularly handsome about him when his features were taken individually, but there was something very compelling. Something that pulled at a woman's interest. Perhaps I should have been afraid—at the least, nervous—but I trusted Colin to not deliberately place me in harm's way.

While I'd been taking my time assessing him, Jase magically appeared next to me. Sawyer turned from me and lasered Jase with a steely gaze that matched the color of his eyes. Jase, every bit as tall as Sawyer, returned his stare with an inflexible one of his own. Until that moment, when those two alpha males were sizing each other up, I'd never realized Jase's civilized appearance was just a thin veneer and how quickly it could be shed.

Looking at him now, it was easy to imagine how lethal Jase's strength could be if he ever chose to use it. It was sexy as hell and gave me the same delicious adrenaline spike I would receive whenever I did something illicit. Like visiting Gramps at his still. Again, not the best thoughts to have in a church basement.

Sawyer broke the silence first. In a mocking tone he said, "Take it easy, Rydan. I'm not here to screw with your woman. Shit, I have enough sensitivity to know how to act in a fucking church after a fucking funeral. Just needed to get a couple things straight with her."

So the guy had a sense of humor, but I'm not sure Jase appreciated it, and Colin was visibly cringing. Sawyer's buddies apparently enjoyed it, judging by the snickers and elbowing going on.

"Sawyer, she doesn't need this shit here, especially not now. If you had something you wanted to get off your chest you should have come to me and left her out of it." Jase wasn't exactly unfriendly but there was a careful watchfulness to his scrutiny.

It was clear the two men knew each other but I'd never met Sawyer before. Not to say I hadn't heard of him. He was a year older than Jase, but I knew all the gossip about how the two of them used to be best buds. Apparently it had been a source of many anxious moments for Jase's parents. But obviously their lives had taken radical turns when they left their teen years behind them.

While Gramps never let me be directly involved with the moonshine trade, it would be impossible to not know who some of the major players were. Sawyer was about as big as you got, and it wasn't just in the shine business. I'd heard whispered rumors of how dangerous he could be. But for some reason my gramps had liked him.

In any case, it didn't matter who knew who; being talked about as if I wasn't there was getting aggravating. "If you two haven't noticed, I'm standing right here, and I don't appreciate being talked about as if I weren't. If Sawyer has something to say, he doesn't have to go through anyone to talk to me. I'm a big girl. I've been allowed to converse with the grown-ups for years."

Colin and the two men who had accompanied him looked stunned. Sawyer's lips lifted the tiniest fraction at the corners in what I guessed was supposed to pass for a grin. Jase was harder to read with his veiled gaze now fastened on me. Apparently most people didn't normally talk to him the way I just had. Jase either, for that matter.

Then again, I wasn't most people and now was as good a time as any for these men to figure it out.

"Fuck, man, let me know when you get tired of her sharpening those claws on you. I'd be willing to let her leave a few scars in my hide." Sawyer left nobody in doubt he was serious in spite of his derisive tone.

Jase never lifted his eyes off me as he said, "Since Charlotte doesn't liked to be talked about as if she isn't here, I suggest you tell her what was so important that you couldn't wait until later."

The tone was mild enough, but the shuttered look in his eyes had me worried I might have finally carried the independence bid too far. It was also disturbing Jase hadn't told Sawyer he wasn't going to get tired of me. But this was me in all my snarky, "*don't think before I speak*," glory. It was better Jase figure it out right now. The lost female of the last couple days wasn't me. Yeah, he'd had peeks at the real me a couple times. But if he couldn't handle my sometimes-smart mouth it was better we both realized it now before this *thing,* we were supposed to have, went any further.

Sawyer scanned the area around us, making sure we were a private island in the sea of people surrounding us. I did the same and noticed everyone, except for Jase's family, were not so much as looking in our direction. The Rydans were still mingling with the thinning crowd, while at the same time plainly keeping an eye out for any trouble Jase couldn't handle on his own.

"We've never met, but I've had business dealings with your granddaddy for a few years. It's because he never tried to fuck me over and helped me out once that I'm even bothering to tell you this." Any trace of amusement there might have been earlier was erased, and the ruthless individual I'd first guessed him to be was back. "Word going around has it you're going to go looking for the person who killed Donley. Same word says you have records of some sort identifying all his customers, along with the runners who made the drops. To save you some time, you can cross me and my men's names off the list. I didn't kill him and none of my boys did either. Colin knows my guys, ask him to ID them if you need help."

Colin met my look straight on, and gave a tiny nod as if confirming what Sawyer had just said. He and I were clearly going to need to have a talk when he drove me home.

"Just so you know, it sure as fuck wouldn't have bothered me to tell you if I'd had anything to do with it." The very flatness with which he made the statement convinced me he was telling the truth.

"Is that it, Sawyer? Sounds to me like you could've had Colin relay the information to Charlotte. Why the face to face? And why here?" Jase was as dispassionate with his questions as Sawyer had been delivering his denial of any involvement in Gramps' death.

Sawyer did that thing with his lips again that I think was maybe a smile. "Here's as good a place as any, and I wanted to see what kind of kin Donley had left. Wanted to see if she's got the kick-ass needed to back-up her mouth. Looks like she does, so I'm gonna clue her in on something else."

"Sooo happy you approve of me and I passed your little test." Man, I wanted to lay into Sawyer and Jase for once again talking like I wasn't there. But if Sawyer had something he thought was important, it probably was, judging the way everyone, aside from Jase, acted like the man was some countrified crime boss.

"Charlotte." The way Jase growled my name he might as well said *shut up.* I didn't like it, but Jase was right. Sawyer was offering help, and I'd a feeling that didn't happen very often. Not for free, anyway.

"There's been some cocksucker moving in on my whiskey territory last couple years. He started out small enough that I didn't take the time to squash him. Things changed a few months back, and now he's starting to fuck up some of my deals. Started using BW as more than a runner and set him up to start buying from some of the moonshiners, your granddaddy included. Whoever it is, he's making damn sure to keep his hands clean by working through a group of low-level butt-fucks that don't know shit when my boys have questioned them. Politely of course." The smile he flashed as he said the last part was so malicious I was glad he was sharing information with me and not hunting for it. "BW's been braggin' how he was going to get his hands on Donley's mash recipes and start his own stills.

"Now Donley's dead he's put a stick in it on the braggin', but something is up with him. Fucker hasn't been shooting his pie-hole off as much as usual. That ain't like him. Because of his daddy being Sheriff, and a private agreement between his daddy and me, I've left him alone. For now. Besides, don't think BW has any more of an idea who the new cocksucker is than any of the other butt-fucks." Nobody was ever going to accuse Sawyer of being delicate.

"Are you thinking BW and this new player had something to do with Donley's death? Why would either one of them want to kill the best whiskey maker around?" Jase's question clearly held a note of skepticism.

"I'm just telling you what I know. And I know shit is about to start happening that ain't been seen in decades around here, and it's going to center around the shine business. Donley's death isn't sitting well with a lot of people in the trade, and this new cocksucker seems to be right at the center of it all. BW's up to his ass in it somehow, and I figured Donley's granddaughter deserved to know. What she chooses to do with what I've told y'all is up to her." With no "nice to have met you," or even a "kiss my ass," Sawyer and his two pit bull buddies turned and walked away.

Jase was silent as he watched the trio leave. When the door closed behind them, he turned his attention to me. His eyes still had a hooded look, which made it difficult to determine what was going on with him. In a neutral tone he said, "After your company leaves tomorrow, give me a call. We have things to discuss concerning all this moonshine business."

Jase definitely wasn't happy right now, and things were only going to get worse if he found out about my lying to him, by omission, about my relatives. He still thought my great-aunt and her daughter were spending the night with me, and I wasn't going to tell him any different. I tried to justify it by telling myself I needed alone time to do some serious searching for the missing records.

To top it off, all the talk about illegal shine in front of Jase felt wrong. There had to be something seriously wrong with me when I was more worried about him being dragged into the bootleg business than about us discussing all of this in a church right after my gramps' funeral. For me, all of my goodbyes had been said last night, and today had been about closure.

Well, the unexpected wealth of information from Sawyer was about closure, too. The kind I'd find when the murderer paid for what he'd taken from me.

CHAPTER SIXTEEN

As I stood and watched Colin pull out of my drive, and head back down the lane to the county road, I felt unsettled and numb at the same time. Definitely in a weird place with my emotions. Standing there, in the heat of the late afternoon sun, I simply wanted to let my mind rest.

I was on information overload from what Sawyer had revealed today and the talk with Colin while he drove me home. To top it off, there was the way Jase had left me at the church. He'd simply walked away after delivering his orders to call him in the morning. I took a deep breath then slowly blew it out and wished my freaking whacked-out mental state could be expelled so easily.

Telling myself I was in that hollowed-out spot a person lands in when a dreaded event has passed, and an uncertain future is staring them in the face, I turned and headed for the front porch. Ruger had beat me to the front door and was whining and digging at it, anxious to get inside.

"Hang on, buddy, I'm coming. It was crappy you had stay outside the church during the reception, but we got enough looks as it was at the cemetery from everyone wondering why the heck there was a dog with me. But you loved him too, didn't you, big boy. You deserved to be there."

The whole time I'd been talking nonsense to Ruger I'd been unlocking and opening the door, preparing to step into the house. The wooden barrier was barely cracked when Ruger pushed his way through and his whine escalated into a deep chested growl. He burst into the house like he was on the trail of hot prey, but the sight revealed as the door swung open froze me in my tracks.

The living room was in utter chaos. Pictures were ripped off the walls, seat cushions were scattered, and the end tables were lying on their sides. Standing in the middle of the doorway, I could only stare in disbelief. I forced myself to move and check out the rest of the house. I picked my way through the destruction, heading for the dining room. The ancient buffet had every drawer in its giant oak frame pulled out and dumped. But it wasn't until I saw how all the family photos had been swiped off the top that the disbelief began to recede and a burning rage kindled in my gut.

There was no longer any hesitation in my step as I made for the mudroom off the kitchen and straight for the door that led to my jewelry work shop. As expected the locked door had been kicked in. The tiny office area off to the side of the open room was a disaster.

The business computer was missing from the top of my desk. Files were flung around the room, as if they had been tossed over a shoulder once they'd been riffled through. Spinning to inspect the behemoth of a safe Gramps had insisted on buying, I was marginally relieved to note that, while battered, it was still intact.

Leaving the work room behind, I hurried back into the kitchen and the answer as to how they had gained entry to the house was easy to figure out. The glass in the backdoor had been shattered, making it a simple matter for the thief to reach in and release the lock.

Again every drawer and cabinet had been searched in the kitchen, the robbers even going so far as to go through my mother's recipe boxes, littering the floor with the cards. Racing into the living room, I headed for the stairs, noting along the way my TV and stereo were gone.

Taking the steps two at a time, I joined Ruger upstairs. He was inspecting each room, growling nonstop. His hair was raised from the scruff of his neck to the base of his tail. I wanted to growl and howl right along with him.

The destruction in my bedroom was on the edge of manic frenzy. The all-encompassing rage still had its talons in me but there was also an overwhelming sense of invasion of my privacy. I slowly walked to where my lacy panties and matching bras were tangled with more practical cotton. Standing there I stared at the jewel tones mingled with common whites and beiges, trying to wrap my head around what had taken place in my home.

While I'd been absent, attending the funeral of my last close family member, scum-sucking bastards had broken into my home and robbed me. I'd heard of such vultures doing this to other bereaved families, but this seemed like a more personal attack than a simple robbery. Whoever had done this hadn't just taken the electronics and anything else they could pawn or sell, but had done a thorough search.

A string of curses, guaranteed to have earned me a week's worth of soap in my mouth when I was a kid, exploded from between my lips. Guess the reprieve was over, and it was now open season on those records of Gramps'. The reason for the search through the recipes was also now clear. It hadn't just been a malicious act of vandalism, the ass-wipe had been searching for the directions and ingredients for the mash used in the moonshine. Like they were going to be nestled in among all the recipes for fried pies and molasses cookies. *Idiot*! I was looking for a freakin' idiot!

The cussing just kept rolling as I thought of Gramps' house and the condition it was probably in. There were still a couple of hours of daylight and I needed to check his place to see if my suspicions were correct.

I dug through the discarded piles of clothes until I came up with jeans and a black tank. Stripping out of my dress, I left it in a wadded mess on the floor with the rest of my clothes.

After straightening from pulling on my boots, I decided to make a quick trip back into the jewelry shop to open the safe. I needed to retrieve my last birthday present from Gramps. A Smith and Wesson 442 Pink 38 Special. I'd been thrilled when Gramps had handed it to me last year. Evan had laughed his butt off when I'd proudly shown it to him. The laughs had stopped after a few rounds of target practice.

After fetching the gun, the last thing I did was tuck the pistol into the waistband of my jeans, where it nestled in the small of my back. I just hoped the bastards were still at Gramps' house by the time I got there. Probably not the smartest wish, but smart wasn't figuring into my drive to shoot someone.

* * *

Jase leaned back against the tailgate of his brother's pick-up. The heat of the day, retained by the metal, soaked into the muscles of his back. Pulling up a booted foot to rest his heel on the edge of the bumper, he tightened his grip around the long neck held in his hand. Tipping his head back he stared at the millions of stars easily seen this far out in the country. Without city lights to dim the view it was a spectacular show. If it hadn't been for the three-quarter moon lighting the predominately truck-filled parking lot it would've been black as pitch.

The owner of Skeeter's didn't believe in spending any unnecessary money on advertising so there was no

blinking neon sign to advertise his bar, and parking lot
lights weren't even a passing thought.

Locals knew about the watering hole located at the
end of a dirt road, and strangers weren't encouraged to
drink with them. Unless the stranger happened to be a
regular's buddy, or out of town kin visiting, it was best if
they didn't venture in. It sure as hell wasn't worth your
life to bring a damn city boy through the doors, no
matter who they were. That's what those new restaurants
located in Copper Ridge, with their sissy bars, were for.

The thumping of the heavy bass leaking out of the
bar seemed to be keeping rhythm for the cicadas as they
whirred their mating songs in the surrounding oak trees.
Course, there was plenty of mating going on in
Skeeter's, too. Both on the dance floor and in the back
rooms rented out by the hour.

It was the chance to question old friends and listen
to gossip of the more illegal sort that had Jase jumping
in Evan's truck earlier to make the trek out to what was
considered the wilder side of night-life for this part of
the country. The draw of a cold beer—or six—on a
sweltering summer night wasn't to be discounted either.

Both attractions had the added bonus of keeping
him from heading over to Char's place. Never mind the
fact that her great-aunt and distant cousin were staying
with her, he was pretty damn positive she wasn't
interested in consolation from him right now. At least
not the kind he wanted to offer tonight. The scene with
Sawyer in the church was stuck in his head and he

couldn't forget the look of interest in Sawyer's eyes when he'd been talking to Charlotte.

It had pissed Jase off, seeing that look of male appreciation coming from Sawyer. Just as it had the other day, in front of the flower shop, when Brent had made such a point of offering to help Charlotte. At least today he'd turned and walked away from her instead of pulling her into a clinch right there in the church basement, staking his claim like he'd wanted to.

This possessive streak he'd developed when it came to Charlotte was starting to get out of hand. It was bad enough to feel a need to mark her as his every time a male looked in her direction, but when he'd spotted BW in Skeeter's it was all he could do to ignore him. He'd wanted to go over and beat the shit out of him. Just the thought that BW might be the one who had caused Charlotte so much pain was enough reason to cripple him. He'd decided to take a breather outside for a few minutes to squash his urge to rip BW's head off.

The crunch of tires over gravel turned his attention in a new direction. Lowering his chin, he watched as a familiar truck pulled into what passed for the parking lot. Eyes narrowing in speculation, he took a pull on the bottle and watched. He had to admit to being equal parts curious as to what the lady who climbed out of the truck was up to, and wondering how she'd managed to show up here. She was supposed to be at home, entertaining some distant relatives. Knowing he was pretty well hidden in the darkness, Jase made a decision not to make his presence known. For the time being at least.

* * *

Shifting to park, I killed the engine and sat for a minute to pull in a few deep breaths. It was a futile attempt at getting a handle on my anger. Sliding my hand across the bench seat, it was easy to locate the tools I'd brought with me. The flashlight was gripped in one hand, while the fingers of my other curled around cylindrical contours in a death grip.

The groan of the truck door, as it swung open, seemed unnaturally loud. Climbing out, rage coiled in my gut wanting to spring free. I was determined to curb my anger and complete the job I'd come here for. Slamming the door closed wasn't a brilliant move when it came to maintaining control, but it sure as hell felt good.

Hoping my quarry was here, I began my search. Stalking across the parking lot, I switched the flashlight on to fan the beam across the collection of motorcycles, trucks and cars, on the hunt for his flashy drive.

There had to be close to thirty vehicles scattered around in no particular order, so it was going to be a matter of weaving back and forth between them. I hit pay dirt on my first pass. Parked close to the edge of the clearing was the flashy truck I was searching for.

Grim satisfaction at finding the bastard I'd come looking for had me taking long strides to the side of the giant four-by-four truck. With a steadiness that gave no hint to the violence inside me, I began to slowly, but oh-so-carefully, spray letters onto the side of the truck's custom paint job.

There was the most satisfying hiss as the paint left the can and settled on the dusty front fender where I began my own personal graphic addition. My occasional pauses to shake the spray can would silence the cicadas. In the silence the rattle of the metal ball bouncing around the inside of the can seemed to call out a *"hey, y'all, come on over here and look at what I'm doing."* The funny thing was, the longer I worked on forming the perfect letters down the length of the truck, the calmer I became. When the last word was complete it was time to stand back and admire my handy work.

Top of my list Fucker

"You forgot to dot the 'i.'"

It would've been cool to say I didn't flinch when I heard Jase's voice, but the reality was I let out the all-purpose *"Shit!"* that happened whenever I was startled. Having gotten the squeak out of me, he didn't say anything else, and I didn't turn around until after I'd moved closer to the Chevy to correct my omission.

"Thanks." I faced him a bit defensively, not really knowing what to expect. He seemed calm enough, but there was an unnatural stillness to his form as he stood in the shadows created by the beam of my light. After the way he'd walked away from me in the church, and now his silent scrutiny, I was beginning to wonder if I'd finally become that mentally unstable woman who was too much trouble to mess with.

Assuming a nonchalance I was far from feeling, I walked over to where he stood and reached out a hand for his bottle. He handed it over, still not saying a word. The beer was cold with a slight bitter bite; in other words, it tasted like crap. Guess I was a true product of the Donley legacy. I'd been raised to appreciate good whiskey from the time it was rubbed on my gums when I was teething as a baby. Passing the bottle back to Jase left me at a loss for what to do next. Lucky for me, he decided to break the silence.

"Are you ready to go home now?"

How the heck did he manage that? I'd heard of poker faces, but Jase had a poker voice. The deep timber of his voice gave me no clue to his mood.

Before I could answer him the door to the bar opened and out walked the proud owner of the monster truck with the creative new graphics. At least with the appearance of BW and a couple of his cronies, I was no longer left in any doubt as to how Jase was feeling. His relaxed but ambiguous attitude took a decided turn towards something darker. It was as if at the sight of the men coming our way, the very air held its breath in anticipation of what was going to happen next.

CHAPTER SEVENTEEN

Jase watched BW exit Skeeter's with his crew. The trio were involved in an engrossing conversation, judging by the close huddle they maintained as they crossed the lot towards BW's truck. His mind wrestled with the fact that he should get Charlotte out of there, while his body made minute adjustments in preparations for battle. A battle he'd been savagely wishing for ever since he'd arrived at Skeeter's and saw BW sitting across the room.

"Go find Evan. Stay with him until I come get you." Jase delivered the words in a harsh whisper. Getting her away from the shit storm that was about to happen was a priority. But there was no denying a primal satisfaction coursed through him at the thought of getting to beating BW until nothing was left but a grease spot on the ground.

Char didn't seem to share his worry about getting caught out here with him, and she sure as hell didn't listen when he tried to get her to leave. When Jase noticed Robbie elbow BW, and point in their direction, he knew the matter was settled. There wasn't going to be any walking away for either of them.

"Well, lookee here, boys. Whatcha up to, Char? Out celebrating your ol' granddaddy's funeral?" BW asked the question with a belligerent bravado, which felt forced for the benefit of his friends. They gave an obligatory chuckle but shifted around nervously.

Jase heard Charlotte's sharp intake of air at BW's words. Meanwhile he was doing his best to remember he couldn't afford to leave her vulnerable to the other two men while he ripped BW's head off.

"Just admiring your new paint job. Gotta admit, it's original." Charlotte's mocking tone was gritted out with not a hint of weakness. He'd known in his gut that when Charlotte was ready to come out from under her grief, and start fighting back, she was going to be hell on wheels. What he hadn't expected was for her to be ready quite so quickly or so recklessly.

All three men stepped around to get a look at what Char was so helpfully spotlighting with her flashlight. Jase took hold of her arm to ease her back farther from the trio. Thankfully she was smart enough to realize being too close to BW right now wasn't the safest place to be.

"Shiiittt! What the fuck did you do, bitch?" BW's high pitched squeal pierced the night. He whirled to stare at Char, his hands clenched into fists by his side. Robbie and Steve stood beside BW, staring in shock. Their disbelief rapidly changed to righteous fury. Whether it was because she'd marked on a buddy's ride or because she'd defaced a primo paint job was a tossup.

"Charlotte's been with me, and not decorating the side of your truck." Jase's low-pitched challenge pierced the intense focus BW had on Charlotte. BW transferred his glare from Char to Jase.

"You think I'm fucking stupid? She's still got the fucking paint can in her hand!" BW's bellowed words almost drowned out the sound of Skeeter's door slamming against its frame as someone exited the establishment in a hurry. Jase just hoped it was Evan coming to see what was keeping him outside so long.

It seemed Char was determined to contribute to the escalating tension, oblivious to the effort Jase was exerting to contain his rage for the sake of keeping her safe.

"What, this can?" Char tossed the spray can to Robbie and the man caught it reflexively. "Looks to me like Robbie is holding it. How do we know he's not the one who did it?"

Robbie froze for half a second, staring down at the can in his hand. His eyes flew to BW, then back to Char. Jase watched Robbie's eyes and could see the exact moment something snapped in the man. Robbie lunged towards Char with the can wrapped in his fist. His arm was drawn back ready to deliver the canister back to Char with a punch from his clenched hand. He screamed at her as he attacked.

"Why the fuck do you people keep dragging me into this shit?" Robbie sounded demented. Out of control. He never made contact with Char.

Jase quickly stepped in front of her before hooking a left handed blow to Robbie's midsection. Robbie doubled over, making an easy target for Jase to follow the hook with a right upper cut to his chin. The blast to his face lifted Robbie upright for a heartbeat before his legs turned to mush. He dropped to the ground as though in slo-mo, knees hitting dirt first, followed by a weaving face plant. With fierce satisfaction, Jase wasted no more time on the crumpled figure on the ground, pivoting to target the next threat.

BW had taken the opening provided by Robbie's attack to make a move on Char. The bastard was circling her, trying to get past the flashlight she was welding like a club. Jase was able to make out Evan running to intercept BW's attempt but Jase was determined to be the one to make BW spit his teeth out. As Jase went to block BW's assault on Char, he was hammered by a body hurtling into his back. A beefy arm wrapped around his neck in a choke hold. Looked like Steve had decided to join the fight.

As Steve tightened his hold, cutting off Jase's airflow, a thunderous roar grew louder by the second. There wasn't time to stop and figure out if it was a result of the loss of oxygen or a more external force causing the guttural throb. Jase's focus centered on breaking out of Steve's chicken-shit attack from the rear.

Digging his fingers in, one hand on Steve's wrist, the other just above the elbow of his attacker, Jase dropped a knee to the ground, managing to flip Steve over his head. Jase plowed him into the ground with a bone jarring brutality. A merciless jab to Steve's throat effectively removed any fight that might have been left in him.

Regaining his feet in a blur of motion, Jase rounded on where he'd last glimpsed Evan closing in on BW. He was relieved to see Charlotte standing to the side, unharmed, but Jase was seriously pissed to see BW backed away from Evan with his hands in the air in the universal sign of giving up.

The coward was sporting nothing more than a bloodied nose. As Jase reined in his frustration at not being able get his pound of flesh out of BW, he was once again slammed by another body. This time he gladly pulled the form closer in a bone crushing embrace. Charlotte didn't seem to mind the bruising arms he locked around her.

The sound of someone slow clapping pulled Jase's focus in a new direction. Loosening his hold on Charlotte, Jase placed her behind him in a protective move. The source of the growling roar he'd heard earlier was made clear when he spied Sawyer leaning up against the side of a Harley. He was flanked by a half dozen more cycles and riders. Sawyer was doing the clapping while the gang with him looked on with a mixture of emotions running the gambit from smirking grins, to cold-blooded stares.

"Sum'bitch, Rydan, looks like you still remember how to fuck up little cocksuckers. And here I was, worried you'd went and turned into one of them hetro-metro fuckers after you moved to the city." Sawyer straightened from his bike and walked towards where Jase and Evan both stood in defensive stances.

Evan barked a laugh, and Jase allowed himself to relax into a more casual stand, going so far as to crack a derisive smile back at Sawyer. "Just like old times, Sawyer. You show up after all the work is done."

Sawyer didn't answer immediately as he paused to watch BW's crew pull themselves together. "Looks like it was light work. I didn't miss much."

Hatred glared out of BW's eyes, but he wasn't willing to make a move now Sawyer and his cronies were there. In his narcissistic stupidity he thought to appeal to the gang by whining his grievances against Char.

"That crazy bitch spray painted my truck."

The announcement caused every man in the parking lot, with the exception of Jase and Evan, to gather beside the marked truck and examine the length of it. Sawyer even went so far as to order one of his men to pull a bike around so they could shine a headlight down the side of the vehicle. The scrutiny of the graffiti by the men didn't have the desired effect BW had hoped for, though.

Deep gutted laughter rolled out of Sawyer. His fellow toughs looked puzzled, giving the impression this was a rare display and they didn't quite know how to react. After a minute though, most of them were doing their own laughing and making less than flattering guesses as to what kind of list BW would be at the top of.

"Shit man, I think I'm in fucking love." Sawyer's flippant declaration was met with a chorus of lewd laughter.

Jase could almost feel the heat of Charlotte's rising anger at Sawyer's cocky attitude. He wasn't thrilled with the lurid suggestions filling the air after Sawyer's announcement, but Jase knew the men making them were more interested in ribbing Sawyer than being disrespectful to Charlotte.

Hell, the kind of women they usually ran with would probably consider their coarse comments as compliments. He decided it was time to make an exit before she could make her displeasure known and further intrigue Sawyer. The man had always been a tough bastard, even as a kid, and he liked his women the same way.

"Hate to break up this party but time to take Charlotte home. She has company waiting on her." At the tiny flinch Char made at the mention of her *supposed* company, Jase knew there wasn't anyone at her house wondering where the hell she was.

"That bitch ain't going nowhere until she fuckin' pays." BW had a seriously faulty sense of self-preservation. Even Robbie and Steve were smart enough to start easing away from him in the hopes of avoiding the fallout.

Any hint of civility dropped from Sawyer. Jase started stringing curses together under his breath at BW's stupidity. He'd seen what Sawyer was capable of when someone pushed the wrong button. From the dead look in Sawyer's eyes, BW had just pushed a whole row of wrong buttons. Jase had to defuse the situation and fast. Sawyer wasn't going to kill the dumb fuck in front of Charlotte if he could help it.

"What the hell do you think is going to happen, BW? You gonna pick a fight with a woman? Get your head outta your ass. You want a fight, well here I am." Jase thumped his chest then spread his arms wide, taunting BW to make a move.

With a look first at Sawyer then back at Jase, BW finally began to realize he was in a no-win position. Jase could see it killed him to back down in front of all those men, but even his pride wasn't going to force him into a fair fight.

Without turning his back on anyone he started walking backwards in the direction of his truck. "This ain't over."

As far as threats went, BW's packed about as much punch as a hissing kitten.

"Count on it." Jase's carried way more promise.

Everyone watched until BW bumped into his truck and slid along its side, searching for the door handle.

"Watch out for wet paint." Char's clear voice rang out with a false sweetness. It broke the deadly tension gripping the group of men she was with. Raunchy laughter returned the group to their former foul-mouthed banter.

The only reply she received was the slamming of truck doors, the sound of an engine being gunned and getting to hear oversized tires grabbing traction in the gravel lot.

"Goddamn, Rydan, take her home before I do." Sawyer sounded more than halfway serious. But he turned and walked away. His gang, following in his wake, moved with a deadly purpose that was a pale imitation of the lethal grace Sawyer possessed.

CHAPTER EIGHTEEN

"So let me see if I've got this right. You lied to me about your relatives staying over. You lied to everyone about having your granddad's records. And you decided to screw with BW because you *think* he's the one who broke into your house."

Jeezz. If I'd thought Jase was the master of the poker voice, then he was the freaking king of male outrage. I had to keep reminding myself he'd just saved me from...hell, I had no clue what he'd just saved me from. But it could have been bad.

While I'd no intention of letting *him* know, I was shaken at the thought of what might have happened to him if first Evan, and then Sawyer, hadn't shown up. Maybe I hadn't thought it out all that well when I charged off to vent my anger. But I still wasn't sorry for the damage I'd done to BW's truck. It was only because I owed Jase for the trouble he'd been put to on my behalf that I gritted my teeth and explained everything to him again. One. More. Time. I was beginning to think the drive back to my house was going to last forever.

"I didn't lie, just didn't tell you my kin had changed their minds about staying. And, I never exactly said I had the files just that Gramps did. And finally, I've admitted the BW thing might not have been smart, but it felt pretty damn good." Thank the lord we were pulling into my driveway.

When the engine went silent so did the interior of the cab. Neither one of us seemed willing to break the quiet. Strange...the whole time we were driving I couldn't wait to get home. But now, sitting here, staring at the deceptive peace of my house, I was sick at the thought of the destruction waiting for me inside. The feel of a warm, callused hand closing over my cold, clenched fist was a serious threat to my control. If he started being nice I was going to break down and cry.

"Are there any more surprises you want to share with me, Charlotte?"

Damn it! The tenderness feathering the dark richness of his voice caused a tear to spill over and trickle down my cheek. Pulling my hand out from under his, I brushed a rough swipe with the back of my hand across my face. I wanted to erase any sign of weakness, but the crude sniffle kind of ruined the effect.

"The house might be a little bit more torn up than I let on to you, and my gramps' house is in worse shape than mine." There, I was back to sounding defensive. Great. At least it beat crying.

"Let's go take a look." The faint slide of a finger caressed my cheek. "Honey, there's nothing in there or at your granddaddy's place that can't be fixed."

Nodding, I opened the door, took a deep breath, and headed for the house. Now the shock had worn off, maybe when I got inside it wouldn't be as bad as I remembered.

My second look at the destruction inside my home wasn't any better than the first. When Jase walked in, his creative cussing might have even given Sawyer a run for his money. Unfortunately, the sight also brought back the male outrage. He'd insisted on calling the sheriff's office, against my wishes, then went right back to his lectures as soon as he'd hung up.

Mom had explained it all to me when I was little. Anytime we did something Dad considered foolish and he started yelling at us, it was just his way of letting the scared out. Thing about Jase letting his *scared out*, he didn't yell. No, he went all dark and, to be honest, pretty darn intimidating. His voice dropped an octave and his eyes got this narrow, flat look to them.

"Just so we're clear. If you ever open a door and the place you're about to walk into is tossed—don't. You call me immediately."

"What if you don't answer?" I couldn't help the challenge in my tone.

"I'll always answer."

"That's ridiculous. What if it's the middle of the night and something happens. What if you're asleep?"

"Then roll over and wake me up." Jase's comment was mighty big talk for a man who'd only ever kissed me once.

I couldn't help the eye roll, or the stab of desire at the image his words provoked. Still, I snorted with derision at his remark. "Remember when I told you if you got too bossy it'd probably start a fight? Well, we're getting awful close to a fight." My words were mild enough, and hopefully Jase realized it was my way of saying "this horse is dead, you can stop beating it anytime now."

A growl of masculine frustration was accompanied by Jase stalking back to stand in front of me. He certainly loved to invade my personal bubble of space. "Charlotte, you could have been killed if you'd walked in on whoever did this. You need to understand what could have happened."

Feeling a little irritated myself, I nevertheless tried to sound reasonable. "Ruger was with me. If anyone had still been in the house he would have found them in seconds. Besides, I took my gun with me when I went to check out Gramps' house."

If possible, Jase seemed to grow even more rigid at my words. So much for me trying to be reasonable. "Do you honestly believe the thought of you toting a gun around is going to make what you did any better? Where's this gun now, and where was it when BW was coming at you outside Skeeter's?"

"I put it in the glovebox when I got to Skeeter's. Didn't figure I'd need it there. It's still in the truck." I was tired of going over and over everything.

"Damn it, Charlotte. Do you even care what it would've done to me if anything had happened to you?"

And there it was. The one question that put a whole new spin on what I'd done tonight. I'd never had a man—at least not one who wasn't related to me—to worry about me before. With one question, Jase managed to make me feel cherished and also guilty over the fear I'd caused. Taking the small step necessary to have me close enough to twine my arms around Jase's waist, I pulled him in. Not stopping there, I buried my face in the hollow just below his collarbone.

"I'm sorry." And I was, deeply sorry for causing him worry. Still, I couldn't promise there wouldn't be any more recklessness from me in the future. There was no sense in lying to him and making promises I might break.

When his arms gathered me even tighter against the solid warmth of his chest, I hoped he understood. I breathed in his maleness. A combination of sweat from his fights, a hint of smoke from the bar and his own unique smell, which had no name but I would remember if I lived to a hundred.

"Baby, you scared the shit out of me tonight."

"I know."

My lips started kissing and nibbling their way to his throat. Between each kiss, "*I'm sorry,*" was whispered.

After every tiny bite, "*I know,*" was softly breathed.

Each caress from my mouth, every mumbled apology from my lips, eased me as surely as it hardened him. His arms loosened to allow his hands to roam in lazy circles across my back. One traced a path up, to tangle masculine fingers in unruly curls. His other traveled south, smoothing along the way, until it had a firm grasp of rounded bottom.

What had started as a means to express remorse over the worry I'd caused was rapidly turning into something more sensual. I swallowed a tiny gasp as Jase fitted me into the juncture of his thighs. His growing arousal nestled in the softness of my stomach. Fire suffused my body but concentrated in a pool at the center of my core.

One more sliding kiss and my lips landed on heated, male, salty goodness at the base of his throat. I rose up onto my tiptoes to allow my mouth carnal access to his straining neck muscles. I continued my assault with sucking kisses, stinging nips, and long languorous licks to the underside of his square jawline. While my lips were busy, my hands were far from idle, having gone on a restless expedition of their own. Working underneath the weathered cotton of his shirt, they wove tiny circles that mimicked the earlier swirls of Jase's hands on my own back. When the fingers of one hand dared to breach the barrier of his denim waistband Jase sucked in a breath and released a curse.

"Goddamn, honey, you're shredding me right now." He followed his declaration by his fist knotting in my hair, and pulling back so he could swoop in and ravage the mouth that had been slowly driving him to the edge of his control. There was no gentle quest for entrance, but a bold claiming with a thrust of his tongue, eager to do battle with the tormentor of his flesh.

I whimpered low in my throat. Not from fear, but need and want. Jase's groan sent vibrations from his chest into my breasts. With a show of strength, he lifted me with one hand, allowing my legs to wrap around his waist. My feet locked behind his back and I wiggled my hips in a desperate attempt to pull myself closer to the bulge contained behind straining material. I craved the heat of him the way an addict lusted after his next hit.

"I'm taking you upstairs and if you don't want this, you need to stop me right now." Jase's dark guttural tone left no doubt he was at his limit. But that wasn't a problem for me, because limits had no place in what I was wanting from him.

"Why aren't we already there?"

His molten laughter cranked my fever several degrees higher. Quite an accomplishment, since I already felt in danger of spontaneous combustion. Jase headed for the stairs, carrying me as if I were no heavier than a living blanket, wrapped around his body. With his first step my thighs tightened instinctively, drawing me even tighter against his swollen cock. We both groaned simultaneously.

"Maybe I better walk." The words panted out of me; normal breathing was a distant memory at that point.

"No, fucking, way." Jase gritted out his reply.

As Jase went to place his foot on the first tread, a loud pounding sounded on my front door. My sob of frustration was drowned by Jase's string of murderous words. The sheriff's office might have arrived to investigate a robbery, but there was a very real possibility they were going to be first on the scene of a murder. Theirs.

"Nowadays a family puts an obituary in the papers and it's like the thieves take it for a personal invite to come on over and rob 'em." Sheriff Cantrell heaved a big sigh, like he was delivering a sermon on the sad state of the modern crook. The man deserved an Emmy for his performance. He was all sorrowful solicitation in his facial expressions, when I knew damn good and well he had no intentions of actually doing anything about the break in.

That he'd showed up this time of night, with one of his officers, was purely for the fact he wanted to control the investigation. That he'd pretty much shut down any suggestion that the break-in was related in any way to Gramps' death just confirmed it. I had my suspicions he'd even dragged Dennis out on the call for a purpose. Sheriff appeared to be trying to limit the number in his own department who were involved with anything that was related to my gramps. Since Dennis was at the original crime scene, Cantrell must have thought it was safe to have him here. Then again, maybe it had more to do with the fact Dennis wasn't from around here, like most of Cantrell's deputies were. Easier to control a man who didn't have any ties to the community.

"What's the bottom line? Are you going to do anything about this? Wait, let me guess. This is just another unfortunate accident and nobody's to blame." I definitely snarled that last sentence out. Jase placed a hand on my shoulder. It was a "calm down" gesture wrapped up as a show of support. He was right and I knew it, but that didn't make me like it.

"I'm going to ignore that, Ms. Donley, and put it down to the grief you're still wrestling with." Cantrell had that infuriating look of a man humoring the little lady in distress. "The scene speaks for itself. They stole the electronics and obviously searched for anything else they could sell. This is getting to be more common, so why would I, or anyone else for that matter, think this was related in any way to your granddaddy's death?"

"Because it's pretty freaking obvious they searched the house looking for those damn files." At this point I was so frustrated it was hard to not just stand there and scream at the idiot. I had my arms outstretched to encompass the room. "Hell, maybe they went through my recipe boxes because they heard about that fucking amazing blackberry cobbler I make."

"Charlotte."

One word from Jase, just my name, had me pulling back from the edge and taking a ragged breath. I needed to get a grip, this wasn't getting me anywhere.

"Cantrell, word's been going around about certain people being interested in not only the records, but in any information about Mr. Donley's *hobby*. This person has been bragging about how he was going to take over Mr. Donley's *hobby*. Using the exact same instructions."

The sheriff and I both stared at Jase. Me, in a *"why the hell are you pussy-footing around about it being BW"* way; Cantrell in a squinty-eyed looked that said he knew Jase was talking about BW, too.

"Dennis, go on back to the kitchen and check out Ms. Donley's little shop while you're at it." Cantrell dismissed his deputy.

My little shop. Looked like the sheriff was wanting to get a cheap dig in at me. Asshole.

Dennis left without a word. Talk about your trained robot.

"You got something to say, spit it out, Rydan. It's just the three of us here now. If you want some plain talking then have at it. Just remember, there's a line neither one of us wants to cross. I've done you people a favor by trying to keep this local and you're too damn stubborn to even see it."

He may have said, *you people*, but I knew he meant *me* by the way his eyes locked on me. Frankly, I didn't give a crap what he thought about me. We all understood he would protect BW, even if he wasn't positive of BW's involvement. Which was just screwed up. BW might be his son, but there had to be a point where even a parent admitted his kid needed to pay for the misery he had caused.

Jase, as he usually did, took charge. "You want plain talking? Then how about this: your son has been going around telling everyone he was going to take over Mr. Donley's business. Mr. Donley ends up dead. BW suddenly quits his bragging. Then just as suddenly, word's out he's in deep shit because whoever he's working for blames BW for not delivering on some promise."

I don't know who was more surprised by what Jase had to say. Most of what he said wasn't news to me, but the little tidbit about BW being in trouble came as a complete shock. Which pissed me off, that I was only now hearing about it. Guess he hadn't had time to fill me in since he was so *busy* chewing me out on the way home from the bar.

I glanced over at Cantrell. He looked like he'd swallowed a bug while listening to what Jase laid out. Looked like BW hadn't been keeping Daddy up to date on current events.

"Now you know as much as the rest of us. I'm giving you a chance to do your fucking job—Sheriff—or I'm going to do it for you." There was no doubt in anyone's mind that Jase had just made a promise he was willing to keep.

Surprisingly, Cantrell didn't start blustering and threatening Jase. He did draw himself up, as if trying to look more impressive. A wasted effort. Hooking his thumbs in the straining waistband of his slacks, the sheriff flapped his lips a few times but no words popped out. He appeared to be wrestling with wanting to say something. He finally gave a resigned shrug, and started talking. "I'm not sorry for decisions I've made over the last week. All of them were made to protect people. Some were mine. Some were hers." Cantrell nodded in my direction. "I'm not about to change any of those choices."

"What does that mean for finding my granddad's murderer?" I glared at Cantrell.

"There was no murder. Remember? Nothing for me to look into." Cantrell glared right back at me for a second before turning sideways, as if to survey the room. "If you want to waste your time playing detective, I ain't gonna stop you. Nobody at the sheriff's office is gonna throw roadblocks up, either. Just don't expect any help from my department."

It was less than I wanted but more than expected. Cantrell appeared to be willing to throw BW to the dogs...maybe.

CHAPTER NINETEEN

Exhaustion should have had me wrapped up in a coma right about now. But here I was, wide awake, standing in front of one of the most beautiful lake homes I'd ever seen. Between the landscape lighting and the floodlights designed to accent unique features on the home, it presented a dramatic statement. Its massive log and stone construction should have been intimidating but, curiously, it felt warm and inviting. Made me feel as if once a person walked through those mammoth wooden doors they would be protected from whatever the world tried to throw at them. It was impressive and sheltering and way too large for just one man.

"Ever think you might have over-built just a little bit?"

"I don't like cramped spaces."

"Well, you certainly aren't going to develop any kinks in that house."

"I never said I didn't like kinks."

His reply may have been delivered on a light, teasing note, but his eyes had gone half mast, his voice dropping into the melt-my-panties range. And just that quick, I was back in my living room at the foot of those steps, remembering how I'd wrapped around Jase like a second skin. My body fired to life, back to where it had been before the sheriff knocked on my door and effectively killed the mood.

I drew in a shuddering breath. My skin felt flushed. I could actually feel my scalp tingling at the memory of Jase's hand fisted in my tangled hair. The want had to be blazing from my eyes. The tip of my tongue flicked out to moisten suddenly dry lips.

Jase's dark eyes fastened on my mouth. He stalked me with a deliberate, slow pace, giving me plenty of time to retreat if I wished. I stood my ground.

I wanted this, whatever *this* turned out to be. Nothing else mattered when Jase had me surrounded with his large frame. There were no holes in my heart that needed filling. Just a hunger for more and more and more.

Jase stopped a sigh away from touching me with his body. He raised a hand and I felt the faint touch of his fingertips, tracing the outline of my ear, sending shivers undulating down my back. One tiny touch was all it took to harden my nipples and have muscles in my pelvic clinch.

"Baby, I'm not going to kiss you until we walk through those doors. Because if I do, I'll be pounding into you against the side of my truck, fucking you up on those steps and screwing you down on the floor of that porch. So if you want to save your ass from being bruised and filled with splinters, I suggest you keep that wet little tongue of yours in your mouth. At least until we make it to my bedroom."

Holy shit! No one had ever talked that dirty to me before, and I wanted every last thing he just outlined. Wanted wild and uncontrolled. Wanted nasty and dirty. Gentle would've been an abomination to the riot of emotions crashing through my system. He stared into my eyes with a clear threat. I stared back for half a heartbeat in clear challenge, then deliberately moistened my lips again with the tip of my tongue.

Breath whooshed out of me as my back slammed into the heated metal of a front fender. My breasts were crushed against granite pecs. A muscled thigh slid between my legs, opening me, allowing me to ride its length with a wanton abandon that should have had me blushing in shame and not groaning in pleasure from the delicious friction. All I could do was grab two hands of ass, and hang on for blessed relief.

His mouth slanted across mine, his tongue demanding entry and mine eager to duel with his. My hair was once again gripped, with little regard for the sting of protesting roots. Jase controlled the exact angle of my head, allowing him access to the darkest recesses of my mouth. He filled his other hand with the aching roundness of my breast. I wanted to scream at the unfairness of the cloth separating flesh from flesh.

Jase tore his mouth from mine, allowing me to draw deep gulps of air into my burning lungs. He buried his face in my neck and delivered sucking kisses to a sweat-slicked throat. His demanding fingers loosened their grasp on my abused locks, becoming cradling and soothing. The hand on my breast was as impatient with the restriction of material as I was and pushed up under my tank. The snick of the front clasp releasing on my bra was a *sweet hallelujah* moment. His callused fingers dragged a path of fire to a distended nipple. The first tug between finger and thumb arrowed a bolt of liquid heat so intense my spine bowed. A curse or maybe a plea exploded from my lips.

"Goddammit, Charlotte, you were supposed to back off at my threat, not push me over the edge. Our first time together wasn't supposed to be banged out on the side of my truck." Jase had abandoned my throat to rest his forehead against mine as he ground the words out.

"Don't you dare stop!" Panic at his slight shift away had me practically begging.

"Baby, I'm so far past the 'stop' sign I'm in another fucking state."

Laughter spilled out of me. Relief, joy, but mainly relief. Jase once more angled his head to take my mouth at the same time as his hand on my breast moved to allow his thumb to strum back and forth across the hardened nub. I moaned *"Yes,"* with a deep sultry slur that didn't even sound like it came from my throat. An answering growl rumbled in the air, growing louder with each passing second.

Jase's body froze. His kisses stopped, as did the delicious torment of his hand on my breast. I, on the other hand, continued to rub the apex of my thighs against the hardness of his leg where I straddled him. Hot callused hands centered on my waist, gripped me, trying to cease my wanton movements. Jase tried to sooth me with a faintly whispered hush.

"Noooo! You said you weren't going to stop!" My disappointment came out in a raw wail. A much louder snarl punctuated my protest.

"Shhh, we're not stopping, just moving the party to a bed. I somehow think the mood would be shattered if Ruger ends up biting me." Jase shushed me with whispered words and a nod in the direction of my growling dog. I felt more than a little foolish at not realizing what all the growling I'd been hearing signified.

Ruger was obviously confused as to why his new best friend appeared to be hurting me. It was just a matter of time before he decided to attack to protect me. I blew out a frustrated breath and tried to relax as much as possible, given my advanced state of reckless lust. Unable to resist one last wiggle of my middle to a jean clad thigh produced a moan I couldn't swallow. That moan ratcheted up the threats from Ruger. I honestly tried to push myself out of Jase's arms at that point. Understood I should be trying to cool down the fever pitch of desire instead of throwing gas on the flame.

"Where the hell do you think you're going?" The question came out on a growl from a human source this time. Jase refused to release his hold on my waist.

"I believe you said something about moving this party to a bed. We'll get there faster if you let me down and we start walking."

"Fast is not on the agenda tonight."

At my giggle, Jase huffed out a quiet, "Shit, honey. You keep making those kitten sounds we're not going to make it to the bed. And I'm going to end up with teeth marks. From the dog."

He slowly slid his leg from between mine. I felt desolate at the loss of his heated contact. I quickly crouched and did my best to reassure Ruger all was well. When I straightened, Jase grabbed my hand and hustled me up the porch steps, pausing only to punch in a code on a keypad and unlocked the front door. Fancy. Convenient. We stumbled through the door and Jase slammed it in Ruger's face. I felt bad for a second until Jase assured me he would let Ruger in later. Much later.

Once inside, I was again smashed between two hard surfaces, one unyielding and one deliciously male. This time I was the one tangling my fingers in thick hair to tug his head down, drawing his lips back to mine. The kiss was primal and wonderful and only lasted a heartbeat before Jase ripped his mouth from mine. He pulled me away from the door and steered me in the direction of a massive wooden staircase. It was a strange race to see who could climb the stairs the fastest without leaving the other behind.

Stumbling into his bedroom and spying his giant bed brought me up short. The only light in the room came from the floor to ceiling windows and wide French doors. Muscular arms slipped around my middle, tugging me close against the furnace of his chest. Jase rested his chin on my shoulder as he wrapped around me, surrounding me with his scent.

"Honey, if you've changed your mind it may kill me but I can still walk away at this point."

"No. I want you. It's just..." My voice trailed off. It seemed like I'd been wanting this, with this one particular man, my whole life. What if I disappointed him? "We're really going to do this. Right?" Even I cringed at the uncertainty in my voice. Why had it been so much easier when it was just happening and I wasn't given any time to think?

"We're going to do *this*." Jase kissed my neck. "Then we're going to do *that*." He nibbled my earlobe. "Afterwards, we're going to do something new." He strung tiny kisses along my jaw before lightly biting. "Baby, we are going to do it all." The husky timbre of his voice increased with each promise. And with each pledge murmured, the craving in me jumped higher. I'd never felt a hunger riding me this hard before. It was scary to want to lose myself in another person to that extent, but there would be no holding back.

Jase stared into my eyes as he eased my shirt up, exposing my body, inch by inch. When he reached my breasts he paused and lowered his eyes to look at them with rapt attention. I raised my arms, without him having to ask, so he could continue to slide my shirt up, my loose bra tangling in the folds. Both were tossed carelessly to the side. My hands lowered to the hem of Jase's tee and began the inching up of material to uncover the washboard hardness of sculpted abs, the flat muscled pecs. When I could raise it no higher Jase reached back over his shoulders to grab the bottom of his shirt and pull it the rest of the way off. The play of muscles was too tempting to resist. My fingers reached out to settle with the pressure of a feather on the undulating valleys and ridges of his abs.

The hiss of his sharp inhalation sounded as loud as a scream in the silent room. Unwilling to stop there with the touching, I ghosted a finger down his flat stomach. Following the faint trail of short, dark hair, until I reached the waistband of his jeans. My finger may have stopped but my eyes continued the journey down to the notable bulge behind the straining zipper.

When my hand went to return to its journey of discovery, Jase stopped me by closing his much larger one around mine and holding it in his clasp. Looking up questioningly at him, I frowned, wanting to continue my exploration. He met my frown with a gentle smile and a slow shake of his head, signaling a no.

"My turn to touch." He backed me up until I felt the edge of the bed at the back of my thighs.

While I'd been content to explore with my fingers Jase had a much better idea of using mouth and tongue. While his hands unfastened my jeans his head descended to a swollen breast. He immediately latched onto a distended nipple, nipping then soothing the sting with swirling laps from a fevered tongue. Whimpers keened from my throat. Somehow he managed to divest me of boots and jeans as well as finish undressing himself, all while lavishing attention on first one and then the other engorged breast.

I have never been the type of female to rhapsodize over a man's endowment but—holy hell—what was uncovered when Jase shed his jeans was worth a line or two. Not that I got much of a chance to explore the enticing length and breadth of it. Jase wasn't wasting any time once our clothes were off, arranging me to his liking. I couldn't help but admire the clench and release of muscle in his arms as he lifted and settled me on top of his high bed.

After Jase laid me on the bed my world narrowed down to touch, taste and greed. He crawled up my body with a lethal grace reminiscent of a predator having brought down its prey, about to indulge in a feast. He settled a thick thigh between mine and his swollen cock didn't just rest against me but pulsed with a heartbeat of its own. I arched my back to press closer.

Jase braced himself with a forearm to keep from crushing me, which gave him the added advantage of being able to trail his free hand down my stomach to the top of my slit. My legs spread wider as I tried to entice him to invade my secrets.

"Please." I pulled back from his mouth to beg. I lifted my hips in a futile attempt to force a closer bond with the insane thickness of his shaft. My nails left a trail the entire length of Jase's back as he started moving down my body.

"Not yet, baby. I've got to taste you." He shifted me into position with one hand under my butt, while the other opened me to his marauding mouth. At the first touch of a sucking kiss on my hooded sex I bowed off the bed in a gasp of wonder. Jase shifted his hand from my butt to my abdomen to press me back to the surface of the bed, controlling me, steadying me for further invasion.

I'd never been this out of control. This starved for the next touch. My hands gripped the bedcovers in a desperate attempt at staying grounded. Jase worked the tiny nubbin of nerves centered at the top of my opening with a skill that bordered on exquisite torture. Just as I thought it couldn't possibly get any more intense I felt him ease a large finger into me. Once more I bowed off the bed at the invasion while panting moans escaped, totally beyond my control.

There was a coiling tension within me, tightening with every stroke. When a second blunt finger joined the first in its rotating exploration, every muscle in the center of my core had me reaching for something that in the past had been a pleasant release, not this uncontrollable frenzy of sensation. Jase was relentless as his tongue manipulated me. I'd never reached this high before, and when that spring was wound that one click too tight the resulting explosion had me screaming out his name.

Pulsating convulsions racked my body. Jase slowly withdrew his fingers and stared into my eyes. I thought it was over, but then he cupped his large palm firmly against my sex, which had the strangest effect of intensifying the rippling waves of pleasure. I'd never realized what he was doing was even possible.

Once the waves slowed to a stop, I lay on the bed in boneless euphoria. Jase once more worked his way up my limp body, but this time with soft kisses, until he was settled between my thighs. He bracketed me with his arms, not crushing me with his weight. Placing tender kisses on my sweat-drenched forehead, he worked his way around the side of my hairline and across my cheek to my lips. As he pushed his tongue inside to connect with mine, the smell and taste of me lingered in his mouth. It was erotic in a way that had never appealed to me before.

Jase shifted on me, reaching for the drawer in the bedside table. When his hand returned with a square foil packet I stirred and held out my hand for the square.

A shuddering exhale erupted from the center of Jase's chest. The packet was passed into my hands and a wildness entered his eyes as a carnal grin slashed across his face. A thrill raced through me at the sheer sensuality of his heated gaze. That stare was all it took to make me feel like I was standing three feet from the sun. If someone had told me the claws of desire could rip into me again this fast after having the most shattering orgasm of my life, I'd have called them a liar.

Jase sat up, allowing me access to his straining erection. I couldn't resist fisting my hand around the base of the hard shaft and dragging it to the blooming head, a bead of pre-cum glistening on the tip. There was an amazing contrast in textures. The velvet softness of skin covered a granite hardness that had me squeezing and flexing my fingers up and down its length. The thickness was fascinating and a little shocking.

"Baby, if you don't stop what you're doing we're not going to need that little packet in your hand." His protest came out in a hoarse whisper.

Shooting a quick glance to his face revealed he wasn't joking, judging by the grimace around his mouth and the beads of sweat on his forehead. Reluctantly I gave up my exploration and rolled on the condom. I couldn't resist teasing him a little. "I thought control was your specialty."

"Sweetheart, you've shattered any hope of me maintaining control."

"Control is overrated. I'm ready for raw." The words had barely passed my lips before Jase had hooked an arm around my waist to flip me over onto my stomach. He lifted me to my knees and I braced myself with stiff arms at the first probe of the broad head of his cock. I was so wet and readied from my orgasm that I was surprised at the amount of pressure Jase was having to apply to slowly push his way into me. The most delicious stretching sensation had me gasping in pleasure. And when he seated himself fully, with a final surge, I rasped out a, "*Yesss*."

A moment was all Jase gave me to adjust to his presence before he began a series of pumps and hip rolls that had my fingers fisting in the covers. Both of Jase's hands gripped my waist as he worked a rhythm as old as time.

I could tell he was getting close to his own release by the quickening pace and the bruising clenching of his fingers. He'd kept up a running dialog, alternating between praises and curses and they were escalating in volume. When he freed a hand to close over my heated core and work me with practiced precision it was too much. The tide pulled me into the center of the sexual maelstrom Jase had created. I was at the crest of a wave when Jase shouted his own release. When the last tremor racked his body Jase draped over me, taking me down to the bed and then rolling us both over onto our sides. He cocooned me in the wrap of his arms and legs. We were both panting as if we'd just finished a marathon.

"Wow." I puffed the word out as I tried to slow my breathing.

"Do I need to ask what the wow was for?" Jase sounded slightly smug. He had a right to.

"Just wondering."

"And what were you just wondering?" He pushed my hair aside and nuzzled the back of my neck.

"If we had completed *this,* and *that,* and were ready to move on to the something new."

A soft chuckle feathered the base of my neck. "Baby, we can do all the *new* you want."

CHAPTER TWENTY

"I'd feel better if you came back with me to your house." Jase leaned against the door jamb with his arms crossed and a steely-eyed look directed at me. He'd been trying to persuade me for the last ten minutes to leave with him. I'd been doing my best to resist.

The middle of Gramps' living room floor was covered with various boxes and papers. I'd collected them from around the house when Jase and I'd worked from room to room, putting the house back in order. We'd found old boot boxes filled with yellowed receipts and papers stuck in the oddest places all around the house. Once gathered, I'd plopped both them and myself on the largest cleared surface—the floor—for sorting.

Whoever had ransacked the place had either found what they were looking for fast, or did a piss poor job searching, due to lack of time. Whichever it was, I didn't hold much hope of finding any clue to where the files had been hidden in this pile. But I couldn't be positive until everything had been gone through. Lord knows, the last few days of my searching hadn't turned up anything. Maybe the thieves really had found what they'd been looking for and this was all a waste of time.

"It's been three days since the break-in and not even a hint of trouble. Come on, you're only five minutes away. Besides, isn't Colin supposed to be bringing those new doors you ordered?" I raised my eyebrows at the mention of the new doors. Jase had insisted on replacing not only the shattered back door of my home, but he'd also ordered new doors for Gramps' house. Colin was supposed to drop them off here sometime later this afternoon.

I'd been staying at Jase's place for the last three nights. Despite heavy hints I should move in, I was determined to get back to my own home as soon as possible. Not that the offer wasn't tempting; Jase was the embodiment of temptation. Just thinking of the nights spent in sexual discovery with him had me ready to melt into a puddle of liquid heat.

"Jase, we need a break from each other. You've not let me out of your sight since the robbery. You've barely let me out of arm's reach." Time to get blunt. My broad hints weren't sinking in. I really did want some space to think over what was going on with the two of us. We'd been on a fast track from the moment I'd literally run into him at the feed store.

"I thought you were enjoying what was happening in my arms." Straightening from the doorway, Jase smirked at me as he lazily walked across the floor to where I sat. He squatted beside me. A large hand reached out to wrap around the base of my neck in a scorching hold. Lowering his mouth to mine, he didn't claim a kiss, as expected, but teased with feather soft nibbles all around the edges of my lips. "Come back with me to your house and I'll remind you just how much you've enjoyed being within arm's reach." Rough, gravely words crawled to the center of my chest. A noticeable increase in heartbeats followed in the wake of the offer.

"Illegal use of a sensual weapon is not going to win your argument for you." I could only hope my willpower was as strong as my verbal refusal to give in. When Jase went all whiskey voiced I usually caved to whatever he wanted.

"Are you sure about that?" Jase used the hand at the back of my neck to pull me in tighter to his lips for a real kiss. Mine parted with no resistance at the first questing lick of his tongue. Dark desire stole into my mouth while the rest of my body awakened to passion from what should have been nothing more than a simple kiss. I was finding out nothing was simple when it came to Jase.

"Come with me."

Those three little words took on a whole new context when murmured by this man. Dang it! He was not going to get his way this time. With a massive show of self-restraint, I shook my head. "This is important to me, Jase. I need some alone time."

I felt like it was necessary for me to prove to Jase, as well as myself, that I wasn't afraid to be alone. I'd never been afraid to be by myself in my life and had no plans to start now. Here lately it was as if the guys were all part of a tag team. If it wasn't Jase hovering over me, it was Evan playing big brother. Colin had even been dragged into keeping an eye on me.

With a final lingering kiss, and an understanding that made me love him even more, Jase nodded. He stood and backed off. "Keep your phone close."

Now that was my man. Giving in, but on his terms. Not leaving without issuing an order.

A faint smile of thanks barely acknowledged his leaving. Shock had me frozen at what I'd just internally admitted to. *My man? Love him even more? Whoa!* This was so different from the girlish crush that had grown into the lustful fantasies of a woman. This had substance and the ability to cripple me. At this point, I was pretty sure there were no options open to me other than letting it play out. I was not going to start going all clingy in the hopes it tied Jase to me for the long haul. Seemed to me those kinds of relationships never ended well. I could only be me, and Jase would have to be the one to decide if that was enough for him.

Forcing myself to focus on the work in front of me again wasn't easy. Channeling the stubbornness of a Donley, I buckled down and immersed myself once more in the mountain of papers. Honestly, some of it was fascinating. It seemed like keeping records had been a trait handed down through the family. There was everything from an unused meal ticket from WWI to a state issued document for the livestock brand the family had used from back in the forties.

It wasn't until a knock sounded on the frame of the open door that I managed to drag my attention away from the wealth of family history spread out before me. Standing in the doorway was Brent, with a stiff legged Ruger keeping a close watch on him.

"Hope I didn't startle you, Char. Hated to interrupt, you were so wrapped up in those papers, but was starting to feel like a creeper standing here waiting for you to notice me." His pale blue eyes were lit with amusement.

"That's okay. Yeah, fascinating stuff. A lot of it's been handed down through the family for years. Most people would've tossed all of it ages ago." I grinned slightly at the thought of the Donleys keeping what most would consider trash.

"But now it's a treasure trove linking you to the past." The words were light enough but there was an edge to them that had me wondering why this topic seemed to have hit a nerve with him. Brent must have noticed my quizzical look, because he began to explain without me asking what the deal was. "In a way, we have a lot in common, Char. We're both the last limb on a family tree that's narrowed down to one lonely little twig. Lucky for you there's a wealth of family history to dive into and explore. The only truly interesting ancestor I'd had wasn't quite so interested in maintaining any kind of link with the trunk of the tree from which she came. At least not in any way tangible, only stories handed down through the generations. Nothing of real substance." Brent paused. I could tell he was visibly pulling himself back from some bitter memories. "Sounded a little envious, didn't I?" He gave a shake of his blond head and a self-deprecating chuckle.

Wanting to lighten the mood, I told him, "Sounded like a lawyer to me, talking about tangible property and substance. You forgot one little detail, though. You have the option of having a family and carrying on your family name. Heck, you could start a forest if you wanted to. But me…well, the Donley name dies with me."

Crap. That certainly brightened the conversation. Not. Feeling awkward, I scrambled to my feet, not wanting to remain sitting on the floor looking up at him. It also gave me an excuse to take a minute to regain some control of my own emotions.

"Whatcha up to, Brent? Did Jase send you out here?" Which didn't seem likely, considering Jase had been pretty clear on not liking the interest Brent had shown me.

"Actually, I can thank Miss Lori for steering me in the right direction. At church this morning I overheard her informing a few of her friends," he paused to wink at me, "that your house was pretty much good as new and you had moved on to putting your grandfather's house back in order."

It figured I'd be Miss Lori's featured attraction for a few days. She'd stopped by yesterday on the pretense of making sure I hadn't fallen into a severe depression over all the tragedy in my life lately. I thought she would never leave. She snooped around the house the whole time she was there. I even found her in the kitchen, going through my phone. She didn't even have the grace to look embarrassed at being caught. The woman had no shame when it came to sticking her nose into places it didn't belong.

It came as no surprise that while she was at my house her questions had less to do with my well-being and were more about what had been stolen. Oh, she also just wondered if I was making any headway in discovering who had killed my granddaddy. Miss Lori assured me she would be more than happy to go over all of Gramps' records with me to help track down the killer. Poor woman had to be about to bust a gut at the thought of all that precious gossip fodder.

"It's killing her to think I have written evidence of sins carried out by the men and women from around these parts and she can't get her hands on it. Ammunition like that would keep her in dirty laundry to flap in everyone's faces for years to come." I smiled back at Brent. "Enough about my turn in Miss Lori's barrel, why'd you track me down, Brent? Have you heard something which might help?" I looked at him quizzically, not really holding out much hope he'd anything useful to share.

"Now I'm afraid you'll accuse me of searching for dirty laundry if I admit to stopping by to see if you had considered my offer to help." There was almost a wishful twist to his thin lips. "It would be in your best interest to have a lawyer going over anything you have of your grandfather's which might pertain to his…let's call it a hobby."

Yeah, why don't we just call it a hobby like everybody else? Not even sure why a flash of anger zinged through me. Maybe it had to do with how hard everyone was trying to diminish a heritage my family had been proud of. They talked about a lifetime of hard work that was dangerous and hard lived as if it were a frivolous pastime of no substance. Didn't matter one little bit they were more than likely doing it for my protection. Still pissed me off.

Reining in my annoyance, I shrugged a shoulder while questioning Brent, "Why would I need legal advice? It's not like I'm going to publish anything I find out. No one is going to be suing me for slander."

"That's not what I'm worried about. There is the very real possibility of legal repercussions if certain federal agencies were notified and they confiscated any and all written records which could lead them to a working still. You've got a lot of people stirred up over Mr. Donley's death. What if someone goes to the state police demanding they look into your grandfather's death, since it's obvious Sheriff Cantrell isn't going to? That same person might not realize how this could all blow back on you. I don't want to see you lose the land that's been in your family for generations. You need me to protect your interests." He certainly looked sincere as he made his case. For some reason, the more justification Brent gave for wanting to help the less I wanted it.

"Wow, it's gone from a hobby to a *working still* now, huh? I don't care who tells what concerning some *supposed* still. Even if they did start nosing around my property, all anyone is going to find is ancient history. Anyone who goes looking for a working still is going to be sadly disappointed." It was easy for me to tell Brent that with confidence. Colin and the others had cleaned out, broken down and removed any evidence of illegal activity from my property. "So, you see, I don't really need your legal advice, Mr. Future Sheriff."

"You don't trust me."

"I don't know you."

Brent ran a hand through his blond strands with a bit of frustration. He paced forward across the room, closer to me, a little too close. I refused to take a step back and let him think he intimidated me.

"Forgive me if I'm wrong but I got the impression you were not only willing to accept my help, but in fact would welcome it."

"That was in finding a killer, which has nothing to do with imaginary moonshine stills." That was a bald faced lie and fooled no one. Gramps' murder had everything to do with moonshine. It was just the more Brent tried to push his way into helping me, the more determined I was to push back. Irrational? You bet. Being female gave me the right to be as illogical as I wanted to be. Just one of the perks.

"You no longer want my help." More of a statement, delivered in a flat monotone voice, than a question.

Why the hell was I suddenly feeling bad? Like I'd hurt him on a personal level. It was ridiculous to feel like I'd let him down in some manner.

"You heard her, Allen. She doesn't want your help."

CHAPTER TWENTY-ONE

Both Brent and I started at the sound of Jase's deep voice. When I scanned the area past Brent, my gaze collided with a pair of stormy gray eyes. They certainly contradicted the bored manner in which he'd addressed Brent. Jase made a show of pulling out his cell and tapping it, as if checking to see if it was working.

Well, that was just plain ol' pissy.

"What's the matter, Rydan? Afraid to let Char make up her own mind on who she accepts help from?" A sneer curled the corner of Brent's lips.

I started reassessing just how smart Brent really was. As he stepped away from me, even his body language changed from relaxed to more of an aggressive stance.

"Sounded to me like she'd already decided she didn't need your help. You appear to be the only one here having a hard time accepting it," Jase said, as he put away his phone. His continued causal posture and off-hand manner of speech was almost an insult when compared to Brent's belligerent attitude.

Now would be a good time for someone to defuse the situation. Looking at the other two made it apparent I was going to have to be that someone. "Jase knows I make up my own mind about matters, Brent." I stuck out my hand and continued talking, "Thank you for stopping by to check up on me. Good luck with your campaign."

Brent examined my outstretched hand before turning his eyes up to mine. The slight tightening of the skin around his eyes let me know he understood this was more of a permanent dismissal than a simple goodbye handshake. I tensed, wondering if he would go quietly. Brent did not strike me as one who liked to be dismissed quite so publicly.

When he shrugged, as if making his mind up about something, then took my hand in his, I have to admit to inwardly heaving a sigh of "*thank the good Lord that's over with.*" I was a little premature in my relief.

He took my hand, but instead of giving it a business-like shake, then turning loose, he turned it over and made caressing strokes with his thumb back and forth across the back. He quirked a gentle smile at me and said, "Ah, Miss Donley, I do believe we would've made wonderful friends. Who knows? Maybe you'll come to realize the value of my friendship in the future."

Jase blocked the door, forcing Brent to stop in the middle of his grand exit. He examined Brent and appeared to find him lacking. Brent's shoulders tensed, as if preparing for an attack. Heck, my shoulders were tense wondering if Jase was going to jump him. But after what felt like a long minute, Jase stepped to the side to allow Brent to pass. Message delivered.

"So, where's Colin?" My attempt to head Jase off from blasting me was feeble at best.

"I thought we agreed you were going to keep your phone close?" And there it was, the first shot of male dissatisfaction with the female concept of following orders.

"I didn't even know he was around until he said something." I tried to not cringe. That was so not the best thing to point out right now. "What was I supposed to say with him standing there watching me? 'Hang on a sec, Brent. Gotta call Jase and make sure it's okay if I talk to you.'" Getting sassy probably wasn't the way to go right now either. It was that filter between brain and mouth problem I struggled with.

"He's interested in you. Hell, he's fascinated with you."

"That's just it, Jase. I don't get a sexual vibe off him at all. I'll agree he seems interested in me but it's only as a friend." That was the puzzling part for me. I honestly didn't feel like he was romantically interested. Still, I felt like it was necessary to blow him off, partly because of Jase, mostly because I'd told Brent the truth about not knowing him.

"Baby, if you don't get a sexual vibe off a guy when he's around you, then he's either dead or gay." Jase walked close enough he could snag an arm around my waist, and haul me against his muscular form. "You gettin' any vibes off me, Charlotte?"

Relaxing into his long length of sculpted muscle was becoming ridiculously easier every time he touched me. Having his hands press me closer to his body was both heaven and torture. What if this didn't last? I couldn't help but believe the scales of neediness were not tipped in my favor. Never a good thing.

Rising on tiptoes, I stretched to reach his lips. Once contact was made I put every ounce of my need into a sensual assault on the perfection of his mouth. When he went from being the recipient to the aggressor, demanding more, I thrilled in the knowledge that in this I was at least his equal. By the time we pulled back to draw ragged breaths, both of us could agree on the vibes being given off.

Bending slightly, in order to rest his forehead against mine, Jase softly chuckled before speaking. "I need to ask those kinds of questions more often."

Laughing, I tried to untangle myself from where I was wrapped around him. It would've been darn embarrassing if he wasn't wrapped just as tightly around me.

"Whoa, where you think you're headed? We were just getting to the good part." Rock hard muscles refused to loosen. I was not going anywhere until Jase was good and ready to let me.

"I still have a ton of papers to go through, and you still haven't answered my question about where Colin is. We keep this up, the poor man will be treated to an Xrated peep show when he walks through the door." I pushed ineffectively at hands which seemed to be everywhere at once, while still managing to keep control of me.

"Colin's not coming. That's why I'm here. He stopped by your house before heading on out this way. I took the doors from him and that means you have no excuse not to complete what you started." He punctuated each statement with random kissing attacks on my neck and face.

Laughing at this playful side of Jase, I still didn't give in and continued to struggle. "I have an excellent excuse. I'm still up to my eyebrows in boxes and papers and you have new doors to install." Boy, did I ever want him to keep pushing me to forget duty.

Going motionless, Jase sobered quickly and framed my face with both of his work-roughened hands. The suddenness stilled my own movement. Worry started gnawing at my confidence. "You almost made me forget why I have to get the doors finished today." Grey eyes searched my face as if watching for the slightest change in expression. "I've got to go to Rogers tomorrow. It's business and if there was a way to get out of it I would, baby."

How ridiculous was it to feel anxious over Jase having to leave? This time when I pushed back from Jase, he let me go. Going for a nonchalance I was far from feeling, I smiled and shrugged. "Well, it's not like you can put your whole life on hold forever, right? We always knew at some point you were going to have to get back to work. You're an important man with an uncle depending on you to help run his company. I can handle my own problems from here on out."

"Son-of-a-bitch, you are the most aggravating woman sometimes," exclaimed Jase, with more heat than expected. "I'm not abandoning you, you little idiot. I'm going to be gone two, maybe three days at the most, and I want you to come with me."

A lightness spread through me. A real smile graced my face and I was afraid it showed just how relieved I was he wasn't walking out on us. "Don't call me an idiot."

"Don't ever look at me like I'm tossing you away again."

"Don't try and read my thoughts. You're a guy. You'll always get them wrong."

Jase reached out and caressed a thumb across my cheek. "But this time I didn't. Did I?"

Lids closed over my eyes, to keep him from reading anything else, like, say, my love for him. But I couldn't prevent myself from leaning into his stroke. "Maybe." It was the most I was willing to concede.

"So, you're going to go with me." He dropped his hand to settle it on my hip. He sounded pretty confident.

"No." And just as I anticipated, the hand that had been easing up and down my hip in a light stroke began to squeeze in a knee-jerk reaction to being told no.

"What do you mean, no?" Yeah, Jase really didn't like it when he didn't get his way. "You can't stay here. Charlotte, do you honestly think once I'm gone everyone who wants to get their hands on those files is going to back off just because you don't know where they are?" Jase flung his arms wide.

"That's why I have to stay here. I'm not going to lose three days sitting in Rogers while you do your boss thingy. Not when I could be here searching." I had my own problems with not getting my way, but I was smart enough to compromise. "In the spirit of cooperation, I'm willing to stay at your house and only come over here during the daytime. I'll bring my gun and promise to keep the door locked the whole time I'm here." I was feeling pleased with myself over all the concessions to keep Jase happy. He didn't seem to look at it in the same light.

"You call that cooperating? Refusing to do the sensible thing and go with me, where I can keep you safe?"

"Hell of a lot more so than issuing an order and expecting it to be followed." He picked the wrong girl if he thought he could get pissy and I would just stammer an apology then meekly do as told. I crossed my arms and cocked a hip.

Men seemed to spend a lot of time running their hands through their hair in frustration when they were around me. Jase was no exception. He paced to the door, braced a hand against the frame and proceeded to stare at anything as long as it wasn't me.

Just when the silence reached the point where I had to strain to keep my mouth shut, Jase swung around to pace back to me. "If you won't go with me, I want more than you staying at my house."

"I'm willing to listen." Dang right, I said it with a heavy dose of self-righteousness. I was the one trying here. Jase gave orders. I'm not even positive he realized it's what he did. Men who were in positions of power tended to forget everyone wasn't on their payroll.

A tiny twitch of an eye was the only sign my dig struck pay dirt. "Will you agree to have someone with you during the day? If Evan can't hang out with you, will you call Colin and see if he's free? Promise to only make the trip out here, or even to your house, only if you have someone to watch your back once you get to where you're going? Otherwise I cancel my trip."

"You've already said this trip was important and you couldn't get out of it." Okay, maybe I was testing to see how important I was in comparison to his business.

"When are you going to understand nothing is more important than your safety to me? Is that what you want, Charlotte? Is all of this your way of getting me to stay with you?" Jase didn't look disgusted with me. If anything, there was an extra tenderness to the slant of his mouth, a softness around his smoky gray eyes.

I was the one disgusted with me. What kind of woman made someone she supposedly loved chose between her and his work? Or anything else, for that matter. A weak one. Nope. Not now. Not ever.

"Of course you're not going to cancel on account of me. I'll be a good girl. But you're going to have to trust me, Evan and Colin to know what is safe while you're gone." I flashed a quick smile at him. "At night I'll be in that fortress you call a home with no need of a guard."

Jase continued to search my face, and I guessed he was satisfied with what he found because he said, "You being a good girl is what I want while I'm gone. When I get back I expect my hell-raiser to be waiting for me."

"Always." Now that was one promise easy to make and keep.

CHAPTER TWENTY-TWO

I sat in Gramps' old wooden rocker, lazily dipping back and forth. The front porch used to be Gramps' favorite spot to sit and relax. It had been a place for me to sit with him and listen to his stories. I wasn't ready to step inside his house and restart my search for the journals, so I sat and rocked and let my mind wander. Ever since Jase went off on his business trip the last few days had taken on a certain pattern.

Evan and Colin had eventually agreed with me on what I considered sensible precautions during the day. They were such pushovers, easy to talk into whatever I wanted, unlike another man who would remain nameless. Those sensible measures included having one of them with me when possible during the daytime, and they were more often than not. When they weren't available, I would check in every hour by phone until I made it safely home to Jase's house and was locked in for the night. It was a pain in the butt, and the guys refused to accept a text, but it beat being under constant guard.

The total non-eventfulness of the past week should have been a relief but it had become a nagging worry. It added to my fears that when the house had been searched the intruders had found what they'd come to steal.

Pushing off with my toes, I rocked and looked across the fields bordering the yard. Ruger was busy sniffing out critters in the tall grasses next to the fence rows. June bugs, with their hard, iridescent green bodies, were giving themselves headaches flying into the porch supports and the side of the house. When I was little, Gramps would tie a thin piece of thread on one of the bug's hind legs, hand it off to me, then laugh the whole time my bug took me for a walk.

So many great memories were wrapped up in this house. Gramps had been born in the back bedroom. The youngest of six children, he'd been the only one willing to stay at home and help his parents as they aged. It was to this house that he brought his new bride. I'd thought that sounded horrible, having to live with your in-laws. Granny had thought it was the most natural thing in the world to do.

All of Gramps' siblings had moved away to work in cities. None willing to stay, work the stills, except my grandfather. The heritage of the Donley whiskey was a source of pride to him. He'd loved this house just as much. Claimed his Maggie had put her heart into making it a home, just as his mother had.

Donna Taylor

It was hard to believe he was now another ghost roaming the empty rooms; that I'd never fuss over him again or make him breakfast. But when I was here, I could almost hear the sound of his voice teasing my grandmother, imagine them walking out onto the front porch together at any moment.

That was why I was certain the journals were hidden here somewhere. To me it couldn't be any more obvious. Gramps probably thought he *had* told me where he kept the "insurance" when he said he kept it close to the heart. But it was a dang big house and had so many additions and renovations over the years there could have been hidey-holes built in a million different spots.

The house also contained one of the biggest secrets our family kept. I looked over at the cistern, built into the corner of the porch connecting to the front wall of the house. Gramps always claimed that old cistern had been hand dug with pick and shovel well over a hundred years ago. Fieldstone had been used to line the large reserve at the bottom and the fifteen feet of shaft. I got claustrophobic even thinking about the men who had been encased inside it during construction. The house's guttering was still connected and still collected the runoff from the roof whenever it rained. All the water collected was directed into the cistern through a single downspout that ran into the side of the structure.

Rainwater was one of the main ingredients in the shine the family called Copper Moon. It was also the water used to cut the whiskey, which gave it its signature smooth as silk, slide down the throat goodness. Gramps always told me that shine was only as good as the water used in the mash. Rainwater was the heart of the Donley moonshine.

Holy horse crap! Talk about a light bulb flashing on. Was I ever right in thinking it couldn't be any more obvious, and I'd still been looking in all the wrong places. The insurance was here. Right under everyone's noses. Well, maybe not everyone's, but it sure as heck had been under my nose the whole time. I pictured Gramps' devilish grin, could almost hear him whisper, *"Took you long 'nuff to figure it out, Sis."*

Catapulting from the rocker, I rushed over to the cistern. The lip came to my waist. A custom cap made out of old oak planking covered the opening. The opening was kept covered most of the time, since the cistern wasn't used on a daily basis. The outside had been cemented years ago and covered in fieldstone in a stacked stone pattern. Beginning with the stones furthest from the house, I worked my way around the perimeter. Running my fingers over each rock I checked for any wiggle, any movement, anything that felt different. There were only a few stones left to inspect, and disappointment was a growing knot, in the pit of my stomach. The last row was both connected to the side of the cistern and butted against the clapboard of the house.

I wasn't sure if I was pleading or praying over the last few rocks I tested, but a steady stream of, *"Please, please, please,"* escaped from my lips. When I finally felt a tiny movement from a rock, I caught my breath and murmured, "Come on, baby. Open up for Momma."

It was a fairly large stone and it took both hands, plus a fair share of wiggling, to pull it from its place. When it finally lifted out I stared at the hole that opened into the side of the house. It wasn't overly large, or even all that deep. But it was enough space to contain a metal box, sitting there, plain as day, waiting for me to collect.

My fingers were actually trembling as I reached out to touch the smooth surface of the container. Pulling it out carefully, I cradled it in my hands as though it were a priceless object as I moved back to the rocker to sit. Now that I had it physically in my hands, instead of tearing into it, I found myself just sitting and staring.

So much fuss over the papers protected by this one piece of rectangular metal.

Right now, half the men in town were worrying over what I was going to do with the information contained inside. Colin had been approached again and again with offers to serve as everything from a negotiator in the sale of it, to a thief who stole it away from me.

Easing the clasp open and raising the lid, the contents revealed dozens of journals tied together, two loose booklets and also a small cache of memory cards in their plastic cases. Picking one of the small plastic covers up, I saw it had a beginning date and end date written on it. Judging by the number of 8GB memory cards in the box, there had to be hundreds of photos here.

After replacing the memory card, I pulled one of the loose booklets from the top of all the tied ones.

Thumbing through revealed page after page of detailed instructions on all the various mashes used in the making of Donley shine. It was fascinating, and I could become easily sidetracked with the numerous personal notes written in the margins beside each recipe. Forcing myself to set the journal aside, I reached for the other loose notebook. Opening it, I began to read.

Names, dates, notes about the type of shine sold and the quantity, all printed out in my gramps' shaky handwriting. Before each entry there was a number and letter combination. Picking up the plastic encased memory card again, I noted the number and letter above the date.

A small twitch of my lips escalated into full-blown laughter. "You wily, old, wonderful man!" I shouted my relief to the skies.

Insurance, indeed!

Jase, I am not leaving something this exciting in a text. Call me back as soon as you have time. The MINUTE you have time. Damn! I wish you were with me right now.

I stared at my phone in disappointment. My first thoughts were to share my discovery with Jase, but he wasn't here and I couldn't even reach him by phone. I had to settle for sending him a text. I hoped that even if he was still in meetings, and couldn't answer the phone, he might be able to sneak a peek at a text. Once the initial rush of the discovery was gone it all seemed a little anti-climactic with no one to share it with. I could call Evan or Colin, but I wanted Jase to be the one who learned about it first.

Checking the time on my phone made me realize just how long I'd spent pouring over the accounts. The first journal I'd studied was the one that appeared to be the most recent. There were plenty of listed customers, but the last entry wasn't for the night of the murder. The last listings were from a couple days prior. I suppose it made sense he hadn't been able to log in the entries for that particular night.

What was equally discouraging were the three empty plastic covers. Those had to be the covers which went with the memory cards of the missing game cameras.

What I had to decide now was whether to take all of this with me back to Jase's house, or to leave it here where I knew it would be safe. Logically, if I took it back to the house I could go over all of it tonight and have a much clearer idea of who the customers had been. I could check to see if there was a pattern to any of the deliveries.

Emotionally, I was paranoid and superstitious enough to be afraid to move it from a proven hiding spot. And there may have been a little bit of wanting to recapture the moment of discovery with Jase. He was going to be home tomorrow. The thought of bringing him here and showing him exactly how I found all of this was bringing back the initial rush.

Deciding to split the difference, I replaced everything back exactly the way it had been with the exception of the last, most current journal. That baby was going home with me. Having finally come to a decision, I called it a night and headed back to Jase's.

My phone began to ring as I pulled into the long lane leading to Jase's home. Relieved to see it was Jase, I answered in an explosion of, "Jase, I found it! Everything! I found it all!" I didn't even give the poor man a chance to say hello. Heck, I'd probably seared his eardrum with my initial squealing of his name as soon as I answered the phone.

"Gawd damn, baby! I knew you'd figure it out. Where were they?" He sounded so proud of me, it made my smile spread almost to the point of pain.

"Oh, no. I'm not about to tell you over the phone. You are still coming home tomorrow, right?" There may have been more than a little anxiety in my tone.

"Baby, I am leaving before daylight. Plan on being home before you climb out of my bed for the day. As a matter of fact, I'm counting on you being right there in the middle of my bed with nothing on but a big ol', *welcome home, darlin'* smile." His voice had gone all rumbly and sexy.

"I believe that can be arranged." Seriously, it was a little ridiculous I'd had to clear my throat—twice—before I could answer him.

"I'm counting on it." Jase chuffed a low laugh.

CHAPTER TWENTY-THREE

Back at Jase's, I burrowed into the plump cushions of the couch with Gramps' little notebook clutched in my hand. I'd been scouring the pages of the journal ever since arriving home. So far there didn't seem to be a clear pattern on any of the buys, let alone the deliveries. Gramps had been the original "*have it your way*" kind of supplier of goods. While he had a great method of recording his sales, if there was a pattern to it, it was apparently going to have to jump out and bite me in the ass, 'cause I sure wasn't seeing any. I started to realize this might be harder than I thought.

Hearing a faint knock on the thick panels of the front door, I shot a quick look at the oversized clock mounted on the wall across from me. It was going on nine, which was a little late for visitors in the country. I walked cautiously to the nearest window which would give me a clear view of the area directly in front of the door.

Standing there, getting ready to press the doorbell again in a second attempt to get my attention, was Miss Lori. Back pedaling quickly from the glass, hoping she hadn't noticed me, I tried to decide if there was a snowball's chance of pretending not to be here. Probably not, what with my truck sitting front and center in the drive and lights on in the house.

Another interrogation by this incredibly nosy woman was not how I wanted to spend the rest of the evening. Sighing to myself, I didn't see any polite way of getting out of this. Figuring I might as well get it over with, I punched the code in to disarm the alarm and was getting ready to open the door when I realized the journal was still gripped in my hand.

Not even wanting to open that can of worms, I hastily slipped the small journal in the waistband of my shorts, settling it against the small of my back. Once I was positive it was safely concealed, I opened the door with perhaps a little more force than necessary.

"Oh, my stars! You startled me!" Miss Lori pressed a hand to her skinny bosom while an oversized purse, hanging off her elbow, banged into her narrow hip.

"I'm sorry, Miss Lori. Kinda surprised to see you out this late. Was there something I could help you with?" I blocked the door, hoping to give her a hint now was not a good time for a visit. But Miss Lori had never been one to take a hint. She gave plenty of them, but never succumbed to a single one herself.

"Well, you can invite me in like a young lady with manners. After all, I did make the effort to come all this way to offer my continued support in your time of need." She had no qualms at pointing out what she perceived as everyone else's rudeness. Too bad she didn't recognize the flaw in her own character.

Giving in to the unavoidable, I widened the door and swept my hand to the side in a silent invitation to enter. Ruger stood at the foot of the stairs, eying our visitor with an intensity, which of course, Miss Lori took exception to.

"I would be much more comfortable if you'd put that animal somewhere he won't be staring at me like I am his next meal." She actually huffed at the end of her sentence. Miss Lori continued to mumble, under her breath, words to the effect that filthy animals did not belong in a respectable home. She was careful the words weren't murmured too low. After all, what good was it to make a complaint if no one could hear it?

Not feeling like it was even worth the effort to argue, I had Ruger follow me through the kitchen into the adjoining mudroom. Neither one of us was happy about shutting him in there. As a matter of fact, I would have happily stayed in the room myself and left Ruger to entertain our visitor.

I realized Miss Lori had followed me as far as the kitchen when I went to retrace my steps to the living room. The woman had already managed to find two tall glasses and was in the process of filling them with ice.

"Can I offer you something to drink?" I fully expected the irony of the question to not even register with her. I was not disappointed.

"You go on into the living room and relax while I fix us something nice and cool to drink. After all it's why I'm here. To take care of you." She shot me a look that I would've labeled as calculating on anyone else. But as quickly as the thought crossed my mind, her expression cleared and she was back to the fussy meddler we all knew and dodged. "I swear, here it is, close to the end of summer, and it's still hot enough to make the devil grin. Now, you go on and relax," said Miss Lori, as she made shooing motions at me with her bony hands.

I clued her in to the pitcher of sweet tea she could find in the refrigerator on my way out of the room. So as ordered, I waited for my tea to be delivered, and resigned myself to an evening of questions I had no intention of giving truthful answers to.

"Now, isn't this nice." She handed off a tall sweet tea to me as she took her seat beside me on the couch. I took a long fortifying drink, wishing it were heavily laced with whiskey. Miss Lori watched me with an overly satisfied smile. I was half afraid she was going to start patting her own back for being such a Good Samaritan by providing me a glass of my own tea.

"Such a lovely home to be staying in while your own is under repair. So thoughtful of Jase to help you. Of course, I know how you young people think nothing of hopping into one stranger's bed after another now-a-days. But I didn't come here to discuss y'all's lack of righteous behavior."

The woman had a talent for wrapping a slap in a compliment.

"What I really wanted to discuss is how naughty you've been lying about those pesky journals of your granddaddy. Pretending you had them all this time. You know dear, you'll go to hell just as quick for lying as you will for stealing." She fired off a severe look of disapproval in my direction. "So much worry they've caused. Now that they've been found, and you truly have them in your possession, we will just make sure they don't cause any more problems for the family."

"I'm not sure what you mean, Miss Lori? What makes you think I've not had my granddaddy's records all this time?" This whole conversation was beyond strange. Miss Lori might be a well-known busybody, but what she was saying went beyond simple gossip she gathered from her tongue-wagging cronies. My brain was starting to act like it wanted to take a little vacay. I was seriously starting to have problems focusing on what was being said.

"Well, dear, I've been a little naughty myself. But if you had just been open with me this whole nastiness could have been avoided." She leveled such a look of reproach I caught myself squirming.

"Wait a minute. What nasshhiness could have been avoided? Missh Lori, none of 'ishh is making any senssss to me. How did you know they were mishhing?" I tried to be forceful but my tongue felt thick and it was getting hard to make it work right.

I'd never notice before how much Miss Lori resembled a walking stick. All thin, long angled limbs and that skinny body of hers. She was rather scary looking, if a person actually studied her. The harder I stared, the more angles and fuzzy edges she acquired. I took another large gulp of tea, hoping to clear my head with a shot of caffeine.

Something was not right here, and my comprehension and vision seemed to be leaving me with each passing second. I was slurring my words, which made no sense. None of this was making sense. What was Miss Lori doing here? I felt myself tipping to the side. Miss Lore neatly snagged my glass before it could slip from my slack fingers. She set it, along with hers, on the large wooden coffee table in front of us, being careful to place them on coasters first.

"Well, young lady, you should really keep your cell phone locked. Such a simple matter to put spyware on anyone's phone. One little app and then nothing is private. For the right person that is." Miss Lori seemed to be simultaneously proud of her tech savviness while scolding me for my lack of phone safety awareness.

"I may have used just a little too much of that liquid in the tea. The boys did warn me not to use too much when they gave it to me, but it was such a large glass of sweet tea." The woman would not shut up, or stop fussing with the pillows behind my back. I kept trying to grab her arm—the edge of the couch—anything that would ground me.

"Just lean back and I'll let the boys in. They can keep you company while I take care of these glasses. We don't want to leave anything sitting around raising pesky questions later. Do we dear?" She pushed me gently back against the cushions she'd been arranging.

I wanted to struggle upright but my body would not cooperate. From where I was sprawled it was hard to keep an eye on Miss Lori as she walked away. Within only a few steps she was out of my line of sight. Voices sounded by the door, masculine laughter followed by the prissy sound of Miss Lori scolding whoever she'd admitted to wipe their feet.

The heavy clomp of boots advancing across the polished walnut flooring drowned the lighter patter of Miss Lori's loafers. What was left of my vision was blurred at best; it was fading in and out at worst. I began to wonder if I was hallucinating when Miss Lori appeared in front of me bookended on either side by a man. It was only as BW hunkered down to peer into my face with a vicious smile that I truly began to understand the shit-pit Miss Lori had pushed me into.

"Surprise, bitch. Looks like it's fuckin' payday."

* * *

Jase felt a sense of having returned to a real home when the headlights from his truck slid across the side of Charlotte's vehicle where it sat parked in his drive. It was the first time he'd felt that way since building the house. He continued on around the driveway, making for the garage. He shook his head in amusement at her stubborn refusal to park in the three-car garage attached to the end of the house. Said her truck wasn't used to the comforts of such a thing and she didn't want to spoil it. He knew Charlotte was the one who didn't want to get used to what she considered a luxury, one she didn't trust would always be hers to enjoy.

As the garage door glided to a close behind his parked truck, Jase's blood heated at the thought of surprising Charlotte when he crawled into bed with her. She wasn't expecting him until much later this morning.

He'd decided at the last minute to drive back home after his dinner meeting wrapped up. It was after ten o'clock before he'd finally made it back to his condo, finished packing and been able to start the trip home. Now it was well after one in the morning and all he had on his mind was that if Charlotte wasn't already naked in his bed, she soon would be.

The first inkling all might not be well on the home front was the sound of barking and a frantic scratching at the door he was about to open. It led into the mudroom, which in its turn fed into the kitchen and the rest of the house. He didn't even think about the damage Ruger had to be doing to the wooden door, all he could focus on was why Charlotte's dog would be trying to dig his way through in the first place.

The door had barely cracked open before a broad head was pushing its way through, to be quickly followed by a sturdy Blue-Merle body. The whining

Ruger put out had nothing to do with "hi, happy you're home," and was more about being in extreme distress.

Pushing past him, Jase noted the alarm system wasn't armed and the door that opened into the kitchen was closed. It was pretty clear Ruger had been trapped in the mudroom for an extended period of time. The lower half of the interior door had been clawed to the point of massive splinters porcupining its surface.

Fear ripped into Jase with a viciousness he'd never had to deal with before. All thoughts of ghosting in to surprise Charlotte fled in the face of a rising tide of fury and conviction something horrible had happened to her.

There were no lights shining on the lower level of the house. Jase started flicking on switches as he made his way swiftly through the kitchen en route to the stairs. Taking the steps two at a time Jase began to bellow Charlotte's name, praying he was wrong and she was curled up safe in his bed.

When he bolted into the master bedroom it was to find a room in pristine condition. As he stared at the empty bed, the one tiny spark of hope for a reasonable explanation for Charlotte to have left Ruger trapped in the mudroom flickered and died. At the thought of Ruger he looked around for him and quickly realized he'd raced up the stairs alone. The dog had stayed below and it sounded like he was doing some major barking at the front door.

Descending the steps as quickly as he'd ascended, Jase joined the crazed dog, who was alternating between barking and howling at the closed door. A quick check confirmed the wooden barrier was locked and that left him with a huge question mark.

There was no good reason for Charlotte to be gone at one-thirty in the morning. She'd expected him back today and he'd promised to be home before she was even out of bed. She'd been over the moon excited about finding the journals and seemed anxious to share the discovery with him.

But now, the only thoughts running through his mind was that those damn pieces of paper were what had placed the woman he loved in danger. And he was the asshole who had left her to face that threat alone.

CHAPTER TWENTY-FOUR

"Tell me again why the fuck Robbie and I didn't tear that sum'bitch's place apart looking for the rest of this shit?" There was a flapping sound, as though someone was waving a notebook around in agitation.

As far as a wakeup call to the land of consciousness and mobility went, that one sucked. Nausea rolled through my guts and gave me something to fight back other than just my fear. Eyelids refused to lift so I couldn't get a visual on where I was. Judging from the moldy smells and the quarreling voices, it was a safe bet I wasn't in Jase's house any longer.

"For the same reason I washed up those glasses before we left. We didn't want to give your damn daddy any reason to believe the bitch was in trouble. You know as well as I do Rydan will be calling in the ol' bastard as soon as he figures out his little bed partner is missing. As it stands, she could have taken off with another man.

Everybody knows how quick she was to spread her legs for Rydan. I made sure of it."

At the mention of Jase, I got a little sicker at the thought of what he was going to go through when he showed up at the house and I wasn't there. The only way I was going to make it through this was to focus on a couple of facts. Jase would be working as hard to get to me, as I was going to be working on getting back to him. Pushing him to the back of my mind, I tried to concentrate on the now.

That had to be Miss Lori talking to BW. I recognized both of their voices. But the cloud of confusion controlling my brain was having a hard time reconciling prissy Miss Lori with the hard sounding woman doing all the cussing. And while I was shocked to find out the sanctimonious busybody was somehow involved, hearing BW's voice added another layer of emotions to the mix. Anger was merging with the fear, and I welcomed it. I was going to need it to help keep the paralyzing terror at bay.

"Goddamn, Robbie! Are you sure you knew what the hell you was doing when you made up that batch of G? Shouldn't the bitch be awake by now?" Seems even BW had the sense to back off from Miss Lori and turn his accusations and complaints on Robbie. And wasn't it great to know there were not two, but three people in the same room, and none of them were on my side?

"Made it the same as always. We've used it plenty of times and the ol' boys we've sold to never had no complaints neither." Robbie sounded more than a little defensive when he answered.

My stomach was still trying to pull a runaway, but at least the longer I was awake the clearer my thoughts became. Right now, my brain was screaming I was in some deep doodoo. Look at me, the genius. Wake up in a strange room—with three psychos and a serious hangover—wanting to barf all over the place, and just like that I figure out I'm in major trouble. Yeah, the hands fastened behind my back was another clue my three companions hadn't brought me here out of concern for my health.

"Shit, Lori, how much of the fuckin' stuff did you give her?" Looked like I'd been too quick to give BW the credit for knowing when to back-off from Miss Lori.

"You might talk to my cousin like that, Billy Wayne, but I ain't your momma and you sure as hell ain't gonna talk to me that way," declared Miss Lori. "Remember, you're the one who called me to dig you out of the shit you're up to your knees in. Jest like you do every time you can't run to your daddy to fix something. Bless your mamma's heart. If it weren't for the fact it would kill her if she ever found out you'd killed someone, I'd wash my hands of you." Ahhh, there was the sanctimonious old lady I was used to.

"Bullshit, Lori. Only reason you're helping me out is same as always. Money. Momma ain't got nothin' to do with it."

It was no surprise BW was trying to blame someone for me still being unconscious when he wanted me awake. What came as a shock was to find out she was a second cousin to him.

Maybe I should have paid more attention to who was related to who when I was growing up. I'd never had to keep up with that sort of stuff, since my parents and grandparents were all the kin I'd had who lived close. Some girls I knew had so many first, second, and third cousins littering the ground they had to look two counties over to find a date. Those girls were regular walking genealogies for this part of the country.

There had to be something severely wrong with me that I was lying tied up on the floor worrying about who was related to who. At this point I was willing to blame whatever Miss Lori had spiked my sweet tea with for my inability to focus on the very real danger I was in.

Upbringing is a funny thing. No matter how much I hated the woman, my raising was so ingrained, I couldn't bring myself to drop the Miss.

The little extra something added to my tea had to be some kind of home-brewed GHB. It sounded like Robbie had been the cook who had supplied Miss Lori with the *Easy Lay* liquid. Figures that Robbie and BW would be very familiar with the date rape drug.

"This is bullshit." BW had hit the limit of his patience and I was damn sure it wasn't a good sign for me. From the sounds and vibration from boots clomping on wood flooring, he was making his way to the corner of the room where I'd been dumped on the floor. Deciding now was as good a time as any to let them in on the fact I was awake, I started struggling into a more upright position. My eyelids were finally willing to get with the program and cracked open wide enough to allow me to see BW on his way over. The groan that escaped my parched lips wasn't entirely faked.

I figured it would be in my best interest to act weaker than I actually was. Acting weak wasn't going to be a problem. The only thing holding the contents of my stomach in was my determination, although the thought of spewing all over BW as soon as he got close enough was very tempting.

"About damn time you started stirring." He actually sounded relieved.

Come to think of it though, if they had overdosed me and I'd died, any hope of finding my gramps' journals died with me. I was certain my being here was all about those records. Looked like I hadn't been paranoid after all when I'd been afraid to remove them from a hiding place that had kept them secure for Lord knows how many decades.

My struggle to push myself into a more seated position was suddenly aided by two bruising hands, fingers digging deep into my shoulders. They jerked me up roughly then tried to leave an impression of my spinal column in the wall they flung me against. The abrupt change in elevation was more abuse than my poor stomach could handle. Slamming my back against the wall was the final tug on the cork of my stomach and all that was needed to get the shindig rolling.

When the first heave hit there was nothing I could do to stop the flood of partially digested food from erupting and spraying both BW and myself. By the time I was geared up for the second disgorging of grossness, BW was scrambling back away from me. His arms were outstretched in an attempt to keep from contacting the contents of my stomach that were decorating the front of his shirt. Curses rolled one after another from his mouth.

Once it was clear there was nothing left for me to bring to the party, BW walked back up to me, squatted down, drew back his ham sized fist and delivered me back into unconsciousness.

My second rising from the darkness wasn't any happier than the first. I was now in worse shape than before, and a little less inclined to let them know I was aware of what was going on around me. The sour smell of vomit-saturated clothes was not my favorite odor to wake up to. It's a sad day when you have to admit the best thing to happen was not having anything left in your stomach to add to your own stench.

Clothing and body odor aside, the pulsating pain in my jaw where BW had landed his blow seemed to be keeping rhythm with the beat of my heart. I had serious doubts the bone was still in one piece, and if by some miracle it was intact, the swelling and bruising would be epic.

Trying to ignore the torment in my face wasn't easy, but it was in my best interest to tune into what all the shouting was about between two of the three crazies I was trapped in a room with. It didn't take long to learn

I wasn't the only one unhappy with the knockout punch delivered by BW.

Miss Lori was giving him hell, and I do mean hell. I don't think I'd been out for too long this time, because she was still screaming at him about how did he expect me to tell them anything if my jaw was broken.

Robbie was staying quiet on the sidelines. It probably had nothing to do with being smart and more to do with waiting it out, in the hope he didn't come under fire from either of the two. While the screaming match was going on, I decided it was a good time to take inventory of my body.

Other than the fact my face felt like half of it might fall off, and my hands were going numb from being tied too tight behind my back, I seemed to be in working order. Talk about being the glass half full kind of gal.

All I needed to do was keep my mouth shut—not as easy as it sounded—and watch for any opportunity I might take advantage of. Miss Lori was the weakest physically, Robbie was the weakest mentally, and BW just needed to have an eye kept on him at all times. He was the wild card who could blow up in the blink of an eye. BW was the only one I was worried might forget he needed to keep me alive, at least until they had recovered all of the records.

It was the magic words, "You're gonna stay here with the bitch," issued to Robbie by BW, that grabbed my attention. The screaming had ended and it looked like BW and Miss Lori were getting ready to leave Robbie here, alone, to guard me.

BW was cussing about needing to go home, wash-up and getting some clean clothes. Sounded like he planned on driving Miss Lori to her house first and, from what was being said, her part in all of this was finished. For now, anyway.

BW would be back later to question me about all of Gramps' journals. I had an idea there would be very little *talking* involved in their notion of persuading me into giving up the records.

"Clean that stinkin' bitch up before I get back." The hate BW felt for me saturated the room with its own stench.

I wanted to let him know the feelings were mutual, but for once I was going to bite my tongue. Because if there was going to be any chance of escape, it was going to have to happen while I was alone with Robbie.

This was the first break I'd had since Miss Lori had knocked on Jase's door.

CHAPTER TWENTY-FIVE

Even after the door shut on BW and Miss Lori I kept my eyes closed. I didn't want to take a chance on one of them walking back in to grab something they'd forgotten and find me awake. It was only after I finally thought it might be safe that I fluttered my eyelids open, as if just now regaining consciousness.

"Save the act. You've been awake for a while now." Robbie had a bitter look on his face. Okay, maybe I'd under estimated Robbie's intelligence.

"Can you help me sit up?" The words came out of my mouth but it didn't sound like me saying them. It was like listening to someone talking around a mouth full of rocks. The excruciating pain threatened to send me back into the darkness.

"You going to throw-up on me if I do?" Robbie sounded worried.

"No. Nothing left to share." Son-of-a-bitch; it hurt to talk. Short sentences were going to be the norm for a while. Being a ventriloquist would've come in handy right then.

"BW wants you to clean-up." Robbie wasn't shy about letting his resentment for BW's orders shine through now the man wasn't in the room. Might be a sore tooth to wiggle there. Something to think on.

"How?" That was better. One word at a time was manageable on the pain scale.

Robbie didn't bother to answer, he just came over and very gingerly pulled me into a sitting position and gently eased me back against the wall. No one could blame him for being leery after the show I'd put on with BW. When I didn't erupt he must have decided it was safe to help me to my feet.

I went to clinch my teeth to keep from moaning but all that resulted in was driving what felt like a half inch drill-bit deeper into my jaw. It was hard on my pride but easier on my face to just let the groans out. Robbie wasn't willing to get too close while helping me rise, so that left me trying to push my feet under me the best I could. Sliding my way up the wall wasn't graceful, and I may have been weaving, but I was standing.

Thankfully he let me stay where I was for a minute, with the wall supporting me. I needed time to build up the nerve to test my ability to take a walk across the room, to the promised bath. Scanning the open space around me, it didn't take long to figure out this had to be someone's hunting cabin. To call it rustic would be charitable.

The room we were in was an all-in-one affair. Kitchen, living room and bedroom. I eyed the bed. It was bare of sheets but the mattress would've been a heck of a lot softer than the floor I'd been dumped on. My hip was reminding me of the drop, as well as the goose egg near my temple. My head must have bounced off the floor when I landed. When I got out of this I was going to look like a rainbow girl but from the darker end of the color spectrum. Black, blue and purple.

Moving past the bed, my gaze settled on the tiny kitchen area. Rough-cut boards fastened to the wall served as shelves and held a few miscellaneous dishes. There were some pots and pans as well, but no handy knife block stuffed with an assortment of possible weapons.

The crude wood table only had one article on it: the journal I'd stuffed in my waistband when Miss Lori had shown up. My attempts to conceal the little book was laughable, seeing how they had figured out the journals had been found. Still, they had to be royally pissed there had only been the one with me at the house. Probably the only thing that kept me alive.

There were two doors to choose from that offered a way out of this open room, both closed. One had to lead to the outside and the other must have shielded the bathroom. Considering the layer of dust on everything, it didn't look like anyone had been here since last fall during hunting season. That didn't bode well for what kind of shape the bathroom would be in, but at this point a bath in a mud puddle would be heaven.

"Cut?" I turned to my side slightly to expose my fastened wrist. This talking in as few words as possible might get tricky.

"Nope."

Guess Robbie was following my lead with the one word sentences. The only way I even had a chance of getting away was if my hands were free. Sucking it up, and trying to move my jaw as little as possible, I struggled through two whole sentences.

"Better balance walking. Won't have to touch me." Heck, *I* didn't even want to touch me, I was covered in so much nastiness. Figured that right there would be incentive enough for Robbie to cut my hands free.

I could see him thinking it over, but it wasn't looking too favorable if the scowl on his face meant anything.

"Git goin'." He jerked his head in the direction of the door that must lead to the washroom.

Looked like he was more willing to take a chance on him having to help me stay upright, than he was on me having my hands free. While disappointing, I was thinking I might still have an ace up my sleeve once we got to the bathroom.

The trip across the coarse oak floor wasn't the most fun walk ever taken, but I managed to make it. If I let on like it was more difficult for me than it was, well, that was my little secret. Once there, I stopped and waited for Robbie to open the door for me. The interior wasn't the Ritz but it was a step up from a mud puddle. A very tiny step.

There was a rusted metal shower stall to the left of the doorway, on the right was a toilet and a pedestal sink with an old-fashion medicine cabinet right above it. Praise the Lord, there was bar soap and toilet paper. But the best feature was the window opposite from where I stood.

"Need bathroom." I again turned, exposing my bindings to Robbie.

"What the fuck you think I brought you in here for, bitch." Robbie was apparently not good at deciphering my abbreviated sentences. The misery of talking was a small price to pay if my plan worked out. And for it to have a chance at succeeding he was going to have to understand me.

"No, need toilet." I glared at his ignorance in not getting the picture without me spelling it out. "Not letting you pull my shorts down to pee. Beside, you washing this off me in the shower?" I looked down the front of me at the upchuck just in case he was too stupid to get my meaning.

Robbie drew back with a disgusted look on his face. Yeah, got his attention. Still, he took his sweet time deciding the only way he was going to get out of scrubbing me down was if he untied my hands.

"I'm leaving the door open the whole time. One move towards that window and it's lights out again. We clear?" He came closer but instead of untying me, he jerked my bound arms up higher. He couldn't raise them much but it was enough to cause the muscles in my shoulders to bunch and send lightning bolts of agony into my abused joints.

My scream at the unexpected move set him to laughing. Somehow I'd always thought Robbie wasn't as mean as BW. Guess there was a reason the two of them had stuck together all these years. They were both sick, sadistic bastards. Made me look forward to what I had planned for him.

Robbie was still chuckling as he finally set to loosening the knots. Tears were streaming down my face from the torture, but what did I care about them? They were just following the path of other tears shed since I'd been taken. Tears from pain didn't make me weak. They were just the fuel needed to feed the resolve to get payback.

Once my arms were free the blood started flowing back into my hands, and along with the blood came the pins and needles to let me know regular circulation was being established again. It took a few minutes of rubbing and kneading before it felt like I had fingers and not sausage links attached to my hands. As soon as they were back in working order, I took hold of the door and started closing it in defiance of what Robbie ordered.

The perverted little prick had taken himself over to the broken down couch and stretched out on it. From his position he could see right into the bathroom. His head was propped up on the filthy arm of the thing. His arms were crossed over his chest. Booted feet rested on the grungy cushions, where they crossed at the ankles. He'd settled in to watch the show, looking mighty comfy.

When he saw the door closing he didn't bother to get up but yelled at me. "I told you to keep the fuckin' door open."

"I'm only shutting it enough so you can't watch me pee. You can give me that much privacy." It was a gamble. I hoped he was too settled in on the couch, after what had to have been a long night, for him to want to make a big deal out of the door. To sweeten the deal I tossed out, "You'll be able to see me get in the shower."

When he didn't say anything else as the door continued to ease towards the frame I breathed a silent of thank you. There was a fine line between closing it too much for his comfort, while at the same time shutting it enough to keep him from seeing what I was up to.

After I'd achieved the perfect balance with the width of the opening, I allowed myself the luxury of bladder relief. Flushing the toilet gave me the noise cover needed to open the medicine cabinet and check for anything useful. Maybe MacGyver could have made something amazing from Band-Aids and a safety razor but me, not so much. Looked like Plan A was all I had.

Taking the bar of soap from the sink I crossed to the shower, making sure Robbie saw it was the only thing I had in my hands. If he was disappointed to see I still had my clothes on when I walked into the stall he didn't let on. Turning both faucet handles to full blast resulted in plenty of water, none of it hot. It was no more than expected, but I still gasped at the freezing temperature.

Determined to tough it out for the sake of being clean, I began rubbing the bar over my clothes. When there was nothing more I could do for them, I started on my body. It was taking a lot of time, which worked for me. There were no towels and the only cloth in the room was the size of a washrag, without it being able to lay claim to such a lofty name.

By the time I was as clean as I was going to get, my teeth were chattering despite it being the end of August. Stepping out of the shower, I left the water running. Glancing over at the couch, Robbie was sound asleep, just as I'd prayed for. It wasn't as much of a miracle as it seemed given how late it had to be. The soothing sound of running water and Robbie's well known laziness was all it took to send him off to dreamland.

I took a deep breath. This next part was going to be tricky.

Wrapping the bar of soap in the rag, I laid it on the edge of the sink. Walking over to the toilet I removed the tank's lid cover and edged back to the partially closed door, making sure not to get behind it. Picking up the bar of soap I hurled it at the window with as much force as I could muster. The sound of the glass shattering was music to my ears. Thank god for cheap-ass single pane windows!

The pounding of booted feet racing across the floor was almost drowned out by the curses Robbie screamed as he ran. When the door bounced back from Robbie's frantic push it was my signal to start the descent of the ceramic lid clutched tightly in my hands. There was a sickening thud that sounded suspiciously like an over-ripe watermelon being thumped then splitting. The sudden silence from Robbie's yelling was deafening. His body crumbled to the floor and I was left holding half a tank lid. I watched the blood start to pool around Robbie's body from his cracked skull.

Precious seconds were lost as I stared at my handy work. If there had been anything left in my stomach I would've been filling the sink with it. As it was, dry heaves bent me double. Telling myself I had to get it under control was easier said than done. It was the fear of BW returning that finally got me moving. I didn't check to see if Robbie was still breathing. There was too much blood for it to even be a possibility.

I did look at his boots to see if there was any hope of them fitting me. When Miss Lori had shown up at Jase's I'd been barefoot. I still was. And I was going to remain so, because what was stuck on those feet would do nothing but slow me down from trying to keep them on. I'd used up my quota of luck. Even Robbie's cell phone had shattered when he'd fallen to the floor.

Not wasting any more time I hurried to the table to retrieve the notebook then headed for the door. Once outside, the dark skies let me know daylight was still a long way off. There wasn't a vehicle to try and steal, since apparently BW and crew had all traveled in the same one. I had no clue where this shack was located or who owned it. All that boiled down to was that I had no idea which direction to go in.

Head in the wrong direction and I could be looking at thousands of acres of forest to lose myself in. Trying to parallel the dirt road while staying close to the woods wouldn't be easy, but what had been so far tonight? If I could manage it though, there was a very real chance for me to stay hidden from anyone coming down the road.

Satisfied this was the best I could come up with for now, I entered the tree-line, trying to remain close enough to the road to not lose it in the dark. I set out determined to stay alive long enough to give Jase a chance to find me.

CHAPTER TWENTY-SIX

"So that's it? The only thing you have to say is Charlotte hasn't been missing long enough for you to start looking for her?" Jase may have asked the questions with a deadly calm but there was no disguising the anger in the stare he leveled on the sheriff.

He'd already questioned both his brother and Colin when the last time they had seen or heard from Charlotte was. From what Jase could gather, she'd made it home safe. Ruger being there confirmed that much. But he'd been the last one to actually talk to her. Both men had wanted to rush over to help in the search. Evan especially was pissed, and claimed Jase was trying to shut him out. Jase had talked them into waiting until he had something more concrete they could do to help, something other than stand around being angry.

The sheriff's office had been his next call. He hadn't expected Cantrell to be the one to show up with— surprise, surprise—Deputy Dennis in tow. Considering the bastard wasn't going to initiate a search, it begged the question as to why Cantrell had even made the effort to come out.

"Look around you, Rydan." Sheriff Cantrell threw out a hand as if trying to draw attention to the room they were standing in.

"There isn't so much as a cushion out of place. Not a rug wrinkled. Not a damn thing that isn't as it should be. The only damage in the whole house was caused by her dog." His pointed finger aimed straight at Ruger, resulted in the dog emitting a threatening growl.

"You forgot to mention the fact that Charlotte isn't in this perfect picture you're painting. Her truck is sitting in the drive, and yet she's not here. You also seem to be missing the point that I'd just talked to her last night, she was expecting me this morning." He'd reached his tolerance level of dealing with the sheriff's deliberate idiocy.

"But by your own admission, she wasn't expecting you this early." Cantrell winked at Jase and tacked on a sly smile. "Who's to say she didn't put that dog of hers in the mudroom to keep it from crapping all over the house while she went off with a *friend* for a few hours? Time probably got away from her and she's cuttin' it close. Probably was hoping to get back here before you got home."

Even Deputy Dennis realized the sheriff had gone too far with his theories. After returning from searching the house for signs of a struggle he'd stood off to the side. He'd made it a point to stay away from the action going on between Cantrell and Rydan. But now he took a step forward, with his hand resting on top of his holstered taser. Dennis was prepared to intervene if it became necessary.

"Get the fuck out of my house." If it were possible for words to slice a man open, Cantrell would've been bleeding his life blood out on the living room floor.

"Now, Rydan, there ain't no call—"

"I said, get the fuck out of my house. I tried to do it the way the law said it had to be done, now I'm going to do it my way." Taking a lethal step in the sheriff's direction, Jase did some finger pointing of his own.

Dennis didn't wait any longer to draw the Taser and aim it at Jase. He then issued a warning, "Don't take another step, Rydan."

Not even bothering to toss a look in the deputy's direction, Jase continued speaking, "I gave you a chance, Cantrell, to do the right thing. We both know you're not going to because that fuck-up you call son is probably involved."

"Not one more step, Rydan, or I'll taser your ass." Command rang in Dennis' words. Sounded like he didn't appreciate being ignored.

Cantrell hooked his fingers in the overtaxed waistband of his khakis and tried to hitch his pants higher over his expanded belly. A tic appeared beside his left eye. When Cantrell went to clear his throat before beginning to talk, the sound came out more along the lines of a high squeak. "Stand down, Dennis. He ain't gonna do anything stupid. Are you, Rydan?"

"Stupid's already been done here tonight, Cantrell. You and your bootlicker need to leave. Now. I've got work to do." Spinning on his heel, Jase walked over to the front door and opened it, is face granite hard. His expression said it wasn't a polite request to leave but a *"get your ass on outta here."*

Blustering, Cantrell tried to make his departure look like his decision. "Well, there's no reason to stay here any longer. No proof there's been any crime committed."

"Before you go, Sheriff, answer me one question." Steel had more flexibility than Jase. "Why is it whenever I call you concerning Charlotte, Deputy Dog here always tags along? He the only one on the force willing to cover for you?"

Sheriff Cantrell ignored the question and walked past Jase out into the dark of the early morning. The deputy bared his teeth in a travesty of a smile, hate gleaming from his eyes, and then he followed the sheriff out.

Shutting the door on what had been a waste of valuable time, Jase pulled his cell phone out. There was one person he knew that would be able to handle something like this and, unlike Jase, he'd never left the area. He'd know every snake hole in a fifty-mile radius, probably even secretly owning half of them.

The phone rang and rang. It was the third call Jase had placed to the same number in the last five minutes.

Just when he expected it to go to voicemail—again—a cold voice answered.

"Whoever the fuck this is, it better be important."

"Sawyer, I need your help."

Jase could hear a woman in the background, calling Sawyer back to bed. She didn't sound any happier than Sawyer had been when he'd answered the phone. Checking the time, Jase saw it was going on three o'clock in the morning. No guesses were needed as to why he hadn't wanted to answer his phone.

"Pack it up, sweetheart, you need to get your ass on outta here and back to your own damn place. I've got business to take care of."

It was clear Sawyer hadn't bothered to move the phone very far from his mouth while he kicked his guest out. Jase could only shake his head at the callous way Sawyer spoke to whoever was his bed-warmer for the night. It didn't sound like she was taking the being tossed out too well from the words he could hear being screamed at Sawyer.

"Stupid bitches. They can't ever tell lust from love." A mocking chuckle, then Sawyer was all business. "What're we doing, Rydan?"

The man might be the toughest bastard Jase had ever known, and all that ran through his mind was, *thank God Sawyer never changed.* It had been years since the two of them had spent any real time together, but here he was, ready to do whatever, not knowing or caring what it might involve.

"Someone's taken Charlotte. I need to find the bastards." Fierce determination marked each word Jase uttered.

"You got a name?"

"I've got a feeling. Cantrell was here and he isn't interested in helping. The fucker looked scared. I think he suspects that kid of his is involved somehow. I called the sheriff's office and Cantrell shows up. Bastard wanted to make sure one of his officers didn't get over zealous and actually do their job. I know you have a deal worked out with Cantrell, and you're laying off of BW because of it. I'm asking you to help me anyway. I'm willing to pay for any information." Jase knew Sawyer was big in brokering information, among other things, and he was willing to pay Sawyer's going rate.

"You trying to fuckin' insult me?"

"I'm saying you don't owe me a thing but you do this for me then I owe you. If you want money, I'll give you money. If you want a favor in the future, it's yours." Old friendship or not, Jase never expected to ask for help from anyone without repaying it at some point. That was something Sawyer could understand.

Letting the matter drop, Sawyer said, "I'll send a couple of men over to watch BW's house, and a couple more over to hound-dog the crappy RV Robbie calls home. As soon as they report back I'll be in contact and we'll meet up."

"I'm out of here and heading to check at Charlotte's house and then over to her granddad's. Want to see if anything's been screwed with at either spot." Jase accepted the fact that having a plan—any kind of plan—was settling and gave him back a sense of control, whether it was true or not.

"Just in case it's not BW's doing, I'm gonna put some feelers out among the bottom feeders to see if there's been talk about any moves being planned against Char." There was a brutal edge to Sawyer's voice. He sounded like this was personal, instead of just a matter of helping out an old friend.

"Sawyer, just so there's no misunderstanding later… When we find Charlotte, whoever has her is mine." Steely resolve with no compromise was the only way Jase knew how to play it.

"Didn't figure it any other way." Approval was a hard thing to win from Sawyer, but it rang through loud and clear over the phone. "And, Jase, hunting people and their secrets is who I am. We'll find her."

Sawyer hung up before Jase could thank him. Jase understood. He'd have claimed Jase was trying to insult him again by offering a thank you.

After hanging up, Jase eyeballed Ruger. "Bud, you're not going to like this but you have to stay here. I promise to bring her back to you."

Ruger whined, as if he knew what Jase had said to him. Jase felt like whining with him. This feeling of helplessness was not something he'd ever experienced before. The full weight of how much he had to lose if he didn't get her back alive was crippling.

Jase made a trip to his gun cabinet and gathered his rifle, a selection of handguns and enough ammo to start a war.

Once in his truck he called his brother up. Evan answered on the first ring. "Meet me at Jim Donley's house. I want to go over the place and see if it looks like they may have taken Charlotte there."

"About damn time you called me. Should I bring a gun?" He could tell Evan was calming down but he wasn't happy about being in the dark. *Well, join the club, little brother.* Because this was fuckin' gutting him.

Jase looked at the arsenal on the seat beside him. "I've got you covered. I'm going to call Colin and have him wait for us at Charlotte's house. If we don't find anything at Jim's we'll go over to her place and check it out."

"I'll be waiting on you." Evan signed off.

Jase knew Evan would be there a lot quicker than him, living so close. He could be counted on to do whatever it took to get Charlotte back. Hell, Evan had done a better job of taking care of her for the last ten years than he had in the last few weeks. Knowing that line of thought would get him nowhere, Jase began running through his mind what could have taken place last night. How the hell had they taken her from his house? He'd been so positive it would be a safe haven while he was gone.

Yeah, he lived out in the middle of nowhere, but there was not one but two safe rooms in the house. One upstairs, one down. Hell, even his own family thought it was overkill. Having a safe room at all was unheard of around here. They were the main reasons he'd been positive Charlotte would be safe.

The alarm meant nothing this far away from Copper Ridge. It was just a signal to head to the safe room if it was ever triggered. From there it would've been easy for her to call for help. It wouldn't have even mattered if she didn't have her cell with her. There were land-lines in each one. But she'd never made it to either one.

The alarm had been turned off when he'd arrived, but he knew it had been on last night when he'd talked to Charlotte. He knew, because the last thing he always asked her before hanging up each night was if she'd set the alarm.

She'd laughed at him, just like every other night he'd asked, then assured him, yes, it was on. Jase placed a hand to his chest to rub at the searing pain centered there. His last words to her were about the fucking alarm and not, I love you. And the thought was killing him.

Pushing all of it to the back of his mind he returned to the puzzle of how Charlotte had been taken. Why had she turned the alarm off? If she'd gone outside, for any reason, Ruger would've been with her and not locked up in the mudroom. That left only one reasonable explanation.

Someone Charlotte knew and trusted had shown up sometime after she'd talked to him. Her abductors didn't have to break in. They'd been invited in the front door. The idea that someone Charlotte knew and trusted had betrayed her cranked Jase from angry straight to homicidal.

Pulling to a stop in Donley's drive, he switched gears from trying to figure out how he'd failed her to concentrating on getting her back. Spying Evan waiting on the front porch, Jase got out of his truck and jogged over to join him.

Both men were grim as Jase unlocked the door. As they headed inside to look around, Jase checked his watch. Forty minutes and Sawyer would be calling. That gave him enough time to see if there was anything to find, both here and at Charlotte's house, before he headed in Sawyer's direction.

Evan wasn't going to like it but Jase was going to ask him to remain here when he left. He was also going to have Colin stay at Charlotte's house to keep an eye on things. There was a possibility whoever had taken Charlotte could show up at either house, and someone needed to be watching in case they did.

CHAPTER TWENTY-SEVEN

I'd given up trying to follow alongside the road in the dark and had been trudging down the middle of the dirt track. The woods were not a forgiving place to try and walk barefooted in the daytime. Start trying to tromp around them in the dark and I was just asking to be left crippled. It was much better to be stone bruised than to end up with a sapling stob remodeling the bottom of my foot.

The sky had been getting lighter, and if a real road didn't show up soon I was going to have to try my luck at walking in the woods again. Last thing I wanted was to be caught out in the open.

The closer it got to daybreak, the harder it was to stop thinking of Jase showing up at the house and realizing I was gone. I told myself there was no way he was going to believe I'd gone off with anyone else, like Miss Lori had hoped. It was my belief in Jase moving heaven and hell to find me that kept me going.

I'd been so wrapped up in my thoughts it took a while before the muted rumble of an engine registered. Panicked at how my inattention might have landed me right back where I'd started, I hobbled for the woods as fast as my ruined feet allowed.

Crouching down behind brush, I watched the slow approach of a huge white pickup. My first reaction was relief it wasn't BW's ride. My second was fear I'd not been quick enough hiding and whoever was driving might have noticed my ungainly attempt to hide.

When the truck jerked to an abrupt stop, I knew my exit from the road had been spotted. I was either going to have to try and run, or pray like hell the person getting out of the strange truck was someone willing to help me. Knowing the running was a non-starter, considering the shape I was in, I went for the praying option while arming myself with a rock.

One of Gramps' favorite sayings was, *the Lord helps those who help themselves,* so if my invocation didn't work, maybe a rock upside the head would. Bashing heads in had worked for me so far.

"Miss Donley? Is that you Miss Donley? You're safe now. This is Officer Dennis Dane. You can come on out." The shout echoed through the trees. "Mr. Rydan is looking for you."

A sob broke free as the rock slipped from my suddenly nerveless fingers. Struggling up from my huddle I waved an arm, shouting, "Here, I'm over here!"

Tears of relief were threatening to hijack my eyes. While I'd been terrified I would never make it to safety, sheer stubbornness to not give up had kept the crying at bay. But now the fear was flowing out of me the tears wanted to follow suit. Blinking rapidly, I rubbed at the few drops rolling down my cheeks with the backs of my hands, being extra careful around my swollen jaw.

Dennis made his way towards me with a big smile on his face. It was impossible to smile back with the swelling taking up half my face, but he had to feel the happiness radiating out of me. It only took him a moment to reach me, mainly due to my having barely penetrated the woods in my hasty bid to hide. Once he was beside me, he gently placed an arm around my waist, giving me much needed support back to his truck.

"Thank God you found me! We've got to get out of here! It was BW. BW, Robbie, Miss Lori, all of them were in on it together. They could be back any minute." The whole time I was babbling, Dennis kept reassuring me everything was going to be all right. That he had me now.

I'd been watching my steps the entire way back to the road, leaning heavily on the officer, I tried to spare my feet further injury. Upon hearing truck doors open, I looked up in surprise that there were others with Dennis. As soon as I raised my head to check out who else was in on the rescue, Dennis' supporting arm became less comforting and more confining.

An abrupt switch from profound gratefulness to abject terror was an overload my abused body wasn't equipped to handle. My legs gave out, and I had to fight the darkness wanting to swallow me. Dennis braced himself to take my full weight.

"Hello, Char. I believe we've come to that point in time where you wished you had realized the value of my friendship when it had been offered earlier." Brent Allen stood beside Dennis' truck with what I would've sworn was a hint of regret as he looked at me.

Standing beside him was a furious BW, if his red face and clenched fists were any indication of his feelings. But there was something else going on with him besides the anger. For once in his life he was maintaining control—sort of—but it was even more than that. He appeared spooked about something.

Turning my attention back to Brent, I couldn't help but think BW had reason to be rattled. Jase had been right. Brent wasn't to be trusted but not for the reasons he'd thought.

Despite knowing it was useless, I began to struggle in Dennis' hold. My efforts had less effect on him than an annoying fly would have. He pulled his handcuffs out and my wrists ended up once again fastened behind my back. My shoulders protested at strained muscles being returned to the same position they'd previously been forced to maintain for hours.

As he half lifted and half threw me onto the backseat, BW made like he was going to follow me in. My trip back to the shack I'd escaped from promised to be a painful one with him as my seat partner.

Before he could climb into the truck, Brent spoke up. "BW, sit up front with Dennis. From the appearance of Char I'd say you've enjoyed her company enough for one day."

BW threw a sullen glare at me but didn't protest the seating rearrangement. That right there let me know whatever part Brent had to play in all of this, he was the boss. This was a major change in the lineup of bad guys; a much deadlier one.

After all the men had settled in the truck, and we were rolling, I turned to Brent and asked, "Why?"

He reached over and patted me on the knee, as if we were a couple of longtime friends out for a Sunday drive. "Patience. We have a lot to discuss, so let's wait until we get to this hunting cabin BW's been telling us about. I promise to explain everything to you."

His calm demeanor, coupled with his gentle smile, was more frightening than any of BW's rants had ever been.

The silent trip back to the cabin gave me plenty of time to come up with all kinds of scenarios for what was going to happen to me during our *little talk.* Of course, he might change his mind about chatting when he got an eye full of my handy work. There was a very real probability of shit hitting the fan when this crew found Robbie's body.

No matter which way I worked it, every supposition ended in my death. But I suppose that had always been the planned outcome for me. I figured that as far as they were all concerned, I was a dead body that just hadn't lain down yet.

* * *

The ringing of his cell phone was a "Thank you, Jesus," moment for Jase, and he made a grab for it with a shaky hand.

"What'd you find out?"

Sawyer wasted no time and went straight to the bones of the facts. "Nobody was at Robbie's piece-of-shit trailer when my boys got there. Didn't find anything worth a fuck inside when they checked it out. The other men who went to BW's had better luck. His truck was gone when they got there but Robbie's truck was out front. BW showed up not long after my guys. Alone. Not ten minutes later, guess who pulls up? Deputy Dennis, and he's hauling the lawyer who's running for sheriff's ass arou—"

"Goddamn! I *knew* the fucker was up to something involving Charlotte!" The blast of Jase's rage cut Sawyer off. "Are they still there?"

"No. They went in the house and about twenty minutes later came out with BW. Little prick looked like he was about to shit his pants. They all climbed in Dennis' truck and took off. My boys followed them to a dirt road that headed off into the woods. Vernon says it dead-ends at a hunting shack about five miles in and is owned by one of Robbie's cousins." Sawyer relayed the information with vicious satisfaction. Something in all this information pleased him.

"Did they see Charlotte?" He gritted the question out. Locking down his emotions was the only way he was going to make it through this and get Charlotte back alive.

"My boys stopped at the head of the road to wait for us. According to Vernon, there ain't but one way out for those cocksuckers. They have to use the same dirt road they drove in on. Those bastards have trapped themselves, and they don't even know it." His cruel chuckle would've made any sane man's balls draw up in his stomach.

"Sounds like you're planning on going with me, Sawyer. I didn't expect anything but information. This is going to get messy and might screw up any arrangement you've got going with the sheriff. He might stop turning a blind eye to your operations." Jase wasn't about to ask for more than Sawyer had already provided. He would welcome it, but thought it only fair to give him an out.

"You trying to fuckin' insult me again?"

"I'm trying to keep your butt out of trouble, but hell, I'd be proud to have your psycho ass with me." Jase felt an overwhelming sense of rightness. He and Sawyer were slipping back into the tight friendship they'd once shared as teens.

"Damn right you are. Meet me on the south edge of town at the old Dairy Bar. We'll double up there in my truck. If you're calling your brother in on this he needs to get his ass here, fast. You need me to dress you for the party?"

"Worry about your own party dress, I'm bringing my rifle and a couple extra magazines. As for Evan, he's working another angle. It'll just be me."

Sawyer let out a low whistle. "Shit, Rydan, you fire of that old 30-06 of yours at close range and you're gonna make one hell of a mess."

"I'm counting on it."

CHAPTER TWENTY-EIGHT

When the rundown cabin came into view, BW finally broke the silence, grousing, "I'm gonna knock that fuckin' Robbie upside the head for letting you get away."

The stress had to be getting next to me, because words popped out of my mouth before I could stop them. "Good luck with that."

All three men stared at me, each with a different expression on his face. BW's was the easiest to interpret, as he always defaulted back to crazed maniac.

Dennis looked at me through the rear-view mirror with the same emotionless look he'd worn whenever he'd tagged along with the sheriff to the numerous crime scenes, beginning with the site of my gramps' murder. I should have known something was screwy when he smiled at me back there in the woods.

And then there was Brent. He cocked his head to the side and studied me as if I'd just become of even greater interest to him. There was speculation in his narrowed gaze.

BW was the first out of the pickup when Dennis pulled up. He made for the warped door at a run. Dennis waited for Brent to pull me out before moving to the opposite side of me from where his boss stood. Both men caught hold of my upper arms and between the two of them, they pretty much carried me into the building.

Once inside they deposited me on the couch. It was a huge improvement over the last time I'd been brought here and dumped, unconscious, on the floor. Less bruising involved. For now.

Turning my head to the side I could see into the tiny room where BW stood, rigid, staring. Just as Robbie had had a clear view into the bathroom from the couch, I had a clear view of Robbie's still form.

I didn't want to look at death lying there on the floor. It was a reminder of how far I was willing to go to protect myself and that brought back the nausea. It wasn't that I wouldn't do the same thing again if forced to save myself. It was the knowing that I'd ended a man's life. And it didn't matter how wasteful that life might have been, because now he would never have the opportunity to change and become better than he'd been.

Pushing those thoughts into a dark corner of my mind, I instead concentrated on BW as he bent to check Robbie for signs of life.

It didn't take him long to catch on Robbie wasn't going to be sitting up and taking any more of his orders. Once the reality, that I had killed his partner, sank-in he stood and started for me, murderous anger twisting his face into a mask of revenge. "I'm gonna enjoy killing you, bitch, every bit as much as I enjoyed killing your granddaddy." He screamed the words at me, then charged in a full kill-frenzy.

At his admission, blind hatred made me forget that jumping up and charging at him, with no weapon and hands 'cuffed behind my back, was not the smartest move to make. Brent made a grab for me and easily controlled my feeble attempts to reach the murderer I'd been searching for. Dennis stepped in front of BW, pulling his gun on him. BW skidded to a halt but his mouth never stopped running. "What the fuck do you think you're doing, man? You're gonna pull a gun on me when that bitch killed Robbie?"

Dennis never blinked and the gun didn't waver. "If Brent says nobody touches her? Then nobody touches her. Sit down, shut-up and speak only if spoken to."

For a split-second it looked like BW was calculating his odds on being able to take the gun away from Dennis. He squinted his little piggy eyes at him and then around the room as if looking for inspiration. But eventually his brain kicked in, or the bravado gave out, because BW moved to the well-worn recliner. As he dropped onto the ripped material of the seat, a cloud of dust puffed up around him.

Being wrapped-up in Brent's arms didn't stop me from trying to squirm away as he spoke close to my ear, "Cousin, this is going to go much easier on you if you stop fighting me and listen to what I have to say."

At the word *cousin*, my mind literally went blank.

It was BW screeching, "What the fuck you do mean, *cousin*?" that let me know I'd heard Brent right.

My stillness was the key necessary to have Brent release me and allow me to turn and face him. "It's not possible." I might have been a little fuzzy on some things in my life but I was damn sure neither Dad nor Mom had any siblings running around popping out cousins.

He stepped away from me to inspect the couch I'd jumped up from in my failed rush at BW. I guess he decided it wasn't up to his standards, because he remained standing. At least the couch inspection had moved him a few feet from me.

"Well, we may be separated by a few branches, but we share a common ancestor. You were lucky enough to come down the male-line of the family tree. I got stuck in a line started by one of the Donley sisters. A female who received nothing of worth because only men in the family, ones who carried the Donley name, were allowed to inherit the true treasure, the moonshine." The bitterness I'd caught a hint of the day he'd come to Gramps' house was a waving flag everyone could see.

"All of this for some shine recipes? You had my granddaddy killed over moonshine?" Sorrow at the waste of it all made my voice tremble.

"I never gave orders to kill Donley. You can thank BW for that piece of idiocy. He was to buy the recipes from the old man, not kill him. But as often happens when you hire a moron, they screw everything up."

"Hey!" BW took exception to being called a moron.

Dennis took the few steps necessary to reach BW and slapped him with the same hand that held the pistol. The weapon opened a wicked looking gash, high on his cheek. BW started to erupt out of the chair but having the barrel of a gun pressed into the center of his forehead changed his mind real quick.

"What the fuck was that for?"

"A reminder to keep your mouth shut. Next time, I'll shoot you."

If there had been any show of anger, a sick pleasure at inflicting pain, anything related to an emotion, it would've made Dennis less frightening. There was no doubt in my mind he would wear the same merciless face if told to pull the trigger on me.

"Getting back to what I was saying," Brent continued, as if Dennis hadn't just threatened to kill BW, "Moron, over there, assured my people he could buy the recipes off of Donley. From what I understand, Donley strung the idiot along, then dropped the little bomb he was retiring and the shine recipes would be going into retirement with him." Brent talked about all that had happened as if it bored the hell out of him. "Instead of contacting my people and letting me handle it from that point on, Moron apparently killed Donley in one of his well-known mad outbursts. It was a huge inconvenience, and one I'd hoped wouldn't be necessary."

It didn't skip my notice he hadn't said he wouldn't have killed Gramps.

"After the deed was done, I was left trying to win your friendship and trust, to the point, where you'd be willing to share information with me. Rydan put a stop to that." Brent couldn't pull off the nonchalance this time, when he mentioned Jase. Some real hate going on there.

"Don't blame Jase. Your natural creepiness was enough to keep me from ever trusting you." Not much sense in holding back if they were going to kill me.

"Careful, Char. If Dennis hadn't made certain to insert himself every time there was an instance involving you, I wouldn't have learned Moron pulled another of his stupid moves and kidnapped you. From the looks of you, he hasn't been too gentle in his treatment. I came out of the shadows to rescue you." The man was delusional if he thought I was going to thank him. "I'd been managing to successfully run my expanding *private businesses* through proxies, until this moron came along." Every time Brent called BW Moron, his uncontrollable madness ratcheted a little closer to the surface. "Lucky for you, I'm a forgiving cousin and willing to offer you a deal which will benefit both of us. After all, blood is thicker than water, even diluted as ours." His smile was just bizarre, almost as if he really thought he was being gracious. "You give me the records, the recipes—all of it—and I'll allow you to live.

To prove how much family means, you can become part of my plans and share in the profits." The freak was positively beaming at me now.

Hearing the offer extended to me was more than BW could handle. He detonated from the recliner like a bomb had gone off under his ass. He started screeching about how it wasn't fair, how he was supposed to be the partner.

The explosive sound of a pistol being fired in the small cabin jerked a scream out of both me and BW. Mine was from surprise. His was from being shot in the knee. He fell back onto the recliner, howling and clutching his thigh above the raw wound. Sobs, which he quickly tried to stifle, shook his body. Guess he finally worked it out that Dennis meant business when he said shut up.

I instinctively started moving away from Dennis. Maybe it was the creak of a floorboard as I stepped back that pushed an alarm button. Whatever triggered it, Dennis spun around aiming right for my chest.

* * *

Jase was the first to exit the truck but his old friend wasn't too far off his heels. Their long strides quickly carried them to where Vernon and Willis waited. The two trucks had been angled to block the narrow road and the last mile of the trip was going to be on foot.

"What are we looking at when we get there?" Sawyer questioned the only man to have been to the place they were headed.

Vernon faced the two men but jerked his head in the direction of the shack. "Been to a couple of keg parties out here. Place is a cobbled up mess. Jest one big room with a john off the backside. It's a small room with a small window. One door in front with a window to the left of it. There's only one more window, on the right side of the shack. Those are the only ways in and out of the place. It's too light out now to not be noticed lookin' in the front or side window but a man might get a look-see through the one in the back."

"Once we get there, I'll go around back and check out the john's window. Jase, you and Willis hang in front. Vernon can watch the side window. Nobody makes a move until we have a better idea of what's going on inside." Sawyer was all business as he laid out the plan.

When Jase used to run with Sawyer in the past, he'd always been amazed how Sawyer dropped the irrelevant name calling and cussing when it was important. Looked like that was another thing that hadn't changed over the years.

But in this instance he had his own ideas as to the men's placements around the outside. "Let Vernon and Willis guard the front and I'm taking the side window."

"You going to be able to keep control if your woman's in there, in a bad way, and you get an eyeball full of it?" Sawyer sounded more than a little doubtful.

"I'll do whatever it takes to get her out alive."

"Yeah, well, if she's in there it'd probably make her happy if you manage to not kill yourself in the process," snorted Sawyer.

CHAPTER TWENTY-NINE

Jase set a fast jog to the cabin with the others easily keeping up. He was through with all the waiting and wondering. In his gut he was positive Charlotte was at the end of this dirt road, and he was getting her back, even if he had to revert back to the bastard he used to be.

When they arrived at the clearing, he and the others melted into the trees surrounding the cabin on three sides. The front of the building had a large cleared area. It was probably a good hundred feet to the cabin from the edge of the forest and another fifty feet across what passed for a yard. A savage grin stretched across Jase's face when he saw how close the tree line was to the rest of the structure.

Winding around the trunks of the huge oaks, Jase worked his way to the side window. He hoped Vernon was wrong and he'd be close enough to get a look into the interior. Sawyer continued on past him, heading to the back of the building.

Since the shack was built close to the ground, the window sill came to just below Jase's waist. The trees crowded the building, being no more than about twelve or so feet away. Distance wasn't going to be the problem when it came to spying on the interior and occupants. It was the years of grime fogging the glass that might screw-up his getting a good look.

Getting as close as possible, while still maintaining his cover, he braced the rifle against the side of an old hickory tree. He looked down the open sights of the 30-06 and tracked each figure until he spotted the one person he'd prayed would be inside.

Charlotte was standing between two other figures. Relief at seeing her alive was only equaled by his overwhelming need to get to her. He had to steel himself against the fierce demands of his body to rush blindly in and start ripping and tearing into anything and anyone who kept them apart.

From what he could make out, Brent was a few steps to the left of Charlotte. He seemed to be the one doing all the talking. She was standing, so he took that as a good sign, but it looked as though her arms were tied behind her back. Seeing that threatened to blow the lid off of his hard-won restraint.

Dragging his eyes away from her, Jase scanned the room, looking for the rest of the men. BW was the only one sitting. What came as a huge surprise was the pistol Dennis had aimed at BW. What the hell was happening in there?

Movement in the forest to the left of him snagged Jase's attention. Sawyer was heading back to lay out the details of what he'd found, and he was grinning like hell. Satisfied he hadn't been discovered, Jase shifted focus back to the scene playing out in front of him, but he was wondering what had his buddy so damn tickled.

As soon as Sawyer got close he breathed a whispered report. "Back window's broke. Robbie's dead on the floor of the washroom. Looks like Char may have taken him out with the toilet lid."

Jase didn't so much as blink at the news, staying rock steady. The gun stayed sighted-in on the center mass of Dennis' body. Since the asshole had a gun out, he was the biggest threat to Charlotte's safety. Jase wasn't taking his eyes off the bastard, and the only reason he hadn't already shot him was because the gun wasn't pointed at Charlotte. All things being equal, Jase was determined to be Dennis' biggest threat to staying alive.

Pride swelled at the sheer grit that was so much a part of his woman. He thanked God she was willing to do whatever it took to stay alive, but it was tempered by his anger at realizing she'd had to kill to protect herself.

Before the two of them had time to start figuring out a plan to get his woman out, BW surged from his chair. He was screaming about something not being fair. Jase didn't even have time to complete saying, "That stupid son-of-a-bitch," before the roaring blast of a gun being fired sounded.

As if it were happening in slow motion, Jase saw BW falling into the chair, grabbing at his leg. He heard Charlotte scream but his focus never wavered from Dennis. He was already squeezing the rifle's trigger when Dennis turned his pistol on Charlotte.

* * *

I didn't have time to think as Dennis trained his gun on me. One second I was looking down the barrel of a gun and the next I watched as the center of Dennis' chest disappeared in a burst of blood and tissue as a couple more deafening explosions filled the room.

Dennis was knocked backwards from the concussion as the rounds slammed into him. He landed at BW's feet. His pistol went skittering across the floor, ending up somewhere under the recliner. BW made a dive for the gun, more worried about being the next one shot than he was about his shattered knee.

A body came diving into the room via the same window the shots had been fired through. Another quickly followed. Both men rolled when they hit the floor, coming up with guns pointed in our direction.

"Charlotte! Drop!"

By some miracle Jase was here. I froze for half a second. That half second was all the time Brent needed to reach me and drag me tight against his body, turning me into a living shield for him to hide behind. He must have had his own gun, because one appeared at my shoulder.

The chaos wasn't over. The front door was kicked open, wood splintering. What remained bounced against the wall. Two more large men barreled in and quickly added their guns to the ones already pointed in mine and Brent's direction.

Brent might have been outnumbered but he wasn't about to give-up. When he saw there wasn't going to be any shooting his way out, he turned the pistol on me. The rounded end bore into my side. I could hear BW firing off one f-bomb after another and scrambling on the floor behind us. The bastard was still trying to get his hands on Dennis' gun.

"One move, by any of you, and I'll kill her."

"Don't be stupid, Brent. There's no way out of here. Let her go and we'll let the law handle the rest of this. You're a lawyer. You should recognize a hell of a deal when you hear one." Jase's voice was starkly brutal, and his eyes promised a coffin was going to be Brent's next residence if he didn't listen.

"You expect me to believe you're going to turn this over to the police after what Char's been through?" Brent's snort made it pretty clear what he thought of Jase's offer.

"Do what he says, Brent, and I'll testify BW was the one who kidnapped me. I'll also testify he admitted to killing Gramps. Right now all you're looking at is holding me here against my will. We can make this all look like it was BW's fault. I'll help you." I held my breath, willing him to agree.

The room went silent except for the sobs wheezing out of BW where he lay on the floor. There were no more sounds of a frantic search. He must have found the gun.

Waiting for Brent to make his mind up was taking an eternity. Finally, Brent's arm started to loosen, and he stopped digging the barrel of his gun into my ribs. I prayed he'd decided to take the deal.

"Call the police, Rydan. I'm not turning her loose until they show up."

"You goddamn, double crossin', sum'bitch!" BW screeched then he started pumping bullets into Brent's back.

I felt it every time one entered his body. The jerks racking Brent's frame, the contracting of his muscles, I experienced each hit as he did. He sank to the floor, taking me with him.

A barrage of bullets signaled an end to BW and the lead peppering into Brent's back.

His dead weight pressed me onto the floorboards, trapping me. I began to shift from side to side in an attempt to get out from under him. Not having the use of my arms was throwing up a serious roadblock.

Before I could extract myself, Brent's body was ripped off me. Jase lifted me from the floor and wrapped me in an embrace that felt like he was trying to merge our bones. Every part of me hurt and the squeezing added to the pain, but I would've endured much worse just to be in Jase's arms.

He rained kisses on top of my head as he rocked me back and forth. Between kisses he murmured, "I love you."

The first time he said it, I was stunned. The second time he said it, the flood gates opened. I wailed like a lost soul that had found its way home. His shirt quickly became a sodden mess where I pressed my face, letting loose gut-wrenching sobs. I struggled to pull my arms out of the cuffs. I wanted to twine them around his solid form, needing that extra sense of touch.

"Shhh, baby. You're only hurting yourself more. Sawyer's found the key. Hold still so he can get you out of those fuckers." Jase tried to soothe me, to stop my struggles. His voice was so ragged it sounded like it had been given a good working over with sandpaper.

"Vernon, you and Willis go get the trucks, and while you're doing that call the others. We're going to need them." Sawyer gave orders to his men. Carefully, he removed the circle of metal from each of my wrists.

As soon as both arms were free, I circled them around Jase's body. I couldn't get enough of him. Thankfully my racking sobs had slowed to the point I felt like I might be able to regain control.

"Get her out of here, Jase. Take my truck when the boys get back. Once you get her home and cleaned up, you need to pack-up and get her away from Copper Ridge until she's healed. As far as anyone is ever going to know, Charlotte was never here, and neither were we. We'll take care of this garbage." Sawyer surveyed the carnage in the room.

"Sawyer, how the fuck are you going to cover up the deaths of four men? They can't just disappear. Hell, one's the sheriff's son. One was running for sheriff. This ain't like covering up the shit we used to pull as kids."

"People see what they are told and expect to see. The boys who broke into Robbie's shit-can of a house found all the makings for a meth lab. Looks like those fucker's were into more than runnin' shine." He jerked his head in BW's direction. "We're going to bring it all here, set it up and let the rumors do the rest. What's one more meth house when there's been so many started in the last few years by pieces of shit like those two.

"My people steer the speculating in the right direction and no one is surprised when, in a few days, the bodies are found. Just your typical drug bust gone wrong. Of course, it's going to be the sheriff-wannabe's own fault for ending up dead. He'd been riding along with a county deputy and interfering in what should have been strictly police business." Sawyer explained the process of erasing what had actually happened with the matter-of-factness of someone used to altering reality to suit their own purpose.

As I listened to how easy the scene was going to be changed, it made me wonder. Just how many times had this been done at other locations where violence had taken place?

"But what about Robbie? The bullets from the guns? What if they trace any of it back to Jase?" I tried to shove back from the security of Jase's body so I could look him in the eyes. I wanted him to see how worried I was about this. That was a mistake.

"Baby, if Sawyer says he can handle it, believe me it's going to be—"

I'd pushed back far enough that Jase got his first good look at my face, and it didn't go over too well. "Goddamn!" Jase was livid.

Taking a step back, he held me at arm's length. He started at my bloodied feet and slowly inspected every inch between there and the top of my head. Each new injury he found produced a darker, harsher cast to his face. By the time he got to the purplish-black mass of swelling that used to be the left side of my jaw, his back teeth were clinched so tightly I could actually hear the grating of tooth against tooth and watch the popping of the muscles in his cheek.

"If I could wake them up I'd peel strips of their hide off with boiling water."

"We killed them too fast, Rydan." Sawyer spoke in a low lethal voice. Guess Jase wasn't the only one who had been inspecting me.

"It's not as bad as it looks."

"Don't." The slow shake of Jase's head warned me to not try and belittle my injuries. I had a bad feeling about where this was going.

"Jase, you can't blame yourself for this."

"Who do I blame, Charlotte? Look at you. Listen to you try to talk. Who left you? Unprotected. Alone."

"You blame BW, that's who. He's the one who started all of this by killing my granddad. Or blame

Brent, for pushing BW to get his hands on the shine recipes. But never yourself." I felt desperate. I needed to make him understand and believe what I was saying. "You saved me, Jase." I raised a hand and lightly traced the rough stubble on his cheek. I searched his face to see if any of what I was saying was getting through. "You were there to save me when I was a kid. After Gramps' death, you saved me from wallowing in grief. Outside of Skeeter's, if it hadn't been for you, BW would've gotten his hands on me then. And today, you saved my life...Jase...it's what you do."

A heavy silence filled the room.

"Hell, Rydan, sounds to me like you've got a full time job keeping your woman out of trouble. So get your asses on outta here and get started on it. Me and the boys need to get started cleaning this shit up. You think we don't know how to clean a fuckin' house without you here?" Sawyer's wicked grin was back.

I had never been so happy to hear Sawyer's special brand of outrageous cussing in my life. It broke the oppressive tension. Now I just had to hold my breath and see what Jase was going to do.

"So, you think we should leave so you can make this all go away?" Neutral. Neutral was better than bleak.

"It won't be the first time, Rydan." The level, no-nonsense look was as good as a billboard. Sawyer knew who he was and there would be no apologies.

The two men stared at each other. It was as if they acknowledged that they may have taken different paths in life but there would always be trails connecting the two.

Sawyer broke the moment with his typical charm. "Don't be thinking we're gonna be huggin' this out, 'cause that shit ain't gonna happen."

Standing there in the middle of so much useless death and beat to hell, I began to smile. Or tried to. My jaw quickly reminded me that it wasn't a good idea.

At my sorry attempt at a grin Jase was back to looking like a thundercloud. He shook his head and swooped down to pick me up in his arms.

"Wait! Stop! What are we going to do about Miss Lori?"

Jase froze. Both men looked at me like they thought I'd finally cracked under the stress. I'd forgotten they didn't know about the role she'd played in all of this.

"She's the one who drugged me and let BW and Robbie in the house."

Jase's arms tensed and his fingers curled into fists. He went from eagle-eying me to exchanging looks with Sawyer. Shit, they were looking seriously pissed that one of the players had gotten away.

"Guys, what're you gonna do? No matter what she did, she's an old lady. Promise me you won't kill her." I wasn't really worried they'd kill her, but figured it was better to get a promise.

"Don't worry, baby. She won't be dead when we get through. She'll just wish she was." Jase wasn't going to be denied some kind of justice.

"Whatcha think, Sawyer? Seems to me it's time for Miss Lori to retire from the post office to a prison for a few years? Stealing certain types of mail from people around here is a damn good way to get your ass tossed in jail." Jase was calm to the point of being indifferent.

"Not a bad idea. It's going to take me a few weeks to set it up but it won't be that much trouble. Damn, Rydan, I'd forgotten you had a knack for coming up with useful shit."

"I know we can't turn her over to the sheriff's office, but this just doesn't seem right. She's old, guys." I didn't have any real hope of changing their minds. Miss Lori had known she was leaving me to die and had walked right out the door without a second thought. Now that Jase knew she'd had a hand in all of this, he wasn't going to be able to let that go.

Sawyer shot a look at Jase and he nodded in agreement to whatever silent question had been asked. Sawyer began to speak, "It may not be right according to state law, but its right according to our law."

I made no more protest as Jase gathered me in his arms to carry me to Sawyer's truck. When we were both settled in the front seat and Jase was driving away, I couldn't take my eyes off him. "I love you." Amazing how three tiny words could hold my entire life in them and I was happy to offer them to Jase.

"I know."

"You know? That's it? That's all you've got?" It felt good to feel free to tease again. I knew that while the rest of the world may never find out who killed my gramps, I knew, and that was enough. "How do you know that I love you?" I couldn't resist challenging him.

"Look at all the crazy shit you've pulled trying to get my attention ever since you were fourteen." His wicked grin pulled at my heart. "And you never did delete me from your contact list. True love, baby. True love."

He was right. True love.

EPILOGUE

"Looks like you're finally getting that fatted calf your mom promised." I looked over at the crowd milling around in the Rydans' backyard. Calling what was in front of me a backyard was like calling Disney World a county fair. The area was huge, and right now it was filled with people and tables, all laden with food. Mrs. Rydan, Martha, threw one heck of a party. Course, this one had been put on hold for a while. Maybe she was making up for lost time.

Jase and I had escaped from the main crowd to a wooden swing, set back from all the action. Once seated, he'd draped an arm across my shoulders and tucked me in against his side.

"It's good to be the prodigal son." He swooped in for a kiss while I was laughing. It was becoming easier to laugh the longer I was with Jase.

We'd been gone for four weeks, and it felt good to be back home. Luckily my jaw hadn't been broken or we'd have had to stay away longer while I healed. A lot had happened in the time we'd been gone, and it was all anyone could talk about tonight. Pretty much everything Sawyer had said would happen had fallen right in place.

Most of the conversations I'd overheard centered on the sheriff's boy being mixed up with drugs. How BW and Robbie had shot it out with one of the county deputies and that nice Mr. Allen. Hearing that part of the story made me want to gag. Everyone was talking about how the sheriff was torn up over the whole thing. He'd even thought about retiring. But with no one running against him for sheriff now, he said it was his duty to continue to protect the people of this county. I might have snorted a little over that.

There'd only been one little hiccup.

Miss Lori had disappeared a few days after I'd been rescued. Sawyer had called Jase to let him know she'd pulled up stakes and left the area. Not just the area, but she had supposedly moved out of Arkansas altogether. One rumor had it that she'd retired to Florida. Others said she had kinfolk in Louisiana and she'd moved down there to be close to them.

I'd been suspicious, at first, that Sawyer had had a hand in on her going missing. But neither of the guys had seemed too happy about it. Besides, like Sawyer had once told me in church: It sure as fuck wouldn't have bothered him to tell me if he'd had anything to do with it. The man certainly had a way with words.

Looking around at the people that were here, there wasn't a stranger in the bunch. Colin was over by the fire pit, where they'd roasted the pig. By the way he was a waving his arms and the men were doubled over slapping their knees, he must have been telling one of his big stories.

I'd told him he was welcome to as many of the stills as he wanted, and I'd even gave him copies of the mash recipes. To know that he was going to continue making Copper Moon was comforting. Gramps would have approved. Made it less final, somehow. He was going to work a deal with Sawyer, and I didn't ask the particulars.

Sawyer had spread the word that he was in possession of the ledgers my gramps used to keep on all his sales. It was a lie. But he and Jase had convinced me it was the only way to keep people from coming at me over them.

I had a lot to thank Sawyer for. The one time I did, he brushed it off, saying, "You trying to fuckin' insult me?" Jase assured me that meant Sawyer liked me.

"Why didn't Sawyer come tonight? Did your parents not invite him?" My questions had more to do with worry over my own standing with Jase's parents than why Sawyer wasn't here.

The Rydans had been nothing but welcoming and seemed pleased I was in Jase's life. It was me that couldn't get over my background. I figured Sawyer and I were two sides of the same coin. His side just happened to be a little rougher than mine.

"He was asked to come but this isn't really his kind of crowd. And yes, it was my mom that did the inviting. Don't tell me that's not what you were wondering." Jase placed a kiss on my forehead. "Baby, they love you as much as I do. As long I'm happy, so are they."

"Thanks. No pressure there."

"Tell you what. Why don't we head to the barn? You can make me real happy and they'll love you even more."

My answer to that suggestion was a fist to his rock hard stomach. That set Jase off laughing to the point people started looking in our direction. Even his parents were watching us with big smiles on their faces.

Evan stopped chatting up Jolene long enough to holler over, "Whadja do to the princess this time, Char?"

Hiding my face against Jase's shoulder was more to smother my own laughter than from embarrassment.

"Shut up, or we won't invite you to the wedding."

My giggles dried-up as quickly as my head jerked-up to stare at Jase. Was he just joking around with his brother or was he serious? Obviously I wasn't the only one floored by what he'd yelled back at his brother. Every eye in that backyard was on us and you could have heard a feather hit the ground.

Jase pulled his arm from around me and stood up. He took my left hand in his, and as I sat there, like a deer caught in the headlights, he got down on one knee in front of me. "Baby, this might seem sudden to some, but you and I both know this moment has been ten years in the making. I told you once that you needed me right then and not in some distant future that would be perfect. Honey, I need you right now, and the future can only be perfect for me if you're in it. Will you marry me?"

I sat frozen. My throat was so tight I couldn't have squeezed a syllable out, let alone a complete word. This was what I had wished for all my life, a love like the one my grandparents had shared, and I couldn't even squeak out a yes.

"Baby? If you don't say something pretty damn quick, I'm taking you to the barn and reminding you how happy I can make you."

That brought a few chuckles from the audience, but most seemed to be holding their breath along with me. Oh, shit, I wasn't breathing. Sucking in a huge gulp of air set me to coughing and choking on my abrupt inhale. Jase started to rise, and seeing him move was the catalyst needed to have me flinging myself at him. He was off balance already and my surprise tackle took him to the ground with me lying on top.

"Yes!" I screamed my answer.

It was the trigger everyone had been waiting to be squeezed and it fired off a round of laughter and shouts of congratulations.

Jase and I were busy sealing the deal with a kiss. I never had to worry about heroes or fantasies again. I had my arms wrapped around a lifetime supply.